Elemental Magic

All-New Tales of the Elemental Masters

Edited by

Mercedes Lackey

DAW BOOKS, INC.

DONALD A. WOLLHEIM, FOUNDER

375 Hudson Street, New York, NY 10014

ELIZABETH R. WOLLHEIM
SHEILA E. GILBERT
PUBLISHERS

http://www.dawbooks.com

First Printing, December 2012
1 2 3 4 5 6 7 8 9

DAW TRADEMARK REGISTERED
U.S. PAT. AND TM. OFF. AND FOREIGN COUNTRIES
—MARCA REGISTRADA
HECHO EN U.S.A.

PRINTED IN THE U.S.A

Elemental
Magic

Contents

Introduction

Elementary, My Dear. . . .

Mercedes Lackey

I hope you weren't looking for the annual Valdemar anthology, because this isn't it. Due to a number of circumstances, we're taking a one-year break from Valdemar to showcase another of my creations instead: the *Elemental Masters* series.

My editor and publisher at DAW actually prefers this series, possibly because it's something other than the never-ending medievalish fantasy series that cross her desk practically every day. I like these books as a break from the medievalish fantasy series as well, for the same reason that I enjoy urban fantasy; it's a chance to integrate magic and the "real world," a great opportunity to play a game of "what if?"

"What if" there is a cadre of people using real magic in our real world, working silently, behind the scenes, and has been for thousands of years?

It's not a new idea of course; lots of people are doing the same thing now, and plenty have done it in the past. My "working construct" of magicians who are confined to using only the Elementals and magic belonging to one of the four classical Greek Elements—Earth, Air,

Water, and Fire—isn't new either, I suspect. But it's a lot of fun, and I like to think I do it well. What is new, or at least newish, is that for my novels I combine this with retold fairy tales—Snow White, Sleeping Beauty, Puss In Boots, Tattercoat, Cinderella, Snow Queen, Tam Lin.

I've confined myself to a specific historical period, setting them in the period between 1870 and 1919. I like that time period a great deal; there was massive change going on during it, much for the good, such as the gaining of women's rights, huge improvements in medicine, scientific leaps and bounds, and some for the worse, such as the beginning of the time when we started actually pillaging the environment without a thought for the consequences. It is also a time when the line between science and "magic" was rather . . . blurry . . . as any exploration of early scientific experimentation and investigation will show. It's very fertile ground for a lot of storytelling, and enables me to change characters with each book while remaining in the same general setting.

However, when we proposed this anthology, I opened things up a bit for my contributors. Even though my books have been set in the UK and Europe, and between 1870 and 1919, I suggested to them that there have been Elemental Masters all through history, and although I wanted to keep the upper limit of 1919, they could go as far back as they pleased. I also suggested that Elemental Masters are not limited to the UK or Europe, and they could take their stories to whatever part of the world they wanted.

I'm thrilled to see they did just that. It was great fun putting this together and reading all the contributions. I'd like to thank all of them now for getting their stories to us in what was a lot less than the usual time before deadline. And I hope you readers enjoy these enough that we can do more!

A Song of the Sea
Diana L. Paxson

Kyria leaned on the rail as the ship left the harbor, balancing easily as the deck began to rise and fall. Behind them, the mainland of Italia fell away as if it were moving and she the one who was standing still. She could see a gleam of golden stone from the acropolis of Kumae, and the painted pillars of the temple where they had made their offerings to Nereus. Several ships had disappeared this spring; it was a sensible courtesy.

Would she ever see Kumae again? She told herself that it made no difference—her home would be wherever Meto was now.

She looked back at the young man who had been her father's student and now was to be her husband. He would be a big man when he filled out, but he was still growing into his bones. He was speaking with one of the sailors, the freshening breeze tossing his light hair. As if he had felt her glance, he looked up and then quickly away.

Their parents had arranged the alliance. Meto's father, a Sikelian merchant who had once belonged to the outer circle of the Pythagorean community, was thrilled to marry his son to the daughter of Archilaus, one of the *mathematikoi* who had learned the Master's secret teachings before a revolution scattered Pythagoras and his students around the Mediterranean like seeds before the wind.

This mating was as rational as one of Pythagoras' theorems. No one had asked Kyria what she thought. She wondered if they had asked Meto.

Block and tackle rattled as the seamen raised the big square sail. The painted meanders rippled like water, then firmed to a tight zigzag and the ship began to move more swiftly. *At least,* Kyria thought as she gazed over the side, *I will spend my last days of freedom on the sea.*

The water over which they were gliding glowed a brilliant aquamarine, the white sand below netted by lines of light. *What might one catch with such a net?* Kyria leaned farther, caught the silver flicker of fish where the purple seaweeds grew and something else—a sinuous gleam as if the water had shaped a form to greet her. She glimpsed a pair of bright eyes and a toothy smile.

"Sea Sister, daughter of Nereus, hail! All honor to you and your father, please ward us on our way!" She found the piece of bread she had stowed in a fold of her chiton and tossed it into the water as she used to do when she was a little girl and still free to scamper about the shore. The strange eyes widened, then Kyria was jerked backward. She came to herself facing Meto's anxious frown.

"Are you all right?" his fair skin grew pinker and he let go of her arm. "You were leaning so far. I thought you were going to fall!"

Concerned for his property? she wondered, but no, a real anxiety darkened his gray eyes.

"I'm fine . . ." she gestured toward the ocean. Her own arms only grew more golden with sun. "It's so beautiful—I wanted to see."

He looked at the water and then back at her. "Your

hair waves like the seaweed," he said suddenly, then flushed and walked away.

Kyria plucked at a strand that had escaped from the knot into which her mother had braided it so neatly that morning. The dark undulations glinted with reddish highlights in the bright sun. She supposed that mark of interest was a good sign. Pythagoreans valued the soul above the senses, but she suspected marriage would be more pleasant if bodies also got along.

If he learns to love me, will he let me walk alone on the shore? She turned her gaze back to the ocean, rolling away in an ever-changing landscape of trough and billow as the ship moved out into the great bay. The Pythagoreans gave their women more freedom than most, but what would it be like in Sikelia? Once she was installed in the women's quarters of Meto's house at Agrigentum, a view from an upper window might be the closest she would ever come to the sea.

The night sky shimmered with stars, reflected in myriad tiny spangles on the sea. Voyaging through such beauty, she wondered why Odysseus had tried so hard to return to Ithaka.

The captain had thrown out the sea anchor for the night and lowered the sail, and the ship rocked gently on a calm sea. To the east, the pointed silhouette of Vesouvios bulked dim against the sky, flanked by the curved horns of the bay, but to the south the sky curved down to the edge of the sea.

In the tent they had rigged just behind the mast, her mother, who had been seasick for most of the day, was sleeping at last. Forward, a flicker of lamplight alternately lit and hid the faces of her father and the other men as they passed the wineskin. Kyria wondered if the wine came from one of the amphorae wedged into the ship's hold.

"Nay, sir," the captain's voice rose above the creak of the timbers. "I've heard the rumors too, but *Wave-Dancer* is a stout ship, and ye've nothing to fear."

"And yet barely half the ships have arrived in Kumae that we should have seen at this time of year," her father replied, his voice too loud, as it had become since his hearing began to fail. "If, as you say, there's no new war, logic tells us there must be some other cause."

"When the Powers of the Sea decide to take their tithe," muttered one of the sailors, "there is nothing men can do."

"Each element has its tone and number. Pythagoras teaches that when there is a balance between Love and Strife, all will be in harmony," Kyria's father replied, and the conversation sank to a murmur once more.

She turned at the sound of a step behind her and recognized Meto's lean height.

"Don't let their talk frighten you—" he said, but his voice was tight.

"I do not fear the sea," she said truthfully, realizing that with every hour she spent on board she felt more at ease.

He cleared his throat. "Would you like to see Jason's ship in the sky?"

"Where?" After it became clear she had no gift for mathematics, her father had stopped including her in his classes. She had not gotten as far as astronomy.

"There's Orion and his dog—" Meto pointed overhead. "Follow the Milky Way to the southeast and you'll see how it runs right into the *Argo*'s sail—" with broad strokes he sketched out the high stern, mast, and steerboard and keel, until her vision shifted suddenly and she could see the great ship sailing over the rim of the world.

For a little while they stood silent before that beauty. *How strange*, she thought, that when Meto was her father's pupil she had seen him almost every day, and except in the classroom, he had hardly said a word. Once they were betrothed, he had not spoken to her at all. But now, in this moment outside of time, talking was suddenly easy.

"Do you think your father is right about the elements?" he asked at last.

"He must be, but I find it hard to imagine numbers experiencing either love or strife!" she replied. His face was a dim oval in the darkness, but he had shown her his soul. Perhaps she could reveal her own. "When I was a child, I used to believe that the Elements existed in a place between flesh and spirit, where beings lived that are the essence of a thing given form."

She remembered how it felt to look into a wave as through a piece of Egyptian glass and wave to the shining maidens there. Had she really seen the daughters of Nereus, or only a trick of the light that gave shape to her nurse's tales? And when she gazed at the sea this morning, what was it that she had seen?

"I believe they exist . . ." he said very quietly, "when I listen to the wind. . . ."

"Meto!" the voice of Kyria's father cut short whatever else the young man had been going to say. "Time to seek your rest! And you, child—what are you doing out of your bed?"

His voice was kind. She knew he cared for her. But how could he stand on this deck and not take a moment to gaze in wonder at the ship that sailed the sky?

*   *   *

On the ocean, nothing is so certain as change. By the next morning clouds occluded the sky and dulled the water, ruffled with whitecaps by the rising west wind. Kyria had gone to the prow as soon as she woke, eager to learn about this new mood of the sea, but her father ordered her back to take care of her mother, who had never much liked boats and now refused to stir from the dubious shelter of the tent.

The wind was too fitful to dare the passage between the Isle of Boars and the southern horn of the bay, and the captain was seeking sea room to weather the island. Kyria could hear fragments of shouted orders over the sound of the wind. The feet of the sailors drummed on the deck as they ran to haul on the sheets and braces, Meto among them, grinning as he gripped the rope and turned his face to the blast. The ship heeled sharply as the big sail was hauled around and *Wave-Dancer* tacked once more.

It was a tortuous, zigzag progress, requiring the most delicate judgment to balance the forces of wind and water. But by nightfall, the storm seemed to be abating, and Captain Libano ordered the sea-anchor cast over the side. Meto did not join the other passengers in the tent until darkness fell.

Kyria was surprised to find herself so aware of his presence. She wanted to ask him if he had heard voices in that wind, but the only conversation in the tent was the counsels of philosophic detachment that her father murmured when her mother's fears outran her control. She wondered why she herself was not afraid. Ships disappeared all the time. It was quite possible that her life would end in these tossing waves.

There is no ocean in Hades, she thought grimly. *If I*

*must die, I will ask the gods to let my spirit remain with
the sea.* But the captain had sounded resolute rather
than anxious, so perhaps it would not come to that, despite her mother's fears.

By the time morning's gray light replaced the darkness they were well out to sea. To their left was a dim
blur that might be land, growing rapidly more distinct as
the rising wind drove them on. Captain Libano grinned
and said that with this wind they would reach their goal
in record time, but the steersman was white-knuckled
with the effort to keep the ship on course.

"What land is that?" Kyria asked one of the sailors
when her mother had fallen into an exhausted sleep at last.

"Surrentum," came the answer, "and a wild, wolf-
fanged coast it is, with sheer cliffs down to the sea. But if
the wind holds, we'll soon be past it."

Kyria kept a tight hold on the railing as the ship
thrashed along, racing surging gray wave horses maned
with white foam. *This must be what it feels like to drive a
chariot,* she thought dizzily as blood sang in her veins.

Presently the wind shifted to the south. The man at
the stern turned the steerboard, and the deck dipped
again as the square sail was hauled around to catch the
wind at an angle that sent the ship speeding eastward
once more. The clouds were beginning to fray.

The air brightened and she blinked at a sudden blaze
of emerald from the sea. Below the distant cliffs she
could make out a white fringing of surf, and more surf
edging three low islands that lay between the ship and
the shore. The wind was still strong, but at least they
could see where they were going now.

That was when she saw Meto halt as if listening. In
the next moment, she heard it as well.

Singing. . . .

It's the wind in the rigging, she told herself, *or the call of a gull.* But no gull ever had a voice so pure. She staggered as the sail flapped suddenly.

"Secure that brace!" called the captain as the sailor she had talked to before let the rope that ran from the end of the yardarm fall. One of the other men grabbed it, and the ship steadied as he wound it tightly around its peg at the stern.

"As for you—" The sailor scarcely seemed to notice as the captain gripped his arm.

"Can't you hear her?" he asked in a conversational tone. "Can't you hear her calling me?"

Now other men were stopping, the confusion in their eyes giving way to wonder. *Wave-Dancer* shuddered as the steersman let go.

"Poseidon strike you! Get back there!" the captain started toward the stern, shouldering past Archilaus, who had emerged from the tent to see what was going on.

Kyria shook her head, trying to sort out the singing from the babble she heard from the sea. Then she saw that Meto had followed the helmsman to the rail. She lurched across the heaving deck, grabbed his tunic with one hand while the other gripped the rail. He did not even seem to know she was there.

"Is there danger?" asked Archilaus.

"Oh, sir, just listen!" Meto's voice rang with joy. "She's singing about the holy numbers—the secrets of music—everything you tried to teach me, but I couldn't understand!"

The philosopher cupped a hand behind his ear, brows bent in frustrated curiosity. There was a splash as one of the sailors leaped into the sea.

"Stop your ears!" Captain Libano's voice cracked. "Gods save us! We've come to the Siren's isle!" Two more men went over the side, and the words borne on the wind mingled with a chorus of lamentation from the sea.

The captain looked wildly around him and gestured frantically to Archilaus, who alone among them stood unmoved. "Sir! Take the steerboard! Hold her as she goes!"

As the philosopher grasped the steering bar, the captain clapped his hands over his ears. The ship wavered, and Meto began to struggle in Kyria's arms. More crewmen were diving overboard, crying out in eager greeting to women only they could see.

Now she could hear words as well—a song of home and hearth and heart's desire—but louder still was the chorus of warning she heard from the waves. She saw her father struggling with the steerboard, but it had been too many years since he had grasped anything but a pen. He went sprawling as the wooden bar wrenched free, and Kyria staggered as *Wave-Dancer* heaved round. The starboard brace snapped with a *ping* as the precise relationship between sail and steerboard failed, followed by the sheetline below. As the yardarm swung, the flapping corner of the sail caught the captain across the chest and swept him away.

In another moment, the portside lines were gone as well. The sail flared forward like a gigantic flag and *Wave-Dancer* followed, prow aimed at the islands, running before the wind.

"Let me go!" Meto tried to push Kyria away. "The voices—now they are telling me how to ride the wind!"

"It's all right—" she tried to soothe him. "Look—in another moment we'll be there!" They were already passing the first island, a round lump surrounded by foam. The larger, crescent-shaped mass ahead of them was approaching with frightening speed. White water frothed around a stony shore, and that was just the rocks she could *see*!

Her father was tying her mother to the mast. He gestured to her to come over, but she could not pry Meto away from the rail. She shook her head. They were all going to drown anyway, and in that moment it seemed to her better to die as Meto's wife than as her parents' child.

"Farewell—" her father cried, "—until we meet again in that sphere where all is Real . . ." He should have looked ridiculous—an old, bony, man with scant silvered hair flying wildly in the wind, but she saw in him a nobility worthy of the Master he revered.

The ship jerked; she heard a groan as the hull scraped stone. Meto's gaze focused at last, and he flung his arms around her. "Kyria—" Everything he had not known how to say was in the way he spoke her name.

Another shock brought the sound of breaking crockery as some underwater fang pierced the hold and wine flooded into the sea. They were still moving forward, but the ship's motion was more sluggish now. Another surge lifted them.

"Sea Sister, help us!" Kyria screamed as a mass of gray stone reared up before them. Then they struck. The deck tilted. She glimpsed the mast torn from its wedging by the impact and whirled overboard, and then the great wave arching overhead.

"*Let go!*" came a voice that was, and was not, within. "*Let go and give yourself to the Sea!*"

Blue hair streamed upward along that endless curve, shining arms reached, she saw the delicate webs between the long fingers of graceful hands. As the wave fell, Kyria released her death-grip on the rail and let it sweep them away.

Kyria's first awareness was the rough prickle of sand beneath her cheek. She lifted her head, forced muscles to move so she could brush it away. Everything hurt. She licked dry lips and tasted brine, flinched at the brightness of sun on sea.

As memory began to return she tensed, but there was no singing. She looked for Meto, and felt a pang of loss whose intensity surprised her as she realized he was not there. She had been washed up in a rocky cove just above the high tide line. Beyond the thin edging of sand the ground rose steeply, covered with dwarf oak and broom and crowned with spindly pines. The gurgling water was retreating now, leaving behind a wonderland of barnacle covered rocks and tidepools where orange starfish clung and the feathery fronds of white and purple anemones waved.

"She wakes . . ." said a small voice from somewhere among the rocks. Kyria spun around and, squinting, realized that what she had taken for a flare of sunlight on the water was a small being, human in shape but with wings that glistened like those of a dragonfly and a slim body scattered with opalescent scales.

"Are you a nereid?" she breathed.

"Nothing so lofty!" there was a ripple of falling water in the creature's laugh. "Only a lesser sprite, Despoina, a nymph of the tidepool, at your service."

Kyria blinked. "Why do you call me mistress?" More laughter came from the rocks around her.

"Because you can see us. Because the daughter of Nereus saved you. You have the favor of the sea. . . ."

"We are happy you live," said another. "The crabs are

outgrowing their shells from devouring all the man-flesh washed ashore."

Kyria's heart sank at the thought of her parents' bodies being nibbled by the creatures of the sea. And Meto—

"Have others washed up recently?" Her voice wavered. "An older man and a woman, and a young man . . . with fair hair?"

Sound washed around her.

"Beyond those rocks—" With a whirr of gossamer wings, the sprite darted ahead, motioning to Kyria to follow. Heart pounding, she picked her way over the tumbled stone. On the other side, a shimmer of light pulsed above a pile of seaweed and broken boards. Closer, she could see shapes in the cloud, like the sea-sprites in form, but transparent as glass. They were hovering above an outstretched hand.

"More dead meat?" Kyria asked tightly.

"No, mistress! The sylphs say he lives!"

Suddenly she could move again. She fell to her knees in the sand and began to tear away the sea wrack until he lay before her, limp as the seaweed, but not as cold.

"Meto! Meto!" A pulse beat in his throat, but he did not stir. She turned to the sprites. "Is there any fresh water here?"

Another subliminal gabble brought her to a little rivulet. She filled a piece of broken amphora from the wreckage, drinking until she felt parched tissues ease, then carried it carefully back to Meto. By the time his shallow breathing gave way to a deeper, shuddering gasp, it seemed to her that hours must have passed, but the sun was only beginning to dip toward the sea.

When his eyes opened, the sylphs chorused in delight.

For a moment he stared without focus. Then he reached up to touch her face.

"You're real . . ." he whispered. "We survived."

For a moment all she could do was smile. Then she pointed toward the sylphs.

"Tell me. When you look over there, do you see anything . . . strange?"

Meto winced as he turned his head. Then she saw his eyes go wide. "You mean you see them too? I've glimpsed them before, but I never dared to tell anyone for fear they would think I was crazed."

The sylphs spiraled upward, greeting him with a shimmer of light and song.

"And over there?" she indicated the nymphs.

"Yes, but not so well. They are not like the other ones."

Kyria smiled. "The ones you see call themselves sylphs. The nymphs are water sprites that came to me. It seems the gods have given to you and me a knowledge of the elements that goes beyond even my father's philosophy. We were never willing to admit we were seeing them before."

Meto levered himself upright. "As soon as we get back to the lands of men, I will make an offering to thank Hera for giving you to me. When our parents arranged the betrothal I was glad, and then terrified that I would betray myself and you would fear me."

"*When* we get back?" She sat back with a sigh, the frantic energy that had fueled her search for Meto gone.

"The Powers saved us. I cannot believe they will abandon us now!"

"What about the Powers that almost killed us?" she objected. "Any ship that comes near this isle will be in danger from the Sirens' song . . ."

He nodded toward the nymphs. "Cannot your friends help us?"

The sea sprite shivered, splattering drops across the sand. "We are no kin to the Sirens. The songs that called your sailors to their death did not come from the people of the sea."

Meto sighed. "It is true. They sang of fertile fields and the sweet scent of flowers on the wind. . . ."

"Ah! That would explain why you heard them so clearly," said Kyria, "but their songs had little power over me."

"Their strength is of the earth and the air—" sang the sylphs. "But since Odysseus defeated them, they fly from one island to another, seeking revenge. The unburied bodies of those they kill pollute this place. We do not want them here!"

That evening, shellfish and the garnet-colored seaweed that grew on the rocks staved off the worst of their hunger. They fell into exhausted sleep on a bed of dry grass beneath the pines, clasped in each other's arms. They woke at dawn, sore and hungry but cheered by the bright day. They were just washing at the little stream when Meto stiffened.

"They are singing again . . ." he said hoarsely.

Kyria ripped at the ragged hem of her chiton and wadded up pieces of cloth to press into his ears. In the next moment the sylphs had descended in a cloud around him, producing a soft humming that muted whatever parts of the Sirens' song he could still hear.

One of the nymphs manifested from the stream. "There is a ship. The evil ones are singing, but the sailors are too far away to hear."

"How can I keep us alive until we are rescued when

at any moment I may be drawn to my doom?" asked Meto, pulling the plugs out of his ears. Kyria nobly did not point out that up to now it had been she who had been keeping *him* alive. "What do the Sirens *want?*"

"They desire what they failed to get from Odysseus . . ." said the nymph, "the love of a living man."

Meto shivered, frowning. Kyria reached out to him, then let her hand fall. Her mother had warned her never to try to talk to a man when he was thinking. A woman could watch a pot, comfort a child, and carry on a conversation, but a man's mind could only focus on one thing.

"We will have to think of something," he said finally. "Even if we plug my ears with wax as Odysseus did for his sailors, so long as the Sirens sing, no ship will be able to get near, and neither one of us will survive."

"In that case," Kyria replied, "while we are thinking, let us give the souls of our lost sailors peace."

The sprites led them to the drowned men. A handful of soil scattered across each body served to release the ghosts before Meto and Kyria covered them with wreckage from the ship—the best they could do for burial. They found Captain Libano, but the bodies of her parents were not there. She tried to hope that some ship had rescued them, knowing it all too likely that they were at the bottom of the sea.

That night they slept curled in their nest of grass once more. But despite the day's labors, she found it hard to sleep, acutely aware of the warmth of Meto's body next to her own. Though they lacked the feast and blessings, they were already bound by law. She had expected that he would want to lie with, as well as beside her. But when he had kissed her on the brow, he turned his back to her and lay still.

He is tired, she thought. *He did most of the work to-day, and he was more harshly treated by the sea.* But he did not lie with the limp abandon of exhaustion as he had the night before. She could feel the tension in his long frame, but if he did not want comfort, she would not pry. And if he did not want to make love to her, she would not beg.

She lay silent, using the branches of the pines to track the passage of the stars, her cheeks wet with tears. Eventually her eyes closed.

When she opened them to the new day, he was gone.

"Why didn't you wake me?!"

The sylphs were absent, but the sea-sprites had come flying in a glistening mob at Kyria's anguished cry.

"You ordered us to leave you alone!" The nymph said sulkily.

Kyria rubbed her eyes and sighed. It was true that when she and Meto lay down the night before she had told the sprites to go away, not wanting to make love in front of an audience. But her anger was all that was holding off despair now.

"Where—" she began, but she did not really need to ask. *Meto has gone to do something noble,* she thought bitterly, but at least he had taken the wax plugs they had made from the stopper of a broken amphora that had washed ashore. There might still be some fragment of his soul he could call his own.

She felt marginally more hopeful when she had bathed her gummy eyes and eaten the last of the sea-weed collected the day before. But her heart raced as she picked her way along the island's eastern shore.

The nymphs had taken to the sea again, leaping like

dolphins through the waves. But soon enough she ceased to need their guidance. From somewhere ahead she could hear the Sirens' triumphant song.

"Daughters of Earth and the flowing river, ancient and fair are we—" trilled the first voice, fresh as the first breeze of spring.

A second voice, golden as summer, continued, "From Earth's womb drawn to dance on the air, and prey upon the sea."

Hardly daring to breathe, Kyria crept forward.

"Leucosia the first, Ligeia the next, and ripe Parthenope!" The third voice was rich and full.

Kyria pulled down a branch of scrub oak so she could see. Before her, a thin layer of soil covered a broad slab of rock, bearing grasses that were turning now from the green of spring to summer gold, edged with yellow broom and scattered with crimson poppies and rockrose. Of the singers, all she could see at first was wings.

They were sitting on an outcrop of dark stone. Leucosia was pale, white-winged, with silvery hair that floated on the breeze. Ligeia must be the one who was all amber and gold, and Parthenope darker, with hair and feathers shading from copper to bronze. About halfway between the Sirens and the edge of the rocks stood Meto, swaying a little to the music, head bowed. His own sylphs hovered in an anxious cloud behind him, too fearful to help, but too devoted to leave.

With his ragged tunic and tangled hair, he should have looked pitiable, but there was something in his stance that reminded her of a patient god. Were they playing with him, or was he resisting their allure? Whatever Meto had intended, it did not seem to be working. But he would be safe if she could get him into the sea.

As she began to ease back, the bronze Siren, Parthenope, rose. Kyria stifled a gasp. The Siren's upper body was as beautiful as her voice, with generous breasts and smoothly rounded arms. Below, she had the feathered thighs and clawed feet of a bird.

"Though shy you are, my fledgling boy, you never will be free!" the Siren sang.

Kyria slid back through the trees and scuttled across the rocks, scarcely pausing when she bruised her feet and scraped her knee. At the edge of the water, the nymphs rose to greet her in a shimmer of glistening wings. She slid gratefully into the waves. The sting of salt-water on her wounds became a tingle and the entire sea began to glow, but she had no time to wonder at it now.

By the time she reached the rocks below the meadow, all three of the Sirens were stalking forward. A sylph darted past Meto's ear, whispering. He cast a quick glance behind him, saw Kyria, then tipped back his head and sang.

"Too fair by far for mortal love, Sirens, let me be!" He had been trained in Pythagorean music, and each note was accurate and pure.

The Sirens halted. Kyria wondered if anyone had ever sung to them before. A billow lifted her onto one of the rocks and she struggled to stand.

"Let goddesses be loved by gods," she echoed him, "and leave this man for me!"

Parthenope's response was more a squawk than song. All three of them mantled suddenly, like hawks in a rage. Clawed feet scored the thin soil.

"Meto, here!" Kyria cried. A wave rolled up the rocks behind her, showering her with spray. "Sea Sisters!" she called as she had once before, "Help me!"

As Meto staggered backward, his sylphs swarmed between him and the Sirens, humming furiously. The Sirens leaped after, powerful wings sweeping them aside, clawing at their prey.

"He is mine, mine, mine!" they screamed. "He belongs to me!"

And screamed again as a great wave rose up before them, and a Voice resounded from the depths, *"No. . . you belong to the sea!"*

Then the whole weight of water fell, tossing Kyria and Meto up onto the land. As it released them, they saw the retreating wave swirl a mass of feathers away. A woman's body gleamed above the billow, then was drawn back under.

"Godly born, you may not die," that deep voice spoke again, "but you shall dwell now in my waters. Earth and air no more shall bear you—become now creatures of the sea!"

Blinking, Kyria glimpsed the supple shapes of the Nereids riding the waves, and beyond them the huge shoulders and bearded face of their father. He plunged his trident into the depths. Twisting and fluttering in the whirlpool were three creatures with the tails of fishes and the upper bodies of women whose flowing hair glistened silver, bronze, and gold.

"If Pythagoras is right about the balance of Love and Strife," murmured Meto, "surely the elements owe us time for love."

Kyria smiled into his shoulder and curved her body to fit his. Looking up through the pine branches, she glimpsed a flicker of white as the piece of sail they had tied to a length of deckboard as a signal flapped lazily. In a moment, she should get up and see what the sea was doing, but it was much nicer to simply lie in Meto's arms.

She must have dozed off then, for when she opened her eyes again, one of the nymphs was hovering before her, stuttering with excitement.

"A ship! Despoina, a ship comes!"

Gasping with mingled tears and laughter, Kyria and Meto scrambled out of their shelter and ran down to the shore. A fishing boat with two rowers was easing around the end of the island, rocking dangerously as Kyria's father stood up and waved.

He was shouting, but all they could hear was the song the sea sang to the wind.

Note: The first discussion of the Four Elements to appear in writing was the work of the philosopher Empedocles, son of Meto, born in Agrigentum, Sicily, in 490 BCE. In addition to being a healer and friend of the Pythagoreans, he was said to be a magician and controller of storms. The Sirens' isles (the Sirenusae) are still there. They may be seen on Google Earth in that dark spot just southwest of Positano, Italy.

The Fire Within Him
Samuel Conway

Poor old Appollonios! His happy, wine-soaked dreams gave way to an awful pounding in his head, as though some very large bird were pecking at his temple, *peck peck peck!* He awoke from the fog to discover that, indeed, a very large bird was pecking at his temple. With a grunt, he flapped his arm to shoo it away, but the bird was back in an instant, *peck peck peck!*

"Oh, go away!" Appollonios cried. "Stop bothering me."

But the bird would not go away. It flittered away from his waving hand only to return right away, its huge black beak pounding at the poor old man's head. Angry now, Appollonios summoned the Fire within him. He did not mean to harm the bird, of course, only to frighten it off, but much to his surprise the bird threw up its wings and a gust of wind rose that parted the flames to either side.

"Aha!" the bird croaked. "So you do have Fire within you!"

"So, what of it?" Appollonios growled. He rubbed his temples, then felt around for his wine goblet. Perhaps a little sip might ease the throbbing, or at least put him in a better mood.

The bird hopped forward and pecked hard at his arm. "Ouch!" Appollonios cried. "Stop that!"

"You must help us!"

"Help you? Why would I want to help such a rude fellow as yourself?"

The bird raised every one of his feathers until he looked like an inky explosion and hopped about. "A crisis!" it squawked. "Catastrophe! Unspeakable disaster!"

"Now, now, calm down," Appollonios said. "What has happened? Is someone hurt, is that what you are saying?"

"Worse!" the bird wailed. "We have been affronted!"

"Affront—? What? Oh, *do* go away!" Appollonios turned his back to the bird, only to feel a sharp peck at the base of his spine. "Ouch! Now see here, you—!"

"Invasion!" the bird shrieked while flailing its wings. "Horrendous invasion! A grievous insult! You must help us!"

"Solve your own problems," Appollonios grumbled.

"We cannot! We have tried, but we cannot turn back the invaders! Only the Fire that is within you can save us! We—mmf!"

Appollonios moved quickly for such an old man, and before the bird could hop away, its beak was clamped tight by a firm hand. "Now, you listen," he growled. "My Fire is not for your war—not yours, not anyone's. I will not help you if you wish me to cause harm to another. Do you understand?"

"Mmff," the bird said.

"Now, if I release this dagger of yours, will you tell me—quietly, please—*exactly* what troubles you? Perhaps I may be of some help after all."

"Mmff," the bird said contritely.

Appollonios released the bird's beak and sat back on his knees. "Now then. Who is this invader?"

"It is a man."

"And what is he doing to your people?"

"He is flying."

There was a rather lengthy silence after that. Appollonios poked a finger into his ear to swab it out and then leaned closer. "I am sorry," he said, "What did you say this man is doing?"

"He is flying!"

There was another rather lengthy silence, and then Appollonios roared with laughter and fell onto his back. "Oh, you!"

The bird beat his wings furiously. "He is flying, I tell you! I saw him! The man is flying!"

"So what if he is?"

"It is an affront! An invasion! Men belong to the Earth! They do not belong to the Air! He has no place with us! You must help us!"

Still laughing, Appollonios rubbed at his eyes. "I think perhaps that both of us were enjoying our wine too much last night. Men do not fly."

"This one does! He has wings."

Appollonios laughed harder and clutched at his sides.

"It is true!" the bird wailed.

"A man? With wings? Flying? Oh, bird, you have put me in a very good mood! I think that I could even forgive such a rude awakening." He sat up and rubbed away a mirthful tear. "All right. I can see that something has upset you, so much so that it has affected the Air that is in your head. Show me this flying man of yours. If what you say is true, I shall give him a good talking to and a kick to the behind, and send him on his way."

The bird leaped eagerly into the air and settled on Appollonios's shoulder. "To the sea-cliffs!" it croaked. "You will see for yourself!"

Hurrying in the direction of the salty air, Appollonios soon found himself standing at the place where the land gave way to Poseidon's realm. "It's quite a long way down," he said as he peered at the frothing waves far below him.

"Not down!" the bird squawked. "Up there! See? See how he mocks us?"

Appollonios shaded his eyes and gazed into the sky. "I see nothing," he said wearily. "Only more of your kind tumbling about and . . . oh!" He squinted. "Oh, my. How can this be?"

It was exactly as the bird had claimed. Rising and falling, turning and banking, a man was riding the Air. Not a man, Appollonios realized, but a boy, a very little fellow indeed, and while at first it seemed that great wings were sprouting from his shoulders Appollonios soon realized that they were a contraption the boy had strapped to his arms.

"Incredible!" Appollonios whispered." Who would have imagined such a thing could work? He really is flying. Look at him go!"

"You must strike him down," the bird hissed.

"Nonsense!" Appollonios laughed. "He's just a boy, and look at how much fun he's having. Surely he is causing you no harm."

"Insult!" the bird shrieked. "Insolence!"

Appollonius brushed the bird off his shoulder with a sweep of his hand. "I shall have no more of this foolishness, now. Surely you can afford to share your realm with one little boy."

The bird landed in a sprawl, hopped to its feet, and puffed its feathers angrily. "One boy today. How many tomorrow? Men belong to the Earth. They do not belong to the Air. This outrage must stop! Here! Now!"

"So what would you have me do? Throw a pebble at him?"

"Burn him, Appollonios!" the bird shouted. "Burn him with the Fire within you!"

"What? Never! Never say that again, you devil. I should kick you into the sea for demanding such a thing of me."

"But you must stop him!" the bird shrieked. "He is not of the Air. What next, if you do not stop him?"

"Why not stop him yourself?"

"We cannot. He is too fast, too nimble for us."

"I will call to him, then. You, there! Boy! Come down here at once! Come down, I say!" He spread his arms helplessly. "He cannot hear me."

"Use the Fire," the bird began but cowered back when Appollonios drew back his foot, "to warm him, I meant. Yes. If he is too hot, he will come to the Earth to rest. Then I shall peck out his eyes."

"You will do no such thing. When he returns to the Earth I will scold him soundly and send him home to his mother. Is that agreed?"

"Agreed." The bird hopped about excitedly. "Agreed!"

"Fine, then."

The boy circled lazily overhead, the shadow of his wings sweeping again and again over the cliffs. It really was remarkable how he had fashioned them. Such an elegant design, so simple, so brilliant, and such a shame to make him take them off. Even so, Appolonios had agreed. Taking a deep breath, he raised both hands slowly above his head. He summoned from within him the most delicate Fire, barely a candle-flame, and surrounded the boy with it.

The bird looked on.

Appollonios's hands traced gentle circles that followed the boy's path through the air. He felt a warm droplet strike his arm, then another upon his forehead. "He's beginning to perspire," he said to the bird. "He should come down any moment now."

The bird said nothing.

Another drop fell upon his fingers and trickled down the back of his hand. To his surprise the trickle slowed, halted, then turned to white before his eyes. It was not perspiration at all. It was . . .

". . . wax?"

High overhead the boy began to beat his arms feverishly. The feathers were separating from his wings and dancing raucously around his body. With every heartbeat the boy's wings faded away while the cloud of feathers grew thicker.

"Oh, no!"

The bird idly preened its chest while the boy fell.

With a desperate cry, Appollonios rushed to the very rim of the cliff. The toes of his sandals dislodged several small stones that tumbled down, down, down to the foaming waves. He stretched his arms out as far as he dared, and then farther still. The boy saw and reached plaintively toward him. Appollonios could clearly see the terror in his eyes, the tiny glimmer of hope that faded to agonized despair as the boy passed so tantalizingly close to the old man's fingertips.

"No. No . . ."

For the last time the boy desperately beat his featherless wings as he plunged down, down, down to the foaming waves below, disappearing beneath them as though he had never been.

Appollonios peered at the waves and prayed to every

god of Olympus that he might see the boy struggling to the shore, but Olympus paid no heed that day, and there was no sign of the little boy who had learned to fly.

The old man hung his head and wept while the waves rolled and roared below, and then he swiped away the tears with an angry fist and spun about to face the bird. "Demon!" he shouted. "Monster!"

The bird shook out his wings and fussed with an errant feather. "Why, gentle Appollonios, what troubles you?" it asked.

Appollonios roared and allowed the Fire to rush forth in a great blast more powerful than he had ever before summoned. Nonplussed, the bird simply flung up its wings and a whirlwind appeared, catching the fire and carrying it skyward in a swirling pillar of heat and light. "Peace, Old Man," it croaked. "There is no need to be unpleasant."

"Unpleasant?" Appollonios stood aghast. "You foul, wretched thing! I will show you what is 'unpleasant' indeed. You murdered that poor boy before my eyes."

The bird tilted his head. Its dark eyes glimmered. "Me?" it said. "I did nothing. I merely asked for your help. It was your Fire that struck him from the sky."

"You tricked me."

"Tricked?" The bird tucked a wing against its breast. "Why, I did no such thing. How was I to know that the silly creature would make himself such fragile wings?"

Enraged, Appollonios summoned the Fire once more, but before he could send it forth his anger melted into sorrow. Falling to his knees, he beat the ground with his fists and sobbed, tears flowing until he could find no more tears within him, while the whole time the bird toyed with a pretty rock it had found. At last Appollonios rose to his feet and mopped at his eyes. "He was just a boy."

"He was of the Earth. He had no business in the Air."

"He was a boy! A little boy, having so much fun. Did you see him as he fell? He was crying. He wanted so much for me to save him."

"Then perhaps you should not have struck him down." Quickly the bird threw up his wings, ready to summon the whirlwind again when it looked as though Appollonios might lash out again with the Fire.

Instead, Appollonios folded his arms and glared at the bird. "You tricked me into murdering an innocent little boy," he hissed. "You have put his blood on my hands. Now I cannot rest until that blood has been washed away."

"The ocean is there," the bird said, pointing with his beak.

Appollonios shook his head. "Oh, no. There is not enough water in Poseidon's entire realm to wash this blood away. My hands will only be clean again when Men march across the sky in columns so thick that you will never again see the clouds past their feet."

The bird raised all of his feathers at once. "You would not!"

"I would, and I shall. Demon of the Air, for your murderous treachery I shall teach men the secret of flight. I saw how those wings were fashioned. That boy was only the first of millions."

With an angry shriek the bird launched himself into the sky. "Beware, Appollonios!" it squawked. "If that secret leaves your lips, we shall intervene. You will never share it!"

"Away with you!"

"Beware!"

"Away, I said!"

The bird beat its wings in a storm of black feathers and darted toward the nearby trees where it melted into the shadows and vanished, leaving Appollonios alone on the cliff-top with the sea endlessly rolling and roaring below.

The face of the boy at the moment of his death lingered in poor Appollonios's dreams through the long night that followed, and followed him into wakefulness when morning came. Eager to right that terrible wrong, he hurried from his home and made his way toward the town as fast as his old legs could carry him. The first person he happened to see was a young woman drawing water from a well. "Hello there!" he called. "Listen to me. I have seen a great wonder. I saw a boy who was able to fly."

The woman's lips were too polite to call the old man crazy, but her eyes were not. "No, no, it is true!" he said breathlessly. "This is what I saw. He had fashioned great wings from . . ."

No sooner had those words escaped his lips than an enormous bird swooped down from above. It dived not upon Appollonios, but upon the woman, who screamed and dropped her water jug as the bird battered at her head with its wings and struck a vicious gash across her brow with its beak. Appollonios tried to shoo the bird away but it continued tormenting the woman until she turned and ran off, leaving Appollonios all alone by the well.

Undaunted, Appollonios continued on his way. Before long, he spied a pair of men working their vineyard. "Ho, Fellows!" he called to them. "I say, please spare a moment. I have quite a story to tell you."

"I hope it is a short one," one of the men groaned as he cracked his spine. "We have a lot to harvest."

"It will take no time at all and you will be glad that you heard it. You see, I saw a boy who could—"

Right away a flock of birds swarmed down from a nearby tree and engulfed the men in a roiling maelstrom of feathers and beaks. Alarmed, they all bolted from the field, leaving the birds to help themselves to all of the juicy grapes that had been left behind.

Appollonios scowled at them as they gorged themselves. "I see your game now," he muttered. "You will not win, you devils."

The birds ignored him, though, and went on gorging themselves while Appollonios turned and hurried toward the town.

The marketplace was as crowded as ever when he arrived. Appollonios nudged his way through the bustle until he came upon a mule driver who was unloading his cart. Quickly Appollonios clambered onto the cart and raised his hands over his head. "Listen to me, everyone!" he shouted. A few people turned curiously in his direction as he waved his arms wildly and shouted as loudly as he could, "You must hear me!"

Slowly, the hubbub of the marketplace settled down. "You may think me a madman or a fool I am certain, but good people, please pay heed. This morning I witnessed something beyond belief. What if I told you that a man could fly if he—"

From every rooftop, from every signpost, from every eave they came, a furious cyclone of wings that filled the marketplace and sent people scrambling for shelter. Appollonios stood helplessly atop the cart as the birds pulled at hair and poked at eyes and screeched in ears, and after only a few clamorous seconds the entire marketplace stood empty.

So it went for the poor old man. He tried to whisper the secret to a friend, only to have that friend suffer a dreadful bump on his head from a rock that fell from the sky while the shadow of wings swept past. He waited for nightfall and tried to tell the men in the tavern, but the night-owls burst through the shuttered windows and struck savagely with their talons and beaks. People began to tell one another that Appollonios was cursed, and it was not long before no one in the town would dare speak to him; most ran off or slammed their doors in his face the moment he opened his mouth.

Haunted every night by the image of the boy's face, he could not bear to stop trying. One morning Appollonios threw his robe about him and began walking in hope that if he could just travel far enough away, the birds would not follow and he could reveal the secret that would cleanse him of his sin. The Fire within him gave him the strength that he needed to journey farther than any man ever had, over mountains and fields, but when he arrived in a new land his first words to the people there were met with a flurry of fury from above. Pecking, thumping, clawing, and cawing, the birds drove the people indoors and left Appollonios alone in the street. Undeterred, he walked farther and tried again, but still the birds were waiting for him.

There was nothing for the old man to do but to travel so long and so far that the vicious demons would forget all about him. Sustained by the Fire within him, Appollonios walked on, through valleys and hills, along rivers and streams, never once opening his mouth. He walked while the sun rose and fell, while the seasons turned, while Men forgot about the gods and invented new ones to replace them.

Fire, it is well known, is a hungry thing, and eventually Appollonios began to feel it gnawing at him from within. The old man's steps were growing ever more slow, and he realized that he might not be able to keep the Fire within him much longer. The time had come at last to settle his debt.

When Appollonios trudged into the next village, he could not help noticing just how oddly the people were dressed. He certainly must have appeared just as strange to them, judging from the whispers and the smirks, which he ignored. He approached a group of men and in a hoarse voice said, "Fellows, I fear that I do not have much time left. You must listen to my story."

The men looked at one another, and then at Appollonios. One spread his arms in a helpless gesture and mumbled something that Appollonios could not make out. "I'm sorry? Please, just listen to me."

The man shrugged again, glanced at his friends then back to Appollonios, and shook his head. They did not seem to understand.

Dismayed, Appollonios turned to the crowd. "Someone? Anyone? I must tell you what I have seen!"

There were more whispers and some furrowed brows, but no hint of comprehension.

Appollonios spied a man who was seated at a small desk and scribbling with a quill upon a sheet of parchment. Desperate, he rushed to the desk and seized the quill from the startled man's fingers. "Look here!" he said eagerly and began to draw. As some of the bystanders leaned in curiously an arm took shape on the parchment, then a hand with fingers outstretched, and then some feathers trailing from the forearm, and then the beginnings of a clever strap . . .

. . . and then the image was obliterated by an immense dropping of lime from above. The men around him roared with laughter and shook their heads while Appollonios stared miserably at the ruined drawing, and a great black shape banked and soared over the rooftops and out of sight.

The Fire surged within him, biting, clawing, gnawing. Panicked, Appollonios pushed his way through the startled crowd and stumbled away from the village. The Fire would not be stilled, its hunger raging, and Appollonios knew that he could no longer contain it. As dusk settled he staggered into a farming field and, spying a great stack of hay, he let the fire roar forth. It leaped upon the hay and gobbled it down, growing huge and hissing in defiance of the old man, its many tongues lashing about greedily for more.

Without the Fire to sustain him, Appollonios felt his strength fade and he fell to his knees. He felt the weight of so, so many years upon him, so great that he could barely breathe. For a moment he thought that rather than drawing it back in, he might instead give himself to the Fire, allow it to consume him, and with him the awful sin for which he could not atone.

Then he realized that he was not alone.

At the edge of the firelight stood two young boys, their eyes wide with worry as they stared at the Fire and then at the frail old man sprawled before it. Right away in both of them Appollonios saw the face of the little boy who had fallen from the sky so many years before, and he burst into sobs.

The boys nudged at one another, shuffled their feet, and at last one drew from his pocket a scrap of cloth which he offered shyly. Appollonios took it from him with a shaking hand and managed to smile. He wanted to thank the boy for his kindness, but he dared not open his mouth lest he draw the wrath of the Air. Without the

Fire within him this was certain to be his last night on this earth, and he did not want to spend it alone. Instead, he patted the ground next to him and turned to gaze at the Fire.

Wary but curious, the boys settled down beside the old man and followed his gaze to the Fire. Free now, it danced with delight as it gorged itself on the haystack. Its joyful voice crackled as it spat out a swarm of sparks that rose in a great swirling column into the air.

Suddenly the old man's attention fixed on those sparks as though seeing them for the first time in his life. His mouth fell open. As he stared at them, the sparks fluttered higher and higher until they merged with the stars on the dome of the sky. They reflected in Appollonios's eyes, and then in his heart. He almost laughed out loud but quickly stifled himself. Furtively, he glanced about. He could not see them but he knew that the birds were watching as closely as ever.

Letting out a loud, lazy yawn, Appollonios smiled apologetically at the boys when they glanced at him. Idly, he plucked a little, dry leaf from the ground, twirling it before his face before tossing it into the flames. He followed it with his gaze as a glowing tongue licked hungrily toward it, but rather than being consumed, the leaf shot skyward, following the trail of sparks and finally vanishing into the darkness high above.

One of the boys noticed and whispered something to his brother. Smiling broadly, Appollonios tossed another leaf and watched closely as the flames seemed to leap toward it, but again were denied as the leaf jumped out of their reach and spun its way into the heavens.

Appollonios said nothing. No birds appeared.

Both boys were watching now as Appollonios flung

two more leaves into the fire, teasing it with such morsels that floated out of its reach before it could devour them. Soon one of the boys, followed shortly by the other, began to toss things into the Fire, their young faces lighting up with curiosity as some were snatched into its jaws while others floated to safety on unseen threads.

There was a rustle and a flutter in a nearby tree, and Appollonios caught the glimmer of two suspicious eyes. He smiled, innocent as could be, then made a great show of folding his hands behind his head and relaxing onto his back. He even let his eyes drift closed—although not quite fully. He watched, and did not move, and did not speak, while the boys played their game.

Satisfied, those eyes disappeared into the darkness. Appollonios lay as quiet and as motionless as he could manage, even though his heart beat wildly in his chest. He felt fresh tears welling when one of the boys, his face glowing with curiosity, rummaged in his pack until he happened upon a sheaf of parchment which he folded into a shape that was much like a boat. Jumping to his feet, he stretched as close to the hungry Fire as he dared, and set the tiny boat free.

Appollonios watched happily as the boat skipped over the tongues of flame and spun its way into the sky, higher, and higher still, and then he closed his eyes. In his mind's eye he saw a little boy plunging helplessly toward the angry sea below, only to be caught up at the last second by a frail folded boat that carried him safely back into the clouds. He knew that these boys saw it, too, that they understood it, and knew that at long last he could let the Fire leave him for good.

Makana

Fiona Patton

The surf slapped gently against the rocks of Kawai Point, tugging at the boy who clung to them as tightly as the tiny *opihi* limpets he was struggling to harvest. The voice of his foster father, engaged in his own harvest a few feet away, whispered through his mind.

"You must practice patience, Makana. The opihi *are wily. They can sense your presence above them, and so you must be wily too. Try to be one with the water all around you; let it ebb and flow through your body. Its rhythm does not disturb the* opihi. *Its natural dance is one they're well versed in. They hunker down when the waves approach, and venture out to feed only when the waves recede. That is the best time to pluck them from the rocks."*

His foster father's expression had softened when he'd spoken of his first love, the waves that crashed against the southern shores of Kaua'i. A fisherman of renown, Kaiko'olokai was strongly in tune with the Elemental power of the ocean. Like the *opihi*, he knew when to hunker down and when to venture out, and he was not afraid to take his outrigger canoe into the deepest of waters. It was he who had heard the call of the waves and gone out during a violent storm twelve years ago to pull a damaged, double-hulled voyaging canoe from the maelstrom, rescuing its only living passenger, a six-month-old boy child wrapped in a warrior's red loincloth. He'd named him Makana-Hinahele, Gift of the Goddess Hina, and had brought him up to love the sea.

But Makana could not be one with the waves, no matter how hard he tried for his foster father's sake, any more than he could be one with the wind or the sun above his head or the rocks beneath his fingertips.

His gaze traveled to a deep outcropping below the low tide mark where he could just make out his foster mother's hair floating on the surface. Born on the rocks of Kawai Point itself, Kapali'i'Ka'ohu was so sensitive to their power that she could feel the touch of an *opihi's* tiny foot on their surface and know when it released its grip to feed. Within the hour the *ipu* gourd she wore slung over her shoulder would be teeming with the wiliest and most prized of all the *opihi*, the *opihi ko'ele*. If Makana remained patient as his foster father counseled, he just might be able to contribute his usual half dozen of the easiest *opihi* to harvest, those that lived above the surf line. It was barely enough to honor the two people who'd raised him as their own. He needed to do better. Especially today.

Allowing the waves to move him back and forth as he'd been taught, Makana resisted the urge to twist his head around to stare at the open water past Kawai Point. Lolani-a-Ailana, eldest son of the premier chief of O'ahu, and his entourage were due to arrive within the hour bearing a proposal of marriage for Nalunani, daughter of Makana's own chief, that would see the two islands allied for generations to come. The ruling *ali'i* from across Kaua'i had made the journey to receive him. A great feast had been prepared, and there would be singing, dancing, and feats of strength and skill lasting for days.

"Makana, have you finished your harvest yet?"

The quiet voice, tinged with just a hint of reproach, pulled him from his thoughts immediately.

"No, Father." Cheeks burning, Makana returned his attention to the *opihi*, staring at the largest of the smooth-shelled creatures clamped to the rock just a few inches from his left hand.

"Move," he whispered. "Go on. You're hungry. You know you are. Move."

When it remained stubbornly motionless, he sighed, cocking an ear to the excited chatter of the people lining the cliffs above him. It sounded like the festivities had already begun, with wrestling or maybe racing. Makana himself was known for his speed and endurance among the village boys his own age . . .

He blinked rapidly, trying to force his attention back to the *opihi*, still frustratingly clamped to the same bit of rock as before.

Time passed. A sudden swell splashed across his face and, gritting his teeth, he resisted the urge to swipe it away. More time passed. The sun beat down on his bare back, drying a patch of salt water between his shoulder blades and sending a sharp, insistent itch skittering along his spine. He narrowed his eyes, refusing to be distracted. The wind whispered across his cheek, the smell of roast boar wafted across his nostrils, his fingers began to cramp, and his left leg went numb, but then he felt the tiniest shudder of hunger-driven movement touch his thoughts. His hand darted out almost by its own volition and the *opihi* lay in the bottom of his gourd.

He grinned.

By the time he and his foster parents made their way back to the village, he'd managed to harvest a full nine *opihi*, more than he ever had before. Each time he'd thought he could sense the hunger of the creatures just before they released their grip to feed. Bursting with pride, he almost missed the long, high call of a conch shell announcing that their guests had finally arrived.

The festivities lasted for seven days. Every morning the *kahuna* and *kaula*, priests and prophets, gathered to make sacrifices and read the signs in the clouds and on the waves. Every afternoon they joined Lolani-a-Ailana and the premier chief of Kaua'i and his family to watch the dancing and judge the games.

Makana himself won three foot races and was named the fastest boy in his village. Presented with a lei by Nalunani herself, he felt a strange tingling make its way across his scalp and turned to see Ka'ohu, Kaua'i's most senior prophet, watching him closely. He made himself scarce for the rest of the day but couldn't shake the feeling that something was about to happen.

On the final morning before Lolani and Nalunani were to leave for O'ahu, Makana stood with a group of friends, craning his neck to watch as the *kahuna* and *kaula* gathered before the village altar. Unable to see over the heads of the adults in front of him, he elbowed a larger boy in the ribs.

"What can you see, Pono?" he demanded.

The other boy elbowed him back. "Your head about to be tossed off a cliff."

Makana ignored the threat with practiced ease. "And?"

"Our chief and his family."

"What are they doing?"

"Talking with Ka'ohu and the O'ahu prince."

"What about?"

"How should I know?"

"Come on, Pono. Your father is the chief's *kahuna nu'i* councilor. You always know."

"Oh, all right." Crouching down, Pono gathered the boys around him in a tight circle. "I heard my father talking with the other *kahuna* yesterday. Word is that O'ahu's chief is deathly ill . . ." He paused. ". . . from an enemy's sorcery."

The boys all gasped, and he nodded his head with grave authority. "This enemy is so cunning that none of the chief's *kahuna* have been able to counter his evil magics or even find him," he continued. "They were just about to give up hope when an *aumakua* ancestor came to Lolani in a dream and told him that only Air, Water, Fire, and Earth magics coming together, in secret," he added in a harsh whisper, "could defeat this sorcerer. Lolani was to journey to the island of Kaua'i to ask Nalunani-a-Okalani to be his wife, and if she returned to O'ahu with him, the vast power of the ocean would follow in her wake. They say that Lolani himself is so beloved of the winds off the Wai'anae Mountains that a cooling breeze follows him everywhere he goes. That's Water and Air."

"I heard," one of the other boys now interjected, "that Nalunani's cousin Keahi is to travel with her. She trained as a *wahine kaua* warrior and a fire priestess of Pele."

Pono nodded. "My father says she's the most powerful *kahuna wahine* in generations. That's Fire."

Once again Makana felt the strange tingling across

his scalp. "And what about Earth?" he asked, rubbing absently at his left leg as it began to grow numb again.

Pono watched the movement with a knowing look. "Earth is hidden," he pronounced. "That's why the *kahuna* and the *kaula* are gathering today, to ask the *akua* for guidance." He straightened. "Now, hush all of you," he ordered with all the arrogance a fifteen-year-old could muster. "They're starting."

Around them, the people stood quietly, the silence broken only by the soft beating of a prayer drum. Makana could almost see the *kahuna pule*, the prayer priest, lifting an *ipu* gourd filled with seawater over the altar covered in fruits and vegetables. If the *akua* accepted these sacrifices, they would have their answer and the Earth Mage chosen to battle O'ahu's sorcerer would be revealed. Feeling a sudden panicked sense of unease, Makana began to back away as quickly as the numbness in his leg would allow. He made it almost to the edge of the crowd before the shouted words "*Amama ua noa!*" halted him in his tracks.

"*Now the prayer has flown,*" he echoed in a strangled whisper. His leg began to throb so painfully that he almost gasped out loud, and a roaring filled his ears so loudly that he almost missed the name shouted out in triumph.

Almost.

"Makana Hinahele!"

"No, no, Kaiko. He's just a child." Tears flowing down her face, Makana's foster mother shook her head vehemently.

"Kapali." His foster father's voice was thick with his own unshed tears as he wrapped her in his arms. "We've always known this day would come. Ka'ohu told us so the very night I carried him in from the sea. Hina gave him to us to raise, not to keep." He turned. "Makana, come here please."

Makana stumbled forward. On the family altar, he saw the red loincloth he'd been found in, but had never been allowed to touch, laid out beside a sacrifice of *'ohua* fish, sea urchins, and coral, all sacred to Hina.

"Ka'ohu predicted that the day you wore this was the day you would leave us. I want you to put it on now."

Makana backed up a step. "I can't, father. Red is for *ali'i*. For the ruling classes. It's *kapu*, not allowed."

Kaiko smiled gently. "Why do you think you've been allowed to play with the boys of our own *ali'i* all these years, hmm? With Pono and the rest?"

"Because . . . because you're a celebrated fisherman, and because . . . because Mother is the most talented *opihi* harvester on Kaua'i. You have great power."

Both his foster parents smiled at that, but Kaiko shook his head. "No, Makana, it is because this design is that of the O'ahu *ali'i*." He lifted the loincloth reverently. "And now it's time for you to join them."

"But I'm no Earth Mage," Makana protested. His left leg began to throb again and he rubbed at it angrily, tears beginning to spring from his own eyes. "I can't feel the rocks as Mother can."

"No, but the earth is far more than just rocks; it's plants, insects, animals, even birds and fish who dwell in the realms of air and water. Some of those you can already feel, yes."

When Makana dropped his head with a stubborn expression, Kaiko touched him lightly on the chest. "Your power is young, untrained and untried, but strong," He smiled again, this time a little sadly. "Very strong. We always knew that if we could just get you to pay attention to your lessons, you would make a powerful *kahuna* one day, or even it seems—" he indicted Makana's leg, "—a powerful *kaula*. Numbness in the leg means a journey is imminent."

"And a tingling scalp means someone is talking about you," Makana answered mournfully.

"That's right. You see, you do pay attention. I always knew you did." Kaiko held out the loincloth. "Come now, there's nothing for it. Take up your past and go to meet your future knowing that no matter where Hina takes you, you will always be *ohana*."

"Always family," Makana repeated woodenly. Kaiko waited patiently and after a long moment, he accepted the loincloth.

He made the journey to O'ahu in a fog of grief and self-doubt. *How can I possibly fight a sorcerer?* his thoughts demanded. He couldn't even walk properly. Although the throbbing in his leg had eased, the loincloth was far too big for him, making him appear bow-legged, and the lei of *ki* leaves his foster mother had draped over his shoulders just before he'd clambered into Lolani's canoe kept jabbing him in the arms and chest. The only way he could possibly win through would be if the sorcerer fell over laughing at the sight of him and Keahi set him on fire while he was distracted.

Around him, the adults either ignored him or left him to his misery, and so it was with a sense of dread that he saw the mountains of his new home rising above the distant clouds.

"You will sleep in the *ali'i* men's hut."

At home, Makana would have continued to sleep

near his foster mother for at least another season, but here Lolani's family had taken his status as both *ali'i* and *kahuna* at face value, treating him as a honored guest despite his youth. Now, lying on a small grass mat, and wearing his old, more familiar brown loincloth, he listened to the sounds of snoring all around him and wondered how anyone ever got any sleep. Stuffing his fingers in his ears, he mulled over his first day on O'ahu.

The celebrations for Lolani's return had been diminished by his father's illness, but the day had still been filled with singing, dancing, and feasting. Makana, unused to sitting beside priests and warriors, and too worried that the sorcerer might make an overt attack against them to enjoy himself, had eaten very little. He'd spent most of his time nervously scanning the gathering, but no one had looked anything like he imagined a sorcerer would. But, since Pono had said that he was cunning, he could have looked like anyone. How an untested and untrained Earth Mage was supposed to . . .

A huge yawn interrupted him in mid-panic, and he shook himself sternly. Nalunani and the others were proper mages. They would know how to find the sorcerer and how to defeat him. All he had to do was not to fall flat on his face while trying to walk in a loincloth far too big for him. Rolling over on his side, he tried to block out the sounds of snoring and told himself to get some sleep.

He wasn't sure what awakened him at first. One moment he'd been dreaming about clinging desperately to the rocks of Kawai Point while a shadowy figure in a red loincloth loomed above him, waiting to pluck him from his home and stuff him into a gourd canoe, and the next he was staring, wide-eyed, into an unfamiliar darkness.

Outside he heard the short, sharp barking of a dog and shivered.

"Dogs howling at night mean a ghost is near," he whispered, then frowned. "But a dog barking? He reached out, much as he had with the *opihi*, and felt the faintest sense of hunger and . . . command? Could a dog command? Rising, he pulled a piece of dried *awa* fish wrapped in a *ki* leaf that he'd saved from the feast from under his pillow, and made his way outside.

The nearly full moon had risen over the mountains, casting plenty of light to see by. Makana wove his way carefully past the darkened huts until he reached the edge of the village, where he saw a small, white dog sitting beside a stand of *'ohia* trees, its gaze disconcertingly direct.

His foster mother's last words as she'd held him on the beach at Kawai Point drifted through his mind.

"Be polite to all you meet. Many people and many creatures are not what they seem."

Feeling a little foolish, Makana bowed. "Hello, little *'ilio*," he said formally. "Would you like something to eat?"

The dog cocked its head to one side, its nose twitching, as he unwrapped the fish and tossed it between its paws. It sniffed at it with exaggerated delicacy, then bent its head and ate. When it finished, it stood, and moving into the trees, glanced back at him.

"You want me to follow you?"

In the moonlight it looked as if the dog rolled its eyes, but once it was certain he was following, it plunged farther into the trees.

The dog took him up a narrow path, overrun with *maile* vines, that wound its way high into the mountains. Many times Makana thought he'd lost it, only to see a flash of white on the path ahead of him, leading him ever higher. The dark trees looming over the path and the unfamiliar sound of night creatures, and probably night spirits, hinted of dangers far beyond a twisted ankle or a fall down a hidden crevasse. He could feel the hunger of hunting animals and even the plants all around him, and once he caught the faintest sense of a wild and savage desire to consume the power of life itself that sent him stumbling quickly after the little dog. It seemed to sense his fear and paused in the moonlight until he caught up, then carried on. Finally, breathing hard, he turned a corner and found a pale-haired girl about his own age wearing a white loincloth standing beside a small path shrine made of stones.

Makana blinked. "Are you *lapu*?" he whispered, "a ghost?"

The girl grinned at him. "No," she answered, inviting him with a gesture to try again.

"*Kupua*?"

She sniffed at him. "I am far more than a nature spirit, Makana," she admonished.

His face reddened. "*Akua*?

"A God? Close, but no." When he looked mystified, she sighed. "I am *aumakua*," she explained with exaggerated patience. "Your *aumakua*."

His breath caught in his throat. "My . . . ancestor?" Then remembering his manners once again, he bowed quickly. "I . . . I mean, I haven't got anything to offer you," he said apologetically. "I gave all I had to the little *'ilio* dog and I . . . oh." He reddened again as he realized what he was saying.

"Yes, the fish was delicious and very nicely offered," she answered with a laugh. "It will do for now. It will do for me, anyway," she amended, suddenly growing serious. "But it will not do for Hina."

"Hina?"

She nodded. "It was Hina who sent me to you." She winked at him. "You may call me 'Ilio for now," she said with a grin, then sobered. "You're in danger, all of you. Once the sorcerer has killed Chief Ailana-a-Hakau, he will turn his magics against Lolani and the rest of the ruling family, then Nalunani and her family. He hungers for power over all O'ahu, and eventually over all the islands. You must stop him."

"But how?"

"Hina will help you, just as she did when you were a baby." When Makana's mouth dropped open, 'Ilio nodded. "The sorcerer is a powerful prophet as well as an Air Mage," she explained. "He had a vision that you would help defeat him one day, and so he sent a flying spirit to carry you away and drown you, but your parents prayed for my help and I for Hina's, and she fashioned a canoe to bring you to safety."

"The red loincloth?"

"Your father's. I brought it to you."

His breath caught in his throat again. "Is he . . . ?"

She smiled at him. "He's alive. So is your mother. When the sorcerer's defeated, I'll reveal you to them, but for now it's far too dangerous. You must remain hidden."

"Earth is hidden," he breathed.

"That's right." She turned. "Now come, we have much to do. The chief will not live another three days. We must fashion a shrine and altar to Hina in sight of the ocean before daybreak, and then you must bring the others to it tomorrow night as the moon rises. Only Air, Water, Fire, and Earth magics coming together in secret . . ."

"Can defeat the sorcerer."

"Exactly."

It took the rest of the night to locate just the right spot, a *leina* on a high cliff overlooking the sea where the dead leaped to enter the realm of the spirits, and then to fashion a shrine and altar a hundred yards up the path from it. Makana worked steadily, building up the floor and walls to 'Ilio's specifications, one layer of stone at a time.

"Your magic will one day be like this," 'Ilio said when he was finished. "Built up layer by layer, each one dependent on the strength of those below, and each one giving stability to those above. Once you've mastered this, from there you can reach out safely to touch the spirits of animals, plants, even the *lapu*. And you won't just sense their innermost feelings as you do now; you'll be able speak to them and even enlist their service. But for now, it's best if you don't reach too far or for too long."

She walked him back to the village, pausing by the same trees where they'd first met.

"Tomorrow you and those who will represent water, air, and fire must gather offerings for every aspect of Hina's divinity: corals, spiny creatures, seaweed, *ohua* fish, leaves from the *ohia* tree and bark from the *wauke* tree," she told him. "Most of these Nalunani can draw from the sea. Set the others to gathering the rest."

"Set?"

She laughed at his appalled expression. "Ask, entreat." She grinned. "Beg. However you do it, the offerings must be ready by moonrise, and they must be gathered in secret; the sorcerer must gain no knowledge of what you're doing. All his powers are fixed on destroying Chief Ailana-a-Hakau, but he has many birds and flying spirits bound to his service, so be cautious."

"I will."

"Then until tomorrow, descendant, keep safe." Spinning about, she took the form of the white dog again and plunged into the underbrush.

The three adults were more willing than Makana had expected. Keahi merely inclined her head. "That's why we came here," she said, pulling her knife.

"It must be done in secret," Makana repeated hesitantly.

Keahi showed her teeth at him in a feral grin. "The *kaula* Pele are never followed," she said, her eyes glowing red. "My harvest will be secret enough." She looked past him. "Lolani, I will collect from the *wauke* tree, you from the *ohia*. It will elicit less talk if you're seen; I doubt you've ever pounded *wauke* bark to make cloth."

As she headed into the trees, the others shared a quick embrace. "You're the chief's son and I your cherished guest," Nalunani murmured in Lolani's ear. "How will we ever manage such secrecy?"

He laughed. "Subterfuge, my intended. We will *slip away* together and then go our separate ways once we're unobserved. No one will come looking for us. It would be rude." He turned to Makana. "Do you remember the cove to one side of the beach where we landed or were you too homesick to take notice of it, little Gift-of-Hina?"

Makana bristled at both his words and his tone. "I remember it."

"Meet Nalunani there. She has the greater harvest, but most can be found in those waters. If you carry them, she can meet me later empty-handed."

"I can do that."

"Good. The *leina* is well known to me. I'll drop my offering off there before we return."

He and Nalunani crossed the village, arm in arm, nodding greeting here and there, then disappeared into the trees together. The knowing expressions on the faces of the villagers made Makana roll his eyes, but he had to admit, however grudgingly, that Lolani's plan seemed to be working.

And he had to admit that, despite the danger, he spent an enjoyable morning helping Nalunani gather the offerings. The cove was cool and soothing, reminding him of home. When she left to rejoin Lolani he felt an irrational stab of jealously, swiftly quelled. She was a chief's daughter set to marry a chief's son, and he was . . ."

"You are *kahuna*," he retorted, startling a small lizard sunning itself on the path as he struggled to bring their harvest to the shrine, "an Earth Mage."

"Untested and untried."

"Oh, shut up."

The four of them came together again at the shrine just before moonrise. As they arranged the offerings on the altar, each one speaking his or her own prayers, they turned to find 'Ilio standing by the *leina*. "*Amana ua noa Hina*," she said solemnly. "Now your offering has flown to Hina.

"Makana," she ordered, "close your eyes and tell me what you feel."

Makana obeyed. At first he felt nothing, just as he had that day on Kawai Point, then slowly he began to sense the lives around him.

"I feel . . . the hunger of little creatures and . . . the hunger of the larger ones who hunt them," he whispered.

"And farther?"

He reached out. "The same, but then . . . a . . . different kind of hunger for . . . power."

"Don't touch that hunger, not yet. Touch the sea, what do you feel on the waves?"

It was harder, he realized, without the earth to anchor him, but there was earth beneath the waves, so he reached down, touched rock, layered his own power like a shrine just above it, then reached out again.

And felt something both soothing and frightening at the same time. Something powerful. Something hungry, yes, but not hungry for food or for power, hungry for worship and hungry to return an all-consuming passion gentled by a love so familiar that it was as if he'd known it all his life, had felt it in the arms of his foster parents, and before that in the arms of his birth parents and before that . . ."

He came back to himself sitting on the ground, tears streaming down his face.

"All the island people are *ohana*," 'Ilio said gently, crouching down beside him and bumping him lightly with her shoulder. "And all are the children of Hina. The sorcerer attacks the very core of who we are, but that core is stronger than anything else in the world."

She turned to Keahi. "Although he's a formidable Air Mage, he's using flying *akualele* made invisible by his power to attack Chief Ailana-a-Hakau. That's where his weakness lies, for although they dwell in the realm of air, they're fashioned of fire."

"Flying fire belongs to Pele," Keahi replied, showing her teeth in a savage grin. "And with Her aid, there's no flying fire I cannot capture."

"What do you need?"

"A simple net made of *maile* vine and strengthened by magic and prayer. My fire spirits will help me fashion it." She laughed as a pair of glowing red salamanders appeared, chased each other across her shoulders, then hung suspended, swinging, from her hair.

'Ilio turned to Lolani. "Hina will make the *akualele* visible, Nalunani will command the waves to slap them away as they fly toward the chief's hut, and Keahi will capture and destroy them. The sorcerer then will send the creatures of the air that he commands against you. You must be ready to combat them. What do you need?"

"Like Keahi, I can ask my own spirits for aid." He whistled and a dozen tiny *elepaio* birds appeared to flutter about his head, each one also landing to hang suspended, swinging from his hair.

"They're a little small for such a great battle," Keahi noted, then chuckled as a dozen black *alala* birds and another dozen *nene* geese joined the *elepaio*.

"They will be needed," 'Ilio said approvingly, "Once his Elemental creatures are defeated, the sorcerer himself will be forced to do battle rather than have his creatures and his *akualele* turned against him."

She now turned to Nalunani. "You acknowledge the Shark God Kamaka'okaha'i as *aumakua*?"

She nodded.

"Call to him. We will need his strength."

"But what am I to do?" Makana asked, afraid suddenly that she'd forgotten him.

'Ilio indicated the shrine. "Hide and wait."

He felt his face flush with embarrassment. "But I thought I was here to fight the sorcerer like the others."

"You're here to *defeat* the sorcerer," she admonished. "Earth is hidden, remember? Be patient," she added when he opened his mouth to protest again. "Build your strength, layer by layer, and wait. When the time comes to act, Hina will come to you, and you will know what to do."

They did not have long to wait. As the moon rose in the sky, they felt the air grow hot.

"I see them!" Nalunani cried and, clapping her hands together, began to sing a song of power to the sea.

The air cooled, grew hot again, became wind, became gale. Explosions rocked the ground as Makana, watching from his hiding place, saw each fireball, wreathed in steam, flung toward Keahi's net by a slap from an ocean wave, caught and slammed against the cliff wall in a shower of sparks. Minute blue-green creatures, finned like fish, spilled from the steam to quench the thousand tiny fires left behind while the salamanders scrambled to repair the net before the next assault. Finally, Keahi wrestled away control of the *akualele* and sent them flying back toward their master.

The wind began to howl as a spinning mass of half-translucent winged creatures tore through the surrounding trees, slashing at their leaves and branches. Makana felt the trees' struggle radiating up through his feet and legs and into his chest as they battled to keep their roots tightly anchored in the ground. As the one nearest the altar shuddered, cracked, and was ripped away, he shrieked in pain and made to scramble from the shrine, but then it was as if a great hand held him in place and a voice—much as he remembered his foster mother's when he'd been a small child—ordered him to stay.

He fought the voice with all his strength, screaming out his denial and rebellion, then fell back, panting, as Lonlani's *alala* birds rushed the creatures in a great flock, rending and devouring them.

The battle raged until the sun turned the sky a radiant pink, and finally the sorcerer himself appeared above the trees. Riding a great vortex of power, he hurled a swarm of glowing white insects from his fingers.

Lolani rose on his own crest of power, steadied by the *elepaio*. He shouted and the *nene* geese dove into the swarms. But the insects were too many and the sorcerer too powerful, and one by one, Lolani's allies were engulfed and destroyed. The sorcerer brought his hands together in a great thunderclap that sent a current of air pulsing out to knock Lolani from his perch and send him spinning out of control. Makana heard Nalunani cry out as her intended hit the ground, and then a great force jerked him from the shrine and the voice commanded:

"RUN!"

Makana ran. Racing down the path toward the *leina*, he heard Lolani shout a warning, heard a new voice shriek in rage, and then the sorcerer was streaking toward him, riding the wind like a surfer. His face was horribly disfigured by fire, and, even as he stretched out hands to snatch Makana up, one of his own *akualele* exploded by his head. The sorcerer dodged the hail of sparks but still came at him, his face suffused with hatred.

Swirls of brown power shot out before Makana's feet, clearing the path of rocks and vines. The sorcerer gained height as the trees whipped about, trying to slap him away, and they burst into the open together.

The *leina* was close, so close, and then Makana was hurtling through the air and down toward the sea. He heard a howl of triumph as his feet left the Earth's domain and entered Air's. The sorcerer streaked in close, and Makana could feel his breath on the back of his neck, but then he heard Nalunani shout out a single word of power and a great wave launched itself into the sky. The last thing he saw was the silvery body of a mighty shark, tattooed markings standing out along its flanks, and then he hit the water hard.

He smelled seaweed, tasted salt, felt the waves move him back and forth, and breathed a sigh of relief. Kawai Point. He was home. He struggled to open his eyes and knew a moment of panic as he was unable to, then calmed as he heard voices.

"I see him! There, clinging to the rocks!"

"I've got him."

"Careful now."

The waves continued to tug at him, but he held on tightly, and finally he felt strong arms wrap about his chest.

"Come, little *opihi*; you're safe now. Let go."

Safe? Somehow he managed to release his grip and felt himself borne away into darkness.

The next time he woke, he was lying on a grass mat before the village altar, the others looking down at him with concerned expressions. Licking lips chapped by salt water, he tried to form words and finally managed to croak out: "Did we . . ."

Keahi grinned at him. "We did. The sorcerer's dead. Kamaka'okaha'i took him for His supper and good riddance."

Deep within him, he felt Hina's rumbling approval and sighed.

The wedding festivities for Lolani and Nalunani lasted for days. Makana had a place of honor beside the chief himself who, now that the sorcerer's *akualele* were no longer plaguing him, had made an almost full recovery.

When he was finally able to get away by himself, he returned to the shrine and, after laying out an offering of fish, sea urchins, and coral, saw 'Ilio watching him from a stand of *'ohia* trees.

Sitting together on the *leina* overlooking the place where the sorcerer had died, Makana thought he could see a faint phosphorescent glow just below the waves. He shivered.

"What do you feel?" 'Ilio asked.

He closed his eyes and smiled as his abilities passed over the spot without a ripple. "Dolphins," he answered.

"Hungry dolphins?"

He smiled in puzzlement. "No, playful dolphins."

"And farther?"

"Whales guarding their young."

"And farther."

"Hina and Her love for her people."

"And still farther?"

He frowned. "'Ilio, I can't . . ."

"And still farther?" she repeated.

He was silent for a long time, then drew in a sudden breath. "I feel . . . a people and their . . . hunger . . ." He shivered again.

"For?"

"For . . . power, for land, our land."

"Are they coming? You are *kaula* as well as *kahuna*," 'Ilio insisted as he raised his hands helplessly. "Prophet as well as Earth Mage. Are they coming?"

His brow furrowed as he bent all his concentration to the faint sense he'd detected far out on the waves to the east.

"Not . . . for many years yet," he said finally, "but yes, they're coming." His eyes opened. "Their hunger is like the sorcerer's, but there're so many more of them. They're coming like a great swell, swamping everything in their path. We have to prepare."

"Yes," 'Ilio agreed. "And for that we need the strength of *ohana*, each generation taking strength from the ones who came before and giving stability to the ones who come after." She stood. "Hina has a gift for you," she said, her eyes twinkling.

She pointed and, far below, Makana saw his foster parents coming along the beach. He stood, his heart pounding with excitement, and then he saw the two people who accompanied them.

"What do you feel?" 'Ilio asked with a laugh as he began to run.

"Joy," he shouted back.

War to The Knife
Rosemary Edghill

Captain Sir Beverly St. John St. Andrew Laoghaire Darwen, a distant cousin of the Duke of Coldmeece, owed to that distinction his present position: He was a galloper attached to Wellesley's General Staff. His friends, of whom he had many, knew him as Learie, and it was said of him that even his enemies liked him. From his mother he had received his fair coloring, his engaging temperament, a thousand pounds a year, and his commission with the 11th Hussars. From his father, John James Peveril Darwen, Baron Noctorum, he had something more valuable than gold and rarer than membership in The Upper Ten Thousand.

He had magic.

Learie had Mastery of the Element of Air. He could summon a storm or dispel one, predict the weather days in advance—and summon the Creatures of Air to aid him.

It was a useful selection of talents for one of His Majesty's Exploring Officers, the brave and sometimes reckless scouts who rode far in advance of their own lines, deep into enemy territory, to observe the enemy's numbers and disposition—and return with that information to their own commanders.

Learie had joined the Army upon his sixteenth birthday, his mother being lately dead and his father having far more interest in books than in people, and had followed his regiment to Portugal that very year. As matters stood, he was likely to see his thirtieth birthday in the same place he had celebrated the previous four: the Iberian Peninsula.

"The rain in Spain stays mainly on the plain . . ." The devil it does. The rain in Spain is like the rain in Portugal: cold, constant, and universal, he thought darkly. It was true that his affinity spared him much of the suffering endured by General Sir Arthur Wellesley's Peninsular Army, but while he could drive off the worst of winter's cold and call cooling breezes in summer's heat, he could not use his gift to shield the whole of the troops, and the suffering they endured (particularly the infantry regiments) tore at his heart. It had been something of a relief to be detached from his regiment and secunded to the General Staff, for its members traveled in as much comfort as one might gain while on campaign, and were assured of the pick of lodgings when the army was quartered in a city or town.

He knew it was a want of feeling on his part, perhaps, to be able to dismiss the suffering he could not cure simply because it was no longer in his sight, but from the day his father had first opened the door to the mysteries of Elemental Magic, he had drummed into the head of his son and only child the fact that this power was not without price.

"You will command your Element and its creatures, my child, but your Element will also command you: Air is changeable and inconsistent, just as Water is subtle, Fire is passionate, and Earth is slow. You must guard against those tendencies in your nature."

As a child of eight, Learie had thought it unreasonable that something you had no say in could influence your entire life. Now, at twenty, he simply thought it unfair, but something that must be endured.

In four long years of battle, General Wellesley's forces had at last swept the French from Portugal. Napoleon's turning his attentions toward Russia had made it easier, for he withdrew thousands of French troops from the Peninsula to fling at the northern bear. Now, only one last obstacle stood in the way of victory: the citadel at Ciudad Rodrigo.

And so, in December of 1811, Learie went riding . . .

It was cold, and the autumnal rains had given way, a few weeks before, to winter's deadly cold. Both Marmont and Dorsenne—formidable enemies both—were in the field, and the British had to reach the citadel before either army, or it would be impossible to take. In order to do that, General Wellesley required accurate information about the two enemy armies, for there would be no success without it.

There were others who could have gone. Gambling was a mania among the officers and men, who were just as liable to stake—and gamble away—favors as gold sovereigns. He could easily have called in a favor or two and sent someone in his place. The mission meant being away from the camp over Christmas—and New Year's, if he was unlucky—and he would miss all the celebrations. Moreover, since he had (without consulting his superiors) left behind, in the care of his batman, every item identifying him as a British officer, if he was captured he would not be offered an honorable parole: he would be hanged as a spy.

But besides his duty, Learie had other pressing reasons to take this mission for his own.

He was hunting.

His father was an Earth Master, who had not left his remote estate on the Scottish border in all of Learie's memory, but he had told him more of his fellow Masters than Learie's tutor in the art, an Oxford don and fellow Air Master, had seen fit to. Dr. Aloysius Shipmeadow had concentrated on the art itself, his instruction brisk, dry, and wholly without context. If he had been left wholly to the good doctor's instruction, Learie would never have known that there were four Schools, that women as well as men possessed these gifts, that their members gathered together in Lodges to share information and do advanced work . . .

. . . or that many such Lodges possessed an officer whose title was Master of the Hunt.

Any ability that was used could be misused, and the Elemental Gifts were no exception. To use them for personal gain, for power, or to do harm meant one's power would turn on its possessor. The best one might hope for was for the power to simply vanish. Though that was bad enough, worse was possible, for an Elemental Mage who misused his powers might do untold damage to those around him before finding the death he so ardently courted. And even that was not the worst, for to bring the fact that magic—true magic—was alive in the world today—and was a birthright that could be neither bought nor sold—would be a disaster more terrible than that of the *Garde Imperiale* marching unopposed through the streets of London. And so, what aid the mages rendered their army was small and circumspect, even though Learie suspected that, did the Elemental Masters of Britain all choose to work together, Boney might have been routed utterly between sunrise and sunset.

And somewhere in all this vast, unfriendly wilderness, someone had decided to do just that.

He hadn't been certain at first. Fire was a constant danger to any army. Cooking was done over open fires, drunkenness was common, and the supply trains carried hundreds of barrels of gunpowder, not to mention fodder for the animals. But in the past several months, there'd been a rash of suspicious incidents. Fires in the French camps. The detonation of stores of gunpowder—also French—that had been safely stored. Grass fires that rendered the countryside a blackened and barren landscape in which the French *forrageurs* could find no supplies for their troops.

Fires that were the work of a Fire Master.

Each Element had its kinship and its opposite. Fire and Air were natural allies, as were Water and Earth. Fire's opposite was Water, as Air's was Earth. Learie couldn't sense the workings of an Earth Master, while someone working Air was as obvious to him as a brass band marching by. And Fire . . . well . . . he'd never met a Fire Master. But somehow he'd known from the very first that this was what he was hunting.

He'd been worried enough to risk a minor summoning, but the sylph who came to his call could tell him little beyond confirming his guess that another magician was using his power to overtly influence the tide of battle. It didn't matter, Learie realized, whether that work aided the British or harmed them. The person responsible must be found.

And stopped.

Somehow.

His father had spoken in passing of Wizard's Duels, where two mages tried their powers against one another in

a Challenge Circle. But when Learie eagerly asked for
more information—for dueling had sounded far more interesting than the tedious work of Shielding that Lord Noctorum had drilled him in before permitting him to attend
Eton—his father would not be drawn to expand further.
When pressed, he said irritably that such things were well
out of fashion, and Learie should be grateful they were.
Nor had Dr. Shipmeadow been any more forthcoming.

I just wish, Learie thought, *that both my tutors had
been less interested in curbing my supposedly frivolous
nature and more interested in telling me things!*

He left his own lines in the darkest part of the night,
slipping past both sentries and picket riders with what
he considered unfortunate ease. Dawn found him
warmly nestled in a hayrick many miles away.

He spent the next several days in a fashion similar to
his boyhood, when he escaped the schoolroom on every
possible occasion to follow his father's gamekeeper
about the estate. That MacGregor was also the wiliest
poacher in the county, teaching the master's young son a
thousand ways to set traps and snares (as well as how to
tickle trout out of the streams), had been something he'd
thought then was unknown to his father. Now, he wasn't
so sure. Surely nothing could take place on his estate
that an Earth Master did not know about. But whether
it was forbearance or indifference, Learie had reason to
bless MacGregor's teachings, for he had brought with
him no supplies save a little grain for his mount.

*If only I had been born with an Earth Gift, instead of
being a flighty ne'er-do-well Air Mage! I'd be able to
sense disturbances to the land, for heaven above knows I
have ridden over it for long enough to develop a sympathy with it!*

If only. Though, of course, Learie reflected philosophically, if he had been born with the Earth affinity, he would probably never have left home at all, for he would have been as firmly bound to the good English earth over which he'd roamed as his father was.

Talking pays no toll, he told himself. *Nor does crying for the moon in a silver cup. I must make do with what I have.*

He just wished he felt more confident about it.

The French armies were essentially where Lord Wellesley expected them to be, and Learie made careful notes of everything he saw. Both of them together comprised a larger force than his own; in total, the French had 350,000 soldiers in Spain, but thanks to the efforts of the Spanish *guerilleros*—and the British Army, of course—most of *L'Armée de l'Espagne* was occupied in guarding its supply lines, rather than in fighting. He wasn't privy to General Wellesley's plans, of course, but it looked as if he'd have sufficient time to reach the citadel before the French could reinforce it.

Learie was on a ridge overlooking the camp—from the ensigns, he thought it was part of General Marmot's force, traveling detached in order to supply itself. It was just before dawn (it was raining, of course), and if he was going to travel any distance today, he had to be on his way before the camp roused for the day. Even if the French stayed put for another day or so—and they might, if they didn't know General Wellesley's plans— there'd be cavalry and infantry drills, *forageurs* scavenging the countryside, and scouting parties.

He was debating between heading directly back—he had what he'd come for, or at least what he'd been sent for—and spending a day or two trying to find the Fire

Master before turning back. His magic had allowed him to make extremely good time on his way here, and it would do him the same service upon his return. He knew what both Doctor Shipmeadow and his father would say: *"Leave the matters of wizards to experienced wizards. You're young yet. And Air, you know, is a flighty Element . . ."*

Learie was *very* tired of hearing that he was scatter-brained, but he realized that he really *didn't* know what to do now. And General Wellesley needed the intelligence he'd been sent to gather.

Then the supply train blew up.

The wagons carrying an army's supplies were always at the center of the camp, both to guard them from theft and so that a unit's quartermaster could easily disburse supplies. He'd noted the gun platforms, covered in canvas against the damp and transported on flatbed caissons, and near them, the kegs and crates of black powder. Harmless until it was poured down the barrel of a canon or a musket. Loose gunpowder burned, but didn't explode; to make the barrels explode you'd have to toss them into a bonfire or insert a length of fuse cord into the barrel and light it.

Or have a Fire Master set it off.

The explosion filled the predawn darkness. It deafened him and made the ground shake. Flaming debris fountained into the sky, starting small fires everywhere it landed.

Learie barely had enough warning to duck down behind the ridge, and what warned him wasn't anything he saw or heard.

It was the sense that someone was using magic. Fire Magic.

As the explosion's echoes began to die, he cautiously raised his head. There! In the stand of cottonwood off to his left. Movement. A lone rider.

He scrambled down the slope of the ridge to where he'd left his mount. Storm was a seasoned veteran of the Peninsula; he'd been startled by the sudden noise, but he hadn't bolted. Learie flung himself into the saddle and touched his spurs to Storm's flanks. The gelding sprang forward as if his tail were on fire, and Learie settled to the chase.

The Fire Master had a head start, but he was riding a beast little better than a pony, one of the half-starved scrubs the peasants (the *rich* peasants) rode, unsuitable as remounts even when the cavalry units were desperate. And Storm was a big Irish Thoroughbred, with power and speed in every line of him.

The wind whipped away the screams and shouts from the burning camp. In the brightening day, Learie had eyes for only one thing: the rider fleeing before him. The Fire Master was dressed in rough peasant clothing, a battered slouch hat pulled low over his face. He rode bareback, over grass gray with hoarfrost, hugging his pony's ribs with his knees. As the thunder of Storm's hoofbeats grew louder, the other rider glanced back once. Learie got a quick glimpse of a pale face and shadowed eyes before the rider turned his attention to coaxing the pony to greater speed.

It was a doomed attempt.

But just as Storm's nose drew level with the pony's flank, the grass beneath his hooves burst into flame.

Learie had been expecting something of the sort. The moment he felt the air spark with magic, he gathered Storm into a jump. The gelding, used to the obstacles of the hunting field, obediently gathered himself and sailed into the air, landing delicately on the unburned turf beyond. Three more strides and he drew level with the pony. Laurie raised himself in his stirrups, and, kicking them free, launched himself at the other rider.

They rolled over and over in the tall grass. The slouch hat went sailing.

The first thing Learie noticed was the cascade of black hair that came tumbling free.

The second thing was that the Fire Master—a woman!—was attempting to knife him in the ribs.

"Here now!" he said indignantly.

"French pig!" the woman spat. "Let me go!"

"French!" Learie exclaimed. "Do I look French to you?" By now he was sitting on her, her wrists clasped in both hands. She hadn't let go of the knife.

"You look like a dog of a pig!" she said. "And I will make you regret the day your mother bore you!"

"Just the one?" he asked lightly. Now that he could get a good look at her, he couldn't imagine how he'd ever mistaken her for a man—or a peasant. Tumbled curls of shining black hair framed an oval face with clear pale skin. Her eyes were black as well, flashing with fury as she attempted to win her freedom. Skin to skin, he could feel the pulse of her Fire Magic like a separate heartbeat. "Look. You can't just go around raising Fire like that. What if you kill someone?"

She stared at him in astonishment.

"I mean—you're Spanish, aren't you? And of course you hate the French. Who doesn't? But didn't your teachers ever tell you, well, the rules?"

"Rules," she said, her voice ugly. "You are English. You play at war as if it is a game. Where were your rules when the French came to Madrid? They came to us as friends, and then named themselves our conquerors! We fought—and they turned the city into an abattoir. The streets ran red with blood as they burned and looted. Nowhere was safe from them. Not even the convents. It was then I understood that the Blessed Santiago had chosen me as his instrument of retribution."

"You were a nun?" Learie asked. She glared at him in disgust. *I guess not.* He wracked his brain to make sense of what she'd said. Madrid had rebelled in the spring of 1808, and Murat had executed hundreds of citizens in bloody reprisal. She looked to be within a few years of his own age. She would have been fourteen or fifteen that year, an age at which many Adepts first gained the use of their gift. But . . .

"Where was your father?" he asked.

"He is English. He had to leave when the French came, but my mother was too sick to travel. He would have taken me, but who would care for her? He left us in the convent, until he returned. But he did not return," she said.

He must have tried to, Learie thought unhappily. But the girl's father—whoever he'd been—might not have reached England at all. Bonaparte controlled the seas, and blockading the ports had been his first step to conquering Spain. The ship might have been sunk. Or her father might never have boarded it. "But, now, look. He must have told you something about your magic. He would have known you were going to have an Elemental Gift when you were born . . ."

"It is not witchcraft!" she cried, renewing her struggles. "It is a gift from God!"

"Well, of course it is—I mean, blast it, no! It's an affinity. A lot of people have them. Mine's Air. And there are Water Masters, and Earth Masters, and—"

"No!" she said. "It is from Santiago, to avenge my mother! Her daughter is dead—but *La Antorcha* will chastise them with tongues of flame!"

La Antorcha. The Torch. This was getting worse and worse; he'd heard that name several times this year—it was the name of the leader of one of the *guerillero* bands. "Oh, please," he said. "Don't tell me you have a troop of crazy Sp—"

Behind him, he heard the unmistakable sound of a pistol's cock.

"If it please you, *señor*, kindly release *La Maestra*," a voice said.

I am not having fun, Learie thought. *How do I know this? Because I have had fun, and this is not it.*

There were six of them. They'd tied his hands behind him and put him on *La Antorcha*'s scrub. She'd taken Storm. The gelding had looked a bit confused at seeing his master riding another animal, but accepted his new rider docilely enough.

"A fine animal," she had said as she swung into the saddle. "I will keep him, as compensation for the trouble you have caused me."

"Oh," Learie had answered, "please. Be my guest."

He had no doubt of his ability to escape at need—and to call Storm to him when he did. That wasn't the problem. The real problem was, *he didn't know what to do.*

The *guerillero* camp was several hours' ride west, a collection of ragged huts crammed into a fissure on the hillside. It was at least a semi-permanent location, judging from the goats and chickens wandering disconso-

lately about. They'd taken his boots, tied his ankles, and
tossed him into the back of one of the huts. Judging from
the smell, it doubled as a goat pen.

Learie leaned his head back against the wall—it
creaked alarmingly—and sighed. He wasn't sure what
he'd been thinking he was going to do. He'd thought the
Fire Mage was a man, of course, but what had he intended
to do when he caught up with him? Lecture him on the
Elemental Mage Code of Ethics? Would that really work
on somebody who was blowing up Frenchmen? *God in
Heaven, Learie. You really don't have a single brain in
your pretty head, do you?* he thought wearily.

His report for General Wellesley was an urgent matter. The General needed to know where the French were
and what they were doing. But the matter of the rogue
mage needed dealing with as well.

If I could just talk to her, Learie thought wistfully. *If I
could just explain. Really explain.*

His lips pursed in a soundless whistle, and he drew all
his experience of Air Magery around himself. Not to
force. Not to compel—neither the Elementals he summoned nor the target of his spell. Just to ask. To hope.
He was afraid he was already half in love with *La Antorcha*, and he could not bear the thought of letting her step
farther along this dark path to madness and death.

Nor could he bear the thought that a Huntsman
might come to do what he knew he could not bear to.

He sat, staring at nothing, as the light that shone
through the gaps in the walls slowly faded into dusk.

"I have brought you food, though I don't see why I
should bother." *La Antorcha* ducked into the hut, carrying a wooden bowl and a wineskin.

"It's because you are good and kind," Learie said.

"I am a fool to waste food on an English heretic who has given his soul to the Devil," she said harshly. She knelt down beside him and aimed the nozzle of the wineskin at him. He opened his mouth, and was rewarded with a thin stream of sour wine.

"No, look," he said after she lowered it. "That's where you're wrong. Common misconception—I mean, it would be if anybody who wasn't one of us knew about it—but you see, the affinity is something you're just *born* with. Like blue eyes. Or black hair."

"I do not believe you," she said. He opened his mouth to argue further. She tried to close it with a spoonful of soup.

"Look," he said desperately, twisting his neck to evade the spoon. "This is all very well and good—God, Satan, St. James, angels, great stuff all of it—but the part you're missing is that if you keep on using your magic this way, *you will die.*"

"Who will kill me, English? You?" she asked scornfully. "You are bound like the sheep for the slaughter."

"No one will kill you," he said, suddenly weary beyond measure. "Your father should have told you. Mine did. There are rules about how you use your gifts. Not like laws and local custom and all that. Rules like if you walk of the edge of a cliff, you'll fall, and if you hold your head under water long enough, you'll drown. See? You can't fight them. You can't argue with them. They just *are*. There are three things you cannot do. You can't use your power for selfish advantage, you can't use it to do harm to others, and you can't use it to kill."

"Huh," *La Antorcha* said. "Then what good is it?"

"That's the point," Learie said, giddy with exhaustion

and the sense he simply wasn't making her understand. "It *is* good. It's *for* good. It's for—when you summon the creatures of your element, and see them for the first time, and know they will always come—as friends, as allies—and you see how beautiful . . ." His throat tightened, and he stopped. "That's what it's for. For doing good. The rest . . . it's perversion. At best, your magic will leave you forever. You'll remember the beauty, but you'll never touch it again. At worst, you'll find yourself twisted by it. You'll hurt everyone you love. You'll destroy everything you care about. You'll beg to turn back time—or die—but you won't. Not until you don't even care." He closed his eyes and let his head drop to his chest. "Then you'll die. And nobody will mourn you. All they'll feel is relief."

"Pretty words," *La Antorcha* said, but for the first time she sounded uncertain. "Why should I listen to you?"

"Did you miss the part where I said I was an Air Master? Forgive me. We haven't been properly introduced. Allow me to present to you Captain Sir Beverly St. John St. Andrew Laoghaire Darwen of the 11th Hussar Regiment, with Mastery of the Element of Air, with which, therefore, I share a certain identity. Meaning I am a useless clown and agreeable buffoon, fickle in my affections, changeable in my emotions, untrustworthy in my passions, but always, *always* entertaining."

He felt the touch of a small, cool hand smoothing back his hair. "I think you are too hard on yourself, English," *La Antorcha* said. Then she was gone.

He lay there without moving for a very long time, then finally turned his attention to the lengthy, but not particularly difficult, process of unknotting his bonds. When he was done, he scooped the litter on the floor of the hut into some semblance of a bed and curled up on it.

"Then you'll die. And nobody will mourn you."

You didn't need to misuse your gifts for that.

You just had to be born to the wrong Element.

Morning came too early—as it always did when he was sleeping rough. Awakened by the gleam of sunlight through the walls, he rolled over, groaned, rubbed his hand over his stubbled jaw, and commenced the laborious process of convincing himself that he really did want to get up. At last, upright, and with most of the kinks worked out of his muscles, he emerged cautiously from his accommodation.

The little settlement was utterly still. Even the chickens were asleep, fluffed grayish balls of feathers huddled in doorways. The Spanish peasant might be up with the sun, but the Spanish *guerrillero* tended to get up with the moon.

He found his boots with his saddle and tack (though his saddlebags, and the supplies they'd contained, were absent). He sat down on the saddle to pull on the boots, then shrugged off his cloak to muffle the rings and buckles of his saddle and bridle. He lifted them carefully, and went looking for Storm.

The gelding was with the *guerilleros'* ponies in the pocket pasture at the end of the crack in the cliff face. There was grass, and someone had determinedly lugged a wooden horse trough here from some (undoubtedly burned-out) village or farm. He wondered how many buckets of water it took to fill it, and where they had been brought from. Storm raised his head when Learie arrived, ears flicking interestedly, and minced toward him, bright-eyed.

"Sorry, old fellow," Learie said. "It's short rations for both of us until we reach home and hearth." He'd flung the saddle over Storm's back and was tightening the girth when he realized he wasn't alone.

La Antorcha stood near the cliff wall, her forearms braced on the back of one of the ponies, watching him. "You'll need a guide," she said when she knew he'd seen her. "To get out of these mountains—"

"Without getting lost?" he asked.

"'Alive,' I had been going to say," she answered.

Learie snorted wordlessly and turned to coaxing Storm to accept the bit.

"I thought you were going to keep him," he said, when they'd ridden a little way down the narrow twisting trail that led back to the plain.

"I could not feed him," she answered, "and he would die. It is the way of English things, I understand."

"Not all of them," he answered. "Some English things can flourish in the most surprising places."

"We shall see, won't we?" *La Antorcha* said.

They rode in silence, first single file, then side by side, until they reached the plains and the road to the south was in sight.

"Now you will go, and you will fight," she said, reining in.

"I will go, and a great many people will fight, I think," he answered. "And perhaps, by our skill and the grace of God, we will win."

"And Spain will be free," she said. "Someday."

"I hope so," Learie said. "And what of *La Antorcha*?"

"There is fighting for *La Antorcha* to do as well," she answered. "And perhaps, when it is done, we will meet once again. But until that day, I will carry your words in my heart. I do not wish to become someone who must die unmourned."

"That can never be," Learie said huskily. "I swear it."

"Then go with God, English," she said. "And we will meet again."

"Burn brightly, *La Antorcha*," he answered. He touched his heels to Storm's sides and put the gelding into a trot.

South.

Into the fire.

Stones and Feathers
Elizabeth A. Vaughan

"Last night, you say?" Lieutenant-General Loftus asked, standing at the window staring at the Tower Green where the preparations for the ceremony had begun.

Colonel Doyle knew that his superior was probably watching some of the men clearing the area of gawking visitors, picking up the worst of the trash and debris, and chasing the damned ravens off. "In his sleep, sir." Doyle said quietly. "Heart, I'm told."

"Damned inconvenient." Loftus said.

"Sir," Doyle hesitated, weighing his superior's turn of phrase. "Because he died in office," he said, tentatively agreeing.

"That too, that too, of course, the poor bastard. Hard for the family to lose the appointment and the right to sell it. Two hundred and fifty guineas lost, true enough. Inconvenient all around." Loftus growled.

Silence was Doyle's safest option, as the Lieutenant of the Tower of London was about to launch himself into—

"Dreadful business, having the Ravenmaster of the Tower die. Damned birds are trial enough, without having to assign a new caretaker." Loftus huffed. "One they may or may not take a piece out of." Loftus stepped away from the window. "On top of everything else I've to deal with—"

Doyle made a quiet but supportive sound, but the Lieutenant-General was just getting started.

"Our new Constable of the Tower, Field Marshall Arthur, Duke of Wellington, just taken office and what's he want? 'Sweeping changes,' he says." Loftus snorted. "Never you mind the dignity of the office, never you mind the traditions over hundreds of years. 'No more commissions bought and sold,' says the Iron Duke. 'From this time forward none but deserving, gallant, and meritorious discharged sergeants of the Army shall be appointed Yeomen Warders of the Tower,' so he says."

"Commands," murmured Doyle.

"Sergeants," Loftus sputtered. "Noncommissioned officers," he continued. "What is the world coming to?" he asked. "Today, in the year of Our Lord eighteen hundred and twenty-six, marks the end of a great and noble tradition. Mark my words, Doyle."

"I will, sir," Doyle offered his assurance. "The ceremony is almost upon us, sir. I believe your aide has laid out your uniform."

"Yes, yes," Loftus finally left the window. "We'll show them a swearing-in ceremony the likes of which they haven't seen, by God."

He continued muttering to himself as he turned to the door.

"And sir," Doyle called after. "About the new Ravenmaster . . ."

"The Duke wants sweeping changes," Loftus growled. "Well then, the onerous task will fall on him. Our new Constable of the Tower can designate his replacement." Loftus stopped, and a smile of satisfaction crossed his face, to be replaced by a very innocent expression. "I'll inform him of the vacancy after we swear in this 'deserving, gallant, and meritorious sergeant.' What's his name again?"

"Thomas Davies."

Tom Davies knelt in the water closet, and heaved his guts out yet again. Not that there was anything to rid himself of, except this horrible upset in his tum.

"What are ya thinking, lad?" his brother's voice rang in his head. *"An Earth Master in London? You're daft, ya git."*

Tom drew a deep breath, risked a sip of water, and spat into the basin. He'd not care to admit it in his presence, but his brother was right.

Oh, he'd expected to be ill. Any city did that to him, to all his family. Earth magic ran strong in their blood, on both sides. Couldn't be helped then, in the cities, with the land paved over, and the filth running through sewers underneath. His ma had sent stomach powders, and he reached for them, determined to settle his gut before the ceremony.

"Some peppermint, and other herbs," Ma had said, her worried eyes saying much more. *"Are you sure there is no other way, Tom?"*

"The place calls to me, Ma," he'd tucked the packet into his kit. *"I must answer."*

He mixed up the remedy with shaking hands, and drank it all down quick, hoping for the best.

He'd taken the Thames as far up as he could, not that the trip was all that easier, what with all that water underneath. But it hadn't been bad till he stepped out on the wharfs. He'd been hit with a wave of weariness, a wrongness that made him sick in mind and spirit.

And gut.

He'd shielded to a fare-thee-well, centering himself in the earth, and drawing as much strength as he could. But the foulness seemed to pierce his shields as easily as a needle through cloth.

Hadn't helped that the ravens were flapping around as he'd walked in, cawing to one another, setting up a stew. Tom shuddered at the memory of the big, black birds, with their sharp beaks as long as a man's hand, and glittering eyes. He'd seen too many of those harbingers of death flapping among the corpses on the battlefields.

His stomach heaved. Tom tried to think of something else.

At least he had a bit of privacy. He'd been given quarters, small and spare. Fair enough, as he was the new man. He'd few needs beyond a place to sleep and a sturdy chair to sit in. A water closet all his own had been a pleasant surprise.

At least he could see to his needs alone, with no hostile eyes on him. The Warders—no, the other Warders—had been less than welcoming. Tom hoped the sounds of his misery had not passed through the stone walls, but no doubt they'd put it down to weakness or nerves. No worse day for a Warder, or so he'd been told, that the day of your oath-taking. Being tested on the history of the Tower, and reciting the oath, all three hundred words and more, before all the Yeoman Warders and the Iron Duke himself; well, that would be enough to put a man off, eh?

He burped, and his stomach seemed eased a bit, but Tom stayed still and quiet. He wasn't fooled. He'd wait to see if it had truly settled before he'd move.

Not that the history was a problem. Tom always loved

the stories of the Tower, loved the past buried deep within its stones. He didn't fear the questioning.

But the oath, now. He closed his eyes, reciting the words he'd learned months ago.

"I, Thomas Davies, do swear to serve the high and Mighty Prince George IV by the grace of God, King of the United Kingdom of Great Britain, Ireland, Defender of the Faith and Crown Prince of Hanover, his heirs & successors lawful and rightful unto, that is, to be a Yeoman Warder of the Tower of London. In all things touching his honor and safety I shall neither myself do, or procure to be done—"

The rest of the words skittered off, slipping from his memory like fish through a net.

Bloody hell.

"Survive the war, and the bloody flux, only to waste away in the cities?" his da had demanded. *"What are you thinking?"*

There was truth in his family's words, a truth that he acknowledged in his heart. After serving his King, he'd earned the right to return to Wight, settle down to the land, using his gifts for the benefit of the earth, and the earth returning his gifts a hundredfold. So it had been in his family since his grandfather's time.

But the call was too strong, and not to be denied.

He'd never have had the wherewithal to buy a commission at the Tower. The news that the Duke was seeking candidates had seemed miraculous, and he'd applied, never thinking that he'd—

Tom shifted slightly, to look out into his room beyond. Where his Yeoman Warder uniform awaited, with its scarlet cloth, stiff with its gold embroidery, broken only by the line of his bar of medals. Tunic, breeches and stockings all laid out for him, and his black Tudor bonnet on his pillow, his short sword beside it.

His heart rose at the sight, even as his stomach really seemed to settle.

He'd take this slow. Slow and steady, like the land and the flow of the seasons. Slow and steady, like the heartbeat of this bit of land and stones. There was a need here, he could feel it. A desperate desire for healing. But what that meant, the details of it, eluded him. The element of earth did not look forward, it concentrated in the present and the past. He could do this. He had to do this.

Which meant getting off this floor and being about it.

A few hours later, he wasn't so certain.

For all the hostility in the Warders, they'd done right by him for the ceremony. They formed three sides of a square on the Green, regal in their scarlet uniforms, swords at their sides. Tom had been marched in to the center, on display to all as the newest Yeoman Warder.

The Duke of Wellington, Constable of the Tower, had begun his remarks. "As a pillar of the centuries, this Tower, this fortress, this palace and prison reigns supreme over all others in the civilized world."

Tom had hoped that the grass of the Green would help him, standing on open, healthy ground. He'd taken his position with hope and sought to center himself. He shifted his stance, and felt the earth below support his body, reaching for the strength to be found there.

But for all he'd strived to shield, for all the strength he'd taken, the sickness rose within him, blinding him with pain.

"Three hundred years older than the Doge's Palace in Venice, or the Kremlin in Moscow. The Vatican is a child in comparison. Older than the Louvre, than the Palace of Versailles, this mighty sentinel has stood, guarding the Thames, guarding our country, since the time of William the Conqueror and Julius Caesar."

Tom drew a slow breath, trying to get his heaving guts to settle. He'd been a fool to apply, a fool to accept. Da was right. He was a daft git.

"For both of those warriors had a military eye, and they . chose their site well, for the strength of its position, protecting sea and land. As King has succeeded King, each has built on the stones, adding stout walls and towers, digging a deep and wide moat–" At this the Duke paused and sniffed. No wonder, given the filth of that water.

Sweat trickled down Tom's neck and gathered on his forehead. He swallowed hard, fighting the rising nausea. It didn't help that one of the ravens had fluttered onto the green, walking around like it owned the place, quorking to itself.

"We must honor this noble Tower," The Duke boomed. "We must set it right, for the glory of—"

A bead of sweat made it into Tom's eyes, setting them stinging. He blinked, trying to clear his vision. The raven paused in front of him, between him and the dignitaries, cocking its head, and studying him with a beady eye. Then it pecked the ground, and for an instant, seemed to peck at a corpse, feeding off the fallen.

Feeding off a corpse—

It hit Tom then, a flash of insight, and it took all his training not to react physically.

He was a proper idiot, he was.

He'd been feeding off a corpse himself, pulling strength from a sickened earth. What had he been thinking, that he'd—

"Change must occur," the Duke said. "But only with an eye toward tradition, and respect for the past. In that way, this mighty fortress will remain, a—"

Tom dropped his shields. All of them, casting them aside. Risky, truth be told, if there were any about with magical abilities and a wish to do him harm. He'd sensed no others, but it didn't matter. Needs must, when the devil drives.

He still felt sick, but now he could see, could feel that it came from without, not from within. The pull was still there, strong, like a fading heartbeat in the land, crying out for something, a need so strong it wrapped itself around him, like a pleading child.

"Soon," he promised.

"For this Tower stands at the center of our hearts and—"

Not much time left. But Tom was a Master of his element; he didn't need much. He raised his shields again, using only his own resources, built them high and just thick enough to—

The nausea abated, and his fever faded with it.

The raven cawed, flapping its wings, the one clipped to prevent flight. He'd forgotten that.

His own strength returned, and with it some sanity as well. Yes, there were hostile looks from his fellow Warders, but there was neutrality there as well, even some support in a few faces. The sun was bright, the sky blue, and his hope soared.

He couldn't do this long, couldn't maintain his shields like this for any real length of time, but for now—

"Sergeant Thomas Davies, stand forth and be sworn," the Constable called.

Tom drew a deep breath, and obeyed.

*   *   *

Three hundred and forty-four words later, Thomas Davies was a Yeoman Warder.

He smiled with relief and pleasure as the Duke of Wellington shook his hand, and offered his congratulations. But this next part, this was for the Warders alone.

The Lieutenant-General ordered him to fall in, and marched the lot of them to the Yeoman Warder's Social Club. There, on a central table, sat the traditional pewter punchbowl, filled to the brim, glasses at the ready.

The Warders milled about, relaxing, offering their hands and welcoming him. Some more welcoming than others, but that was fine. Colonel Doyle's was one of the welcoming ones, with a hearty handshake and a genuine smile.

Tom was thankful that the ordeal was over, that his shields were holding. He'd time enough, to earn their trust and respect.

The bartender was filling glasses, handing them around. Tom took his with pleasure.

The Lieutenant-General cleared his throat and the room went silent. "In our tradition, I'd ask you all to raise your glass to the health of Thomas Davies, Yeoman Warder," he lifted his own toward Tom.

All the glasses were raised. Tom blushed with the pleasure of it.

"Mind you that it's at your expense," Colonel Doyle whispered.

Tom laughed ruefully, and nodded. He'd already known he'd be handed the bill.

Loftus hesitated for a moment, then scowled at his glass. "Change may be here, and more coming, but in this one thing, there shall be no change. We'll preserve this, at the very least." He raised his glass to Tom again. "May you never die a Yeoman Warder," he boomed.

"Here, here," came the supporting cries, and glasses were once again drained in his honor.

"My humble thanks," was all Tom could manage, but it was enough. Now, the Warders could relax, talking, re-filling their glasses. Tom fully expected pats on the back, and offers of stories of their experiences.

But even beyond the camaraderie that was filling the room, here, in the Tower of London . . . the stones within were speaking to him. The past, the present deep within the foundations of this place, they called. Muted, by the shields, but still there, in the back of his head.

A sense of satisfaction spread through him.

"Congratulations, young Davies," the Lieutenant-General was before him, smiling. "A Yeoman Warder, and a promotion your first day," the man's smile grew teeth. "By order of the Constable of the Tower himself."

"Promotion?" Tom asked.

"Aye." The Lieutenant-General slapped a falconer's thick leather glove against his chest. "You're the new Ravenmaster."

Fire's Children
Elisabeth Waters

"Albert! Luke! Go light the altar candles!" The crucifer sounded nervous, which wasn't surprising because the service was due to start in ten minutes and the Rector, Father Pearce, wasn't here yet.

Luke and I each grabbed a candle lighter/snuffer, and Luke lit the wicks on both of them. All the other acolytes knew I wasn't very good with fire. This was embarrassing for two reasons: My father and my twin were both Fire Magicians and couldn't understand why I had problems with things they could do easily; and El, my twin, was a much better acolyte than I was and everyone knew it. Unfortunately, our mother's return from Switzerland had meant the end of El's career as an acolyte.

I made sure that I was on the Gospel side of the altar, because the Epistle candle had to be lit first. The Gospel candle is never supposed to burn alone. Luke lit his candle, and I tried to light mine. Unfortunately, the Altar Guild had put in new candles since last week, and I couldn't see the top of the candle. For all I knew the wick could have been buried in the wax, which would make it almost impossible to light. Out of the corner of my eye I could see Luke trying to decide whether to come help me. Before he could move, however, a ball of light exploded at the top of the candle. I quickly pulled the lighter away before its entire wick melted and slid the wick back into the tube to extinguish it. The light subsided to a normal candle flame as Luke and I turned to go back to the sacristy. I took a brief look to my right as we went and saw El smirking at me from the front pew. Normally I would have found that annoying, but first, she *had* helped me, and second, it was the happiest I had seen her look in two weeks. As I entered the sacristy, where Father Pearce was hastily vesting, the crucifer handed Luke and me our torches before picking up the processional cross. I hoped that nobody else had noticed El using her magic. I knew Mother hadn't noticed; she didn't believe in magic, and she didn't really know either of us.

Mother was consumptive, so Father, who was a doctor, sent her to Switzerland to be cured when El and I were three. Between the soot in the air from burning coal and the frequent fog, London was no place for anyone with bad lungs. The mountain air in Switzerland had done wonders for Mother, even if her recovery had taken nine years. She remembered, however, that she had given birth to twins, but not twin *boys*—something El and I had pretty much forgotten. At the moment, she was barely speaking to Father. And El was barely speaking to anybody.

El and I understood what Father had done. Between his medical practice and his duties as a Fire Adept with the White Lodge, he didn't have patience for the fuss of raising a girl. Actually, he didn't have much patience at all. So when he was left with no wife and two small children, he raised us alike—as twin boys. He shortened Eleanora to El and told anyone who asked that it was short for Elihu (which actually *is* a family name). El and I went to the same schools and learned the same things, though she was much better at mathematics, which she loved and I hated. Mother said that mathematics were unladylike, which was one of the *nicer* things she had said to El since her return—as if any of this was El's fault. I really missed having El as a fellow acolyte. She was so much better at it than I was, and she was good at covering up my deficiencies.

Now El sat stiffly next to Mother and Father in a pew at Christ Church. She was wearing a pale pink dress with a matching bonnet to hide her short hair. I didn't have to see her to know that she was miserable. I stood next to the last pew in the nave, resting the base of my torch on the floor and carefully mirroring Luke's position. The crucifer stood just ahead of us. When the introit ended and the opening hymn began, the crucifer would lift the cross, and we would raise our torches and process down the aisle, followed by Father Pearce, who stood behind us. From here I could see that the altar candles were now different heights. It looked as if about four inches of the Gospel candle had burned when El lit it. Ooops.

The introit, being sung *a capella* by the usual tenor soloist, seemed to me to get longer each week. I wondered whether he was singing to glorify God or just to show off. Maybe it was both.

While I was waiting for him to finish, I looked through a blur caused by the heated air just above my candle's flame and wondered what was wrong with me. El could light candles with her magic, even when seated in the congregation unwillingly pretending to be a young lady, while I had trouble lighting even a previously burned candle from the flame on the end of the candle lighter. If there was such a thing as an anti-Fire Magician, I seemed to be one.

After the reading of the Gospel, Luke and I took the torches back to the sacristy and extinguished them. We wouldn't need them again until the recessional, when all we had to do was carry them and follow the crucifer. The middle of the communion service was my favorite part; I had no problems with the collection plate, the bread, the wine, or the water. Especially the water; I like water.

In London, the water is at least more wholesome than the air—usually. We've had epidemics of cholera, and Father often sees dysentery among his charity patients. He volunteers at a hospital for the poor, and he frequently takes El and me along to assist. Again, it's something she's better at than I am.

But I enjoy handling the water during the service. It feels alive to me in a way that fire does not. The other acolytes help me with fire, but they all seem happy to let me do the ablutions: a carefully choreographed routine in which I pour water from a cruet over Father Pearce's fingers while holding a small silver bowl beneath them, and then turn slightly so that he can take the towel draped over my left forearm to dry his hands. This ritual washing of the hands is purely symbolic; if his hands were dirty, this would not clean them. But before he consecrates the bread and wine so that they become the body and blood of Christ, his hands have to be symbolically clean as well. We finished the ablutions, Father Pearce and I bowed to each other, and I put the bowl, towel, and cruet back on the shelf at the side.

Our family stayed after the service to meet with Father Pearce. It was horrible, even though nobody was angry with me. Father was angry enough for everyone in the room to feel it, and Mother was furious as well. And I hate it when people around me are angry. I sat in a chair, shaking, and kept my mouth shut.

Father Pearce wasn't angry with El, either, but he was *very* upset to learn that she was a girl. Apparently there's a rule in the Church of England that says girls can't be acolytes. He told her she could join the Altar Guild when she was older, but I could tell she did not find that to be the consolation he obviously intended. Still, she thanked him politely, and she pointed out that the Bishop couldn't blame him; there was no way he could have known she wasn't a boy. Christ Church didn't even have our baptismal records; we had been baptized at the estate of our mother's family, out in the country, so the records were in the parish church there.

He then tried to mediate between our raging parents, with limited success. Mother was determined to leave Father—and to take El with her. It was finally agreed that she and El would visit her family in the country. Father allowed this on the grounds that it would be better for her lungs, and that's what he could tell anyone who had the impertinence to ask why his wife had left him so soon after her return. As for Mother's argument that this would give Eleanora a place to learn to be a proper young lady, Father wasn't enthusiastic about losing his best pupil and assistant, but he couldn't say *that* in front of Mother, who would have thought him insane—and she already thought that raising her daughter as a boy was both crazy and cruel.

From the look on El's face as Mother promised her lots of pretty dresses and lessons in music, dancing, and embroidery, it looked as if the cruelty was coming from Mother. El had no more interest in those things than I did.

El hugged me hard, and I hugged her back. Being separated from El was inconceivable; we hadn't been apart from each other since we were born.

Mother practically dragged El from the room before we could say a proper goodbye—although I felt as if I were choking and probably couldn't have said anything anyway. I felt as if half of my soul was going with them. Maybe it was.

Father scowled after them. "El will be wasted in the country; she's been doing good work in my practice, and she shows the potential to become an Adept. Why did the one with real talent have to be the girl? The White Lodge doesn't take women!"

I was astonished to hear him mention the Lodge in front of an outsider, but Father Pearce's reply surprised me even more. "You'll have to find a teacher for her wherever she ends up. She needs to learn more control; she melted several inches of one of the altar candles this morning."

Father looked at me, and I said miserably, "I couldn't light it; I think the wick had been covered by melted wax, but it was too tall for me to see. El lit it for me."

Father glared. "You do have *some* magic; I can feel it in you. You should certainly be able to light a candle with a lit taper; boys with *no* magic manage that!" He sighed. "I'll step up your lessons; now that I have only one of you to teach, I can concentrate more on you."

This made me feel the way El had looked when mother was promising her embroidery. I didn't seem to be able to learn *anything* from Father. While El was there, it hadn't been as noticeable, but if he was concentrating on just me . . . I repressed a shudder. Father and Father Pearce exchanged a few more comments that I didn't hear, and then we went home.

The next few weeks were very strange. I spent hours with Father in his workroom, trying to light a candle: a process that left him scowling and made me very thankful that it was Lent and the church had only the two altar candles to light. I wasn't looking forward to Easter, when there would be dozens of them.

I accompanied Father to his surgery and to the hospital. Although I don't have El's talent, I was moderately useful as an extra pair of hands.

But not only did I miss my twin, I was starting to fear that I was losing my mind. Whenever I went out alone, I saw things. Creatures. I'm not talking about Elementals like salamanders; I'd seen them as long as I could remember. I think they lived in the fire in our nursery. But now I saw tiny naked women—with long hair covering at least part of their bodies—splashing in the pond in the garden near our house or perched at the top of every rain barrel I passed on the way to school. I watched the boys with me carefully, and I could tell that none of *them* could see the creatures. And when we all went down to the river one afternoon, the women were there too, but this time they had seaweed draped around their bodies. They called to me: "young magician"—and I was thankful that none of the other boys heard *that*. I really hoped it was just that I was reaching the age when boys started thinking about naked women, because if those creatures were *real* . . .

*   *   *

Lent came to an end, school was out, and I was busy at church with the various services for Holy Week. Father was busy with his medical practice; there was a sudden increase in dysentery in London.

Although I was serving as an acolyte on Easter Sunday, I wasn't one of the ones who had to deal with all of the candles. On Easter everyone in the parish came to church, including the "Easter Lilies" (the people who come only at Christmas and Easter), so we had extra acolytes and extra Altar Guild ladies.

The only thing I had to handle for the Easter communion was water, so I was feeling pretty relaxed—until I picked up the water for the ablutions. It felt as if it were twitching in my hands, despite being contained in a glass cruet that was *not* moving, and it looked to me as if it were full of red flecks. I must have been seeing things, because not even the most inexperienced new Altar Guild member would put out something that really looked like that. But a new lady might not know to boil and filter the water . . .

Father Pearce's hands were clean; the ablutions couldn't make them physically cleaner. But pouring *this* water over his fingers could make them spiritually clean and physically dirty, right before he distributed consecrated—and contaminated—bread to everyone in the parish. It would be a nightmare, an epidemic. I could *not* let that happen.

Father's lessons had been all about pulling power through me and pushing it out to light the candle. I found myself doing the same thing now, except that instead of trying to call up fire, I pushed power through the cruet, visualizing pure, uncontaminated water. I felt dizzy, the stopper jiggled in the top of the cruet, and the crucifer hissed, "Don't just stand there!" I blinked and looked again at the cruet. The water looked clear, and it felt pure. I quickly removed the stopper, gathered up the bowl and the towel, and crossed to Father Pearce to do the ablutions. He looked at me oddly, but I thought it was just that I had been slow about it. The rest of the service was normal.

After the service I was absolutely starving. I had never been so hungry in my life. Father and I had been invited to the house of some friends of his for Easter dinner, and I tried very hard to behave properly, despite my desire to eat everything in sight. I obviously didn't quite succeed, because the man sitting next to me made a joke about growing boys with hollow legs. But then he had one of the footmen give me second helpings, so I guess he did just think I was a growing boy. Still, it's a good thing that Easter dinner is a feast.

That night I dreamed of those little naked women again. I was sitting next to the pond in the garden, with my pajama legs rolled up and my feet in the water, and they were frolicking around me like a pack of puppies, excited because their human had returned. I could hear their voices still in my head: "magician, Water Master . . ."

I woke suddenly, remembering something Father had said when he first started teaching us. There were four elements; he had mentioned that briefly before concentrating exclusively on Fire. The other three were Earth, Air, and Water, *which was Fire's opposite!* So an anti-Fire Magician would be . . . a Water Magician. If I were a Water Magician, no Fire Magician could teach me properly. That might be why I couldn't learn anything from Father!

It was just dawn, and nobody was around to stop me. I dressed quickly, slipped quietly out of the house, and almost ran to the pond in the garden. I knelt next to it and cautiously dipped one hand into the water while trying to think friendly thoughts. The water rippled as the creatures swam to me. "Hullo," I said tentatively. "Can you answer me something? Am I a Water Magician?"

The water in the pond positively churned as the creatures started rolling about, hooting with laughter. "Answer me!" I snapped.

The laughter stopped instantly, and every face turned toward me. "Yes, Master," they chorused.

Ooops. Did I just command *them?* I forced a smile. "Very well. You can go back to laughing at me now, if you wish." There were a lot of smiles, along with just a few giggles, as most of the creatures vanished into the water.

I need to talk to somebody. Not Father, though. Maybe Father Pearce? That reminded me about the water at church. Somebody should do something about that. Actually somebody should have done something about that yesterday—or even earlier. I headed for the church.

The doors were unlocked, and Father Pearce was leading Morning Prayer. I hadn't realized I'd spent that much time at the pond. I knelt in a pew at the back of the nave, lost in my own thoughts. *I am a Water Magician.* I wasn't a miserable failure who couldn't learn even the simplest things; I had been trying to learn to master the *wrong element.* I was different from Father and El. Much as I loved them, I wasn't like them. And it would be a waste of the gift God had given me to try to be.

I did not want to be a disappointment to Father—

although I suspected that was unavoidable—but I realized that I didn't want to be like him either. For all the love and respect I had for him, it had not escaped my notice that he was quick-tempered (probably a Fire trait, because El was too) and arrogant, and those were not things I admired or wanted to see in myself. I didn't want to grow up to be the man Father was. *I need a different teacher.*

The small congregation had left, and Father Pearce stood next to my pew. "Albert? Is something wrong?"

"The water," I blurted out. My thoughts were still too chaotic to be put into coherent sentences. I felt as if my world had been turned upside down and backwards. In a way, I guess it had. "Yesterday. The water in the cruet was bad."

Father Pearce nodded. "Yes, it was," he said. "I went to the well last evening and cleaned it."

"Are you—?"

"I'm a Water Adept," he said quietly. He smiled. "I've been wondering how long it would take you to come to me."

I took a deep breath. "Can you teach me?" I asked.

He nodded. "Yes, Albert; I can. I'll be happy to teach you."

"And I'll be happy to learn from you." I knew that Father Pearce could teach me what I wanted to learn: not just how to use Water Magic, but also how to grow up to be the man I wanted to be.

For the Sake of Clarity
Cedric Johnson

There was nothing special about the town of Forest City. The entire span of the Rocky Mountains was dotted with such mining towns, and Colorado had its fair share. Nestled into a small pass and miles from anything resembling a real city, Forest City was like every other town created by the rush for gold and silver. A railroad line had been laid to bring people in from far and wide, as well as to haul away the wealth pried from the earth. With people came the buildings, and Forest City had its general store, its town hall, a hotel, telegraph and newspaper offices, a school, dance halls and, of course, saloons.

There was nothing special about Forest City.

There was, however, something special about Thaddeus Wohltat—though few people knew it, and fewer still admitted it. For all appearances, he was a simple man fallen on hard times. Thaddeus had been meandering up and down the main street for most of the day without purpose. He was, in fact, simply killing time.

But as the afternoon steadily turned into evening, the air grew colder still and eventually Thaddeus wanted out of the cold. He found himself next to a single-story wooden building with a simple sign that bore the single word, *SALOON*, to which he started walking.

"Perfect," he said as he walked toward it, wrapping his threadbare coat tight around himself. "A no-name establishment for a no-name magician."

The saloon had few patrons this early in the evening. Most of the town's miners were either still working, sleeping, or at other establishments. Not counting the man behind the bar, Thaddeus made the number an even half-dozen. No one made note of this, or paid him any attention. The bartender spared him a brief glance of acknowledgment and went back to cleaning glasses.

Thaddeus paused in the doorway for a moment. Even though he had no friends or acquaintances in this town, he'd come to expect at least a casual greeting from the other establishments. The almost complete lack of reception made him feel entirely unwelcome. But the feeling soon passed as he continued to be ignored. Thaddeus relaxed and walked to the bar, choosing a stool that was a comfortable distance from the other patrons, but close enough to get the bartender's attention.

"What can I get you?" asked the bartender, still focused on his cleaning.

Thaddeus looked up at the collected bottles of liquor along the wall behind the bar. He wasn't one that partook in alcohol very often—better to have a clear head in case a need for magic ever arose, was his thinking—so he really didn't know what to ask for even if he was in a position to be choosy. It was all brown water to him.

He reached into a pocket of his coat, dug out the small handful of coins he had left and placed them on the bar. "Whatever this will get me," said Thaddeus.

"That'd get you a swift kick out the door in most places," said the bartender, not bothering to keep the sneer out of his voice. "It's not going to get you much more around here, either."

Thaddeus let out a quiet sigh, but managed to keep any expression off his face. "You are absolutely right, sir," he replied. "I should have expected no less nor any more than that." He stood up and managed to give the bartender a faint yet cordial smile. "You may keep it anyway, my good man. I have no need of it any longer."

Thaddeus turned and walked toward the door without a second thought. But something about their encounter, something about the man's bearing and demeanor, had apparently struck a chord of sympathy with the old bartender and made him call out to Thaddeus as he reached the door.

"Come, sir. Have yourself a drink. It's to be a cold night, by all the signs. Stay a while and fortify yourself against it before departing."

Thaddeus paused with his hand on the door, turned and looked back at the bartender warily. But the old man was good to his word, and drew a beer that he placed on the counter with a genuine smile. He glanced at the other patrons, but none showed any sign that this was some sort of prank—or moved for that matter.

Still a bit cautious, Thaddeus returned to the bar and sat again. The beer was waiting there in front of him, the coins he had left on the bar untouched. He left them alone, to show he wasn't taking advantage of this strange generosity. It was a drink bought and paid for, after all.

"Thank you, good sir," said Thaddeus, taking the beer and sipping it. As far as he could tell, it was simply beer, with nothing added to it to insult or harm him. "Though forgive my asking, and my curiosity. Why the change of heart?"

The bartender shrugged. "Nothing in particular, sir. Sometimes you meet a man, and the first thing you do is despise him, often with no good reason. And out here, even in this new age, a man can't be too careful of strangers."

A shot glass appeared next to the beer, filled with what Thaddeus could only guess to be whiskey. "And you, sir, you appear to be the good sort of chap after all," the bartender continued. "A bit down on your luck, perhaps, but that's nothing new out here. I would like to hear your story. Call it curiosity."

Thaddeus had recovered from his initial shock and had relaxed a bit. Taking another sip of beer, he said, "I'm not really sure where to begin . . ."

"You could start with your name."

Thaddeus chuckled. "Fair enough. Thaddeus Wohltat, at your service. Though I doubt I could provide you much service these days. Originally from Philadelphia, I came here to Colorado to make my fortune. What came after that, you've likely heard many times. Fickle investors, unscrupulous partners, and claim jumpers have left me with nothing but the coins on your bar and a train ticket back to Philadelphia."

Thaddeus paused and ventured to take a sip of the whiskey. It burned, but not in an altogether unpleasant way. "After tomorrow, I'll have neither of those. I'll return home and, if any luck remains with me after this, return to work at my old profession."

"And what might that be?" asked the bartender.

"A magician," answered Thaddeus quietly. "Earth Magician."

Those four words did what his entrance and the bartender's generosity completely failed to do; the other patrons stirred and murmured, two of them getting up and leaving the saloon entirely. Thaddeus couldn't help but notice the disturbance, and glanced up at the bartender to see if the old man's generosity would vanish as quickly as it had appeared.

The bartender's next words were cautious, but not hostile. "Don't get many of your kind around here, these days."

Thaddeus nodded carefully. "Indeed, fewer choose to follow the path of magic with every passing year. I'm certainly not the first seeking to find his fortune by locating and collecting the elements of the earth. Magicians are not immune to the desire for wealth, after all."

"And you thought Colorado could use another Elemental Master, did you?" asked the bartender sourly.

Thaddeus shook his head. "Oh, I'm no Master. Not by any stretch of the imagination. I know the ways of only a few spells. I managed to conjure an Elemental only once, a very small one, and even then could not control it and had to beg my colleagues to unbind it for me. A total disaster, that was."

Thaddeus threw caution to the wind and drank down the entire shot of whiskey. "And my one talent," he continued in a raspy voice, "the one thing I am good at, that I thought could help me find my fortune . . . worthless. No one cares. Gold and silver, that's all these people care about. All the wonders of the earth, and that's all they want. Gold and silver. Bah!"

"What would that be?" asked the bartender, his curiosity getting the better of him, "Your talent, that is."

"Quartz."

"Beg your pardon?"

Thaddeus took a deep breath and looked the old man unsteadily. "Quartz, my good man. I have the ability to sense, locate and identify any type and quality of quartz. No other magician in living memory has made that claim!" He took a long sip of his beer and muttered, "Of course, now I have a pretty good idea why no one has . . ."

The bartender looked a bit confused. "Yeah, no wonder you went broke. Why would anyone want the stuff?"

"WHY WOULD—" Thaddeus coughed and flustered. "It has plenty of uses! Quartz can harness the energy of the earth for use in a multitude of spells of any element. And it has uses for ordinary folk, as well. It is used for fine jewelry, cut crystals in many colors of the rainbow." He pointed a slightly unsteady finger at the bartender. "And did you know . . . they're even using it in the latest phonographs!"

The bartender raised an eyebrow. "I'll take your word for it, sir," he said, pulling away the empty shot glass and barely touched beer. After a moment's pause, he added, "So that's really it for you, then? Giving up this search for your fortune in quartz, not doing any more of your magic in these parts?"

Thaddeus nodded. "Completely done, old boy. Come this time tomorrow, I'll have nothing left of Colorado but the dust on my clothes. I'll have said farewell to the Rocky Mountains."

There was a lengthy pause after this proclamation. The bartender broke the silence by refilling the shot glass, drawing a fresh beer and sliding both in front of Thaddeus. There was an unusually large smile on the old man's face as he said, "All the best to you then, Thaddeus Wohltat. Here's to leaving nothing but memories that'll fade, and to magicians who know where their place in this world is."

* * *

When Thaddeus awoke, it was with a sudden jolt that had him sitting upright in his seat without a hint of grogginess. He didn't know what caused it. There was nothing he could recall dreaming that would have startled him, and there was no danger from his surroundings. In fact, he was completely alone in the saloon he'd wandered into the evening before.

Thinking back, he tried to recall exactly how much he'd had to drink. It wasn't enough to cause him any discomfort, but obviously enough to make him unable to find a proper bed. He was also aware that he had other matters to attend to that were more important. Namely, he had a train to catch, and he had no idea what time it was.

Thaddeus stood up and made a tidy pile of the bottles and papers scattered around him on the bar as a small courtesy to the owner. Making his way outside, he looked up and saw that the sun had only just cleared the mountains. Thaddeus was relieved that he hadn't lost much of the morning. Still, he wasted no time in wrapping his thin coat tightly around him to ward off the morning chill and walking briskly toward the train station.

Even though the town was small, it still took Thaddeus a few minutes to reach the station, as it was almost on the opposite end from the saloon. As he arrived, it was clear that there were no trains there. He didn't know if this meant he was early or late, since there were no clocks to be seen. He approached the ticket booth and cleared his throat to get the clerk's attention.

"Beg your pardon sir, do you have the time?"

The clerk glanced up from his newspaper. "Haven't you got a watch?"

Thaddeus sighed. "I do, but at the moment it's at a pawn shop in Buena Vista. So it doesn't do me much good."

The clerk scoffed and returned to his paper. "Quarter past nine," he said, paying Thaddeus no more attention.

Thaddeus' shoulders slumped. He had missed his train after all. "I don't suppose there's any chance the #34 to Denver is running late this morning?" he asked.

"Train arrived and left spot on time, sir," answered a new voice behind him.

Thaddeus turned around and tried to look less startled than he was. The rugged man needed no introduction; the brass star pinned to his chest said it all. That alone wasn't what startled Thaddeus. It was the fact that the sheriff's hand was resting on the grip of his pistol, ready to draw.

"If you had been on it, there'd be a heap of trouble going down the telegraph line and waiting for you at the next stop."

Thaddeus blinked and found it hard to swallow. "What trouble have I caused, sheriff?" he asked nervously. "I can't recall anything I've done against the law . . ."

The sheriff shook his head and replied, "You haven't done anything yet. But if you were on that train, you would have. It means you would have left town with an outstanding debt, and although that might not mean much to you city folk, it means quite a bit out here."

"N-no . . ." stammered Thaddeus, "I get the meaning, and I've done everything I can to settle my accounts before leaving. I'm just at a loss as to whom I owe, sir."

"The saloon keeper you just left," answered the sheriff, "Seems you had quite a bit last night. I take it that you didn't bother to read the bill he left you."

"I—I—" Thaddeus stammered again. It seemed the bartender's generosity was only a show. He couldn't recall being told that he had to pay for his drinks. There had been several papers on the bar when he awoke, and it was true he hadn't stopped to read any of them. He simply wanted to make his train and be on his way home.

"I can make good on my bill," he said. "I just need to contact a few people first."

The sheriff stared at Thaddeus. It wasn't a cold stare, but it certainly didn't have any warmth in it either. "See that you do, Mr. Wohltat. And don't stray far from town. If you haven't settled by sundown, you'll be spending the next several nights in a cell. Just something for you to keep in mind."

Thaddeus smiled as best he could and nodded to the sheriff. The smile vanished as soon as the other man was out of sight, replaced by mild panic. Thaddeus had told the lawman a complete lie. There was no one in the entire state who would give him any more money. He wasn't even all that sure there were any on the East Coast, either.

He walked away from the train station and, like the day before, paced up and down the streets of Forest City. Every name he could think of, every claim partner he'd lost, none of them would help him out. He was sure of that.

Thaddeus found himself at the end of a road heading north into the wooded mountains. "Fitting," he said, though there was no one there to hear him.

As he stood there, cold and alone, an answer came to him almost like a revelation. If anyone had seen the smile that crept back onto his face, they would have said it was a bit of a crazy one. Looking out at the snow covered peaks, then back at the town, and then back at the mountains, it became clear in his mind what it was he had to do.

Thaddeus ran.

By the time the sun was almost touching the western slopes, Thaddeus was completely lost and exhausted. Although he'd headed in a mostly northeastern direction, with all the steep slopes and trees in his path, he would be amazed if he had made more than ten or fifteen miles.

He long ago stopped questioning what possessed him to run in the first place. It was madness, pure and simple. A sane man would have owned up to his debt and made an arrangement to work it off. A sane man would not have run into the wilderness without any supplies nor any plan. Still, he kept running, sure that he would hear horses and gunfire behind him at any moment. The sheriff and his men would probably look for him along the roads first, but it wouldn't take them long to realize he wasn't on any of them and to start searching the mountains.

Thaddeus' lungs were burning. It was the only thing that kept his mind off the numbing cold in the rest of his body—his already inadequate coat had been torn to shreds by the pine trees, so he'd abandoned it hours earlier. He vaguely hoped that someone hunting him would find it and aid in his capture. Spending several nights in a jail cell would be better than freezing to death in one night out here.

The first stars of evening were coming out now, and Thaddeus couldn't push himself any farther. He stopped to catch his breath before facing the decision that could save his life or end it: keep going, hoping to stumble upon even the smallest sign of civilization, or find whatever shelter he could here, and hope that the early November night wouldn't leech the last of the warmth and life from his body.

As he pondered his equally grim options, a loud *crack* echoed from the northeast. Thaddeus bolted upright, sure that a posse had finally caught up with him. But he didn't hear any sounds of men or horses approaching. A moment later, there was a low rumbling and the same *crack*. It didn't sound like gunfire or a mining explosion. Curiosity got the better of Thaddeus, and he headed toward the sounds.

The trees thinned out, and the ground sloped down into a valley. There were no signs that this place had ever been seen by man, though that seemed unlikely. It was 1901, after all, and prospectors had been over most of the Colorado Rockies by now.

But something else had caught Thaddeus's attention more than the pristine beauty. There was magic here, very strong Earth magic. He could feel it throughout his numbed body. But surely, with a place this strongly steeped in Earth magic, he would have felt it, even faintly, in Forest City. So it couldn't have been the valley itself, rather something in it that had recently appeared. When the rumble and *crack* repeated, he saw it.

It was a sight that took away what little breath he had regained. Down in the bowl of the valley, two great creatures were doing battle. Mesmerized by the sight, Thaddeus began to descend toward them without thinking.

The larger of the two was a giant, terrifying bull, dark and shimmering and easily three times as big as a normal bull. As Thaddeus carefully approached, he recognized the shimmering as the fading light reflecting off crystal. His senses tingled, telling him it was indeed a large beast made out of quartz. An Elemental perhaps, or a golem of some kind. He'd never heard of either being made of quartz crystal. Whatever it was, it snorted, stomped, and paced in front of its adversary, acting like a normal bull in every way.

Its adversary was as magnificent as the bull was terrifying: a stag of perfect white fur, shining with an inner radiance that was just short of blinding. It was easily twice as tall as even the largest elk any man had ever seen, but it was still clearly a creature of flesh and blood. But as Thaddeus watched only several dozen yards away, the size difference didn't stop the stag from pressing the attack. It circled around the bull, stamped the ground, and charged.

The ground rumbled as bull and stag ran at each other, heads lowered. Thaddeus knew what would come next. The beasts collided, their horns interlocking with the same *crack* he'd heard before. They struggled for a moment before the bull threw its head back and sent the stag flying backward. It landed only a few yards from Thaddeus, who was rooted to the spot. The stag got to its feet, snorted and shook its head, and then prepared itself for another charge.

Thaddeus wasn't sure what possessed him to speak just then. Just being near the white stag and in the presence of such strong Earth magic filled him with courage he had never felt before.

"Wait!" he shouted, "There, where the legs meet the torso. The two edges of crystal come together. Strike there, and the quartz will shear clean in two!"

The stag's ears flicked back, snorting once. Thaddeus was sure that he'd been heard and understood. He would know very soon if such was the case, as the stag lowered its head, stamped the ground, and charged once more.

The bull stood its ground as before, waiting for the stag to get close. Its dark horns lowered once more, ready to meet the stag again. In the last few seconds, the bull rushed forward and the ground rumbled under its hooves. But this time instead of the loud *crack* of their horns meeting, the stag darted aside, ducked its head, and brought it up as hard as it could exactly where Thaddeus had told it to.

The bull reared up on its hind legs with a mighty bellow that rang throughout the valley. Just as Thaddeus had predicted, the quartz crystal of the bull's chest split at the leg from the force of the blow. The stag had seen this, too. It ducked its head once more and then lunged up as hard as it could, driving its horns into the bull's chest.

The roar that followed was deafening, but final. The beast fell to the ground and shattered. Tiny fragments of quartz flew everywhere, and Thaddeus panicked and threw himself face-first onto the ground with his arms over his head. But that turned out to be the least of his worries. A few seconds after the bull fell, the ground itself began to tremble, shaking with a fury Thaddeus had never felt before. Birds for miles around took to the air and cried in alarm. The tremor lasted nearly half a minute, as if the earth were letting out its pent-up fury.

It was over as quickly as it had begun. The birds settled and the valley was quiet again. Thaddeus was alone with the stag and what remained of the bull. Thaddeus approached carefully. The stag was kneeling on the ground a few yards away from the remains; its radiance had all but died away. Its brilliant white coat was covered in gashes from the explosion of quartz crystal. Some of the shards were still embedded in its hide.

Thaddeus knelt beside the stag. His brain whirled as he tried to think of anything he could do to help. Perhaps some Earth magic that could at least lend some energy to this creature and help heal it.

The stag seemed to sense his thoughts and shook its head with a snort. It nudged Thaddeus' hand towards the remains of the bull. Thaddeus nodded, stood up, and approached them. To his continued shock, what he saw instead of a pile of smoky quartz was a large man— seven feet tall if he was an inch, but a man nonetheless. If not for the fine robe, Thaddeus would have taken him for a simple mountain man.

The hem of the robe caught Thaddeus' attention. The old runes and wards sewn into it told the true tale; this was no mere Earth Magician. This was an Elemental Master. *And you thought Colorado could use another Elemental Master, did you?* The bartender's words came to Thaddeus clearly, and with them their true meaning.

Glancing back at the stag, he realized that he'd just witnessed nothing less than a grand battle between two Earth Masters. Not only that, but he'd helped in it. As selfish as it was, he wanted something to remember this moment by. In the fading light, Thaddeus caught a glint of gold. He looked closer and saw a chain around the Master's neck. As he did so, his sensing talent flared up within him. There were shards of quartz all around him but this was something that stood out even from that.

Pulling the end of the chain out from under the Master, Thaddeus saw a pendant made of the same smoky quartz. Holding it up, he saw that it had been carved into a bull. It must have been the Master's focus. He couldn't possibly take such a thing, even if the Master had no further use of it.

Thaddeus was startled by the stag suddenly at his back. He hadn't even heard it stir. The stag insistently nudged him to his feet. Thaddeus still had a firm grip on the pendant and the chain broke as he rose. But before he could protest, the stag lifted him up and began to run. Thaddeus clung desperately to its horns and clumsily mounted the animal.

With a horn in one hand and the pendant in the other, Thaddeus held on for dear life as the stag ran through the night at incredible speed. He lost all sense of time, and even dozed off a couple of times. But each time he jolted awake to find that the stag had him firmly on its back, not letting him fall.

It wasn't until the sky began to grow brighter in the east that Thaddeus felt a different sensation. Whenever he actively tried to sense quartz, he had to concentrate on one area at a time. Now, with the Master's focus in his hand, he had a sense of a very large deposit of it off in the distance. More curiously, the focus was letting him know where it was.

Thaddeus said, "More to the east. There, where the slope folds in on itself."

He wasn't sure exactly why he had instructed the stag, but it obeyed without hesitation. The feeling grew stronger the closer they came to the spot, and he was sure it was the right thing to do, even if he didn't know why.

The stag topped the slope and entered the tiny valley behind it. There was nothing here that Thaddeus could see; the area was clear of any trees and the northern face was sheer and insurmountable. But he was sure this was where he was meant to be. The quartz sense vibrated within him stronger than it ever had.

Thaddeus slid off the stag's back and looked all around him. As he did, the animal slumped to the ground. Alarmed, Thaddeus turned around and knelt beside the stag. The wounds it had received from the exploding quartz hadn't stopped bleeding, and it had been running at full speed all night with Thaddeus on its back. After all that, he couldn't just let the magnificent creature die.

"Please, let me help you," begged Thaddeus. "If there's any spell I can cast, even just to give you the energy . . ."

The radiance that Thaddeus had first seen surrounding the stag flared back into life. It died down just as quickly, but as it receded, the stag took the form of a young man. When the light died completely, he smiled at Thaddeus.

"You've already done more than I could alone," said the Master quietly. "I truly thank you."

Thaddeus was taken aback. "I don't understand, Master. What is this all about?"

The Master reached up and placed his hand on the one with which Thaddeus held the focus. "Find the treasure within the mountain, and all will be explained."

With those words, the Master's hand fell to the ground and he began to sink into the ground before Thaddeus' eyes, returning to the earth.

Numb, Thaddeus stood up and looked at the sheer mountain face. Not knowing what else to do, he grasped the focus and approached the face, reaching out with his quartz sense. Almost immediately, he was drawn to a particular spot on the rock wall. The focus glowed briefly and the rock slid back as easily as a door.

"Enter, Master. For you are safe here." The voice came from the rock itself, but Thaddeus heard it speak inside his head. Rattled but determined, he set off down the tunnel.

The tunnel quickly opened into a grand hall. As he entered, crystals in the walls lit up like torches. The hall was a wonder to behold, carved from the earth itself by powerful magic. His sense drew him in farther, until he came to a dais covered in ancient runes.

"Step onto the platform and you shall have your treasure, Master," said the voice.

Thaddeus was hesitant, but his quartz sense was stronger than ever before, and the focus drew him closer. Taking a deep breath, he stepped onto the dais. Immediately it began to sink into the ground. He closed his eyes and gripped the focus tightly, willing out his fear.

He opened his eyes again when the stone stopped sinking. Thaddeus blinked and rubbed his eyes to make sure what he was seeing was real. It was like the hall above, only each alcove held huge quartz crystals in every possibly color, larger than Thaddeus had ever seen, and each pulsing with great magic. He wandered over to each, marveling in their size, beauty, and power.

At the far end of the hall there were two great chests, made of perfectly clear quartz. Thaddeus peered into the first one and let out a low whistle. Inside was a delicately carved crystal mansion, complete with grounds and miniatures. It radiated magic as well, and Thaddeus could only assume that it was created in such a way. Such fine detail would be painstaking, if not impossible, simply by hand.

Thaddeus reluctantly turned away from the tiny wonder and looked at the second chest. He stopped dead in his tracks once more, his breath caught in his throat. Lying inside was a woman, pale yet beautiful, her skin like milky quartz. Thaddeus leaned in closer, his heart thumping. He couldn't tell if she was a real person, or some kind of magical construct. Looking closer, Thaddeus saw a faint rise and fall of her chest, and a ribbon of her blouse fluttering slightly. She was breathing, which meant she was very much real and very much alive.

Suddenly her eyes snapped open, wide with panic. Thaddeus leaped back out of reflex. But the woman quickly calmed down and said, "You've come to save me! Please, break the latch and let me out, I beg of you!"

Thaddeus didn't think twice. Finding the latch, Thaddeus cast a quick spell to make his hand as solid as stone and brought it down as hard as he could. The latch shattered at once and Thaddeus put all of his strength into moving the chest lid. It slowly slid over and fell to the ground with a dull thud. The woman sat up and threw her arms around Thaddeus' neck as he lifted her out.

"I knew someone would come for me," said the woman, lifting her head to gaze happily into Thaddeus' face. "I did not know who, but I knew someone would. Oh, thank you, Master Mage!"

Thaddeus flushed. "I'm no Master, Miss . . ."

"Clara."

"Miss Clara. Just a poor fool magician in the wrong place at the right time."

Clara laughed. "So you say. But only a powerful Master could have defeated the lord of this place."

"I did not defeat him, Miss Clara. I only aided in his defeat," replied Thaddeus. He quickly recounted the events of the night before with the bull and the stag.

Tears formed in Clara's eyes. "My brother is dead? I'm truly alone now."

Thaddeus couldn't help himself and wiped away the tears. "The stag, the other Master . . . he was your brother?"

Clara nodded and answered. "Yes, he was. My family has lived here for many generations. When our parents died, my brother and I shared the estate. But he loved me and would grant me full control of it upon my marriage.

"Not long after, a stranger appeared on the grounds one night. His name was Marco, and he was the Master who controlled this place. He wanted my hand and asked my brother for it, but was refused. My brother could sense something dark within him, and wanted to protect me. Marco would not be denied. He came to me himself, begging me to let him prove his worth. But I would hear none of it, having already been warned by my brother.

"That night, as I slept, Marco came to me as if in a dream, leading a white stag. He told me that I had until morning to change my mind, otherwise I and everything that was mine would be his regardless. Still I refused, calling out for my brother. Marco laughed and pointed at the stag, saying that my brother had already refused.

"I tried to scream for help, but my voice would not come out. Marco chanted more words of magic, and I fell into sleep again and dreamed that he had taken the entire estate, help and all, shrunk it to a crystal miniature and sealed it away in his great hall under the mountain."

Thaddeus held Clara in his arms and said, "Now you find that none of it was a dream. Oh, Clara, I wish there was something I could do."

"There is," answered Clara. "I saw much in my dreams. Marco had taken the miniature estate from the dais and placed the souls of all the people into these crystals. Perhaps if you were to reverse his actions . . ."

Thaddeus beamed. "Yes, it might be possible. I'll try at least, for you."

Working quickly but carefully, Thaddeus freed the crystal model from it's chest and placed it on the dais. He took a step back and with Marco's focus firmly in hand, reached out his quartz sense to the giant crystals. When he had them all in his mind, Thaddeus began a very simple spell to break rock. It normally wouldn't affect quartz crystal, but with his sense amplified by the focus, the vibrations that crumbled rock were altered. The crystals began to shake and, after a moment that left Thaddeus sweating slightly, shattered in their alcoves.

There was a rush of released energy that flowed towards the dais. The crystal miniature absorbed it all and lifted itself up off the dais, up the hole and vanished in a flash of light. Shaking and panting, Thaddeus turned back to see Clara smiling even brighter. He could see by her face that he had succeeded. He returned to her side and took her outstretched hand.

"My dear Thaddeus," said Clara, "You've done what no other magician could, not even a true Master. You've returned me and all that was my family's to the world. And if you would have them, I would gladly give them both to you. You would never be a poor magician again."

Thaddeus laughed and led Clara to the dais to begin making their way home. "And I would be a fool to turn you down, my beautiful Clara. And that would leave me as simply a magician."

As they returned to the surface and were greeted by

the morning sun, Thaddeus could see nothing wrong with that.

The saloon doors creaked open, followed by heavy foot-steps. The bartender glanced up from his washing, slowly dried the glass in his hand, and picked up another before saying, "Quite the tremor last night. Don't get many in these parts."

The sheriff stopped a few feet from the bartender, close enough to speak low and still be heard. "That was a mighty big gamble you took, Ephram. You're lucky it paid off."

"Had to be done, Silas," replied Ephram as he reached under the bar and brought up an old bottle. Uncorking it, he filled two shot glasses. "Marco made sure that no one of the family line could break his curse. Thaddeus Wohltat was the only other magician for miles around. It had to be him."

Silas picked up a shot glass and Ephram did the same. After a silent toast, Ephram added, "For what it's worth, I did hate to put a nice young man like him into such hardship. An underskilled magician against a Master . . . Just not right, Silas. Though I'm curious, how did you get him to head north?"

"That was my own gamble," answered Silas. "Luck—and just a little bit of magic to steer him in the right direction."

Ephram smirked and nodded. "So I take it the estate has also been restored?"

Silas put down his glass and refilled both his and Ephram's. "In all its former glory. We can go home now, if you want. And the bloodline will go on. Clara has taken quite a liking to young Thaddeus. That's good, because that's something neither of us—nor her brother, God rest him—could rightly do, either."

Ephram tossed back his drink and fixed Silas with a steady gaze. "Does this mean we'll be bringing Mr. Wohltat into our Lodge?"

Silas picked up his shot glass and raised it in a general toast. "That's up to him. We'll watch over him, regardless. Clara is happy with Thaddeus just the way he is. That's more important than making sure he becomes a proper Master right now."

The sheriff drained his glass and set it on the bar. "It all comes down to what kind of man he wants to be. Can't say what that'll be, but I do know this: He'll do right by us no matter what, because that's the kind of man he already is."

To Ride The River-Horse
Dayle A. Dermatis

Myfanwy leaned out the window as far as she dared, balanced on the precarious knife-edge between yearning desire and abject fear.

She didn't like heights, not one bit. Even now, with her hands firmly against either side of the wooden frame that lined the opening in the stone, her stomach tilted and rolled.

Far below, the broad expanse of the River Taff—the object of her longing—glinted in the rare Welsh sunlight.

Her tightly controlled terror of high places wasn't the only thing that contributed to Myfanwy's unease. The fact that Aunt Siwan could come through the door at any moment and catch her was frightening enough on its own.

Siwan wasn't really Myfanwy's aunt. Myfanwy was reasonably sure that they weren't even related and, indeed, that "Myfanwy" wasn't her own real name. Myfanwy didn't look a smidgeon Welsh; she didn't have the pale blue eyes or jet-black hair or slight stature of those who surrounded her. Instead, her eyes were liquid brown and her hair was a lush gold that seemed to have a radiance of its own.

Not to mention, she had an extraordinary abundance of it.

When it wasn't braided and coiled around her head, it fell in thick waves to her feet. Siwan had cut it several times, lopping off the braid at the nape of Myfanwy's neck, but it always grew back. Instead of selling them for wigs, Siwan placed the heavy hanks of hair into a trunk; a curiously nostalgic gesture that had seemed out of character for Myfanwy's aunt.

Myfanwy didn't know why Siwan wanted to keep her hair, anymore than she knew why Siwan kept her confined to this tower unless she was closely supervised. She didn't entirely know why Siwan wanted to train her in the arts of Water magic but not let her practice by herself.

Not let her communicate with the undines and naiads and river-horses that she could see playing way down there in the wide River Taff, or even sometimes see in a cup of water or in her bath.

Myfanwy wasn't allowed alone with a cup of water or her bath, or any other water, for that matter.

Siwan was a Fire Master, someone who could summon the Elementals of Fire. She wasn't, Myfanwy mused, the best person to teach a person with an aptitude for Water— yet another thing Myfanwy wasn't allowed to know.

All she knew, right that moment, was that she wanted nothing more than to raise an undine out of that glittering ribbon of water. But if Siwan found out, she'd be punished severely.

Even that didn't stop her from reaching out a hand to the distant river . . .

She was so intent that when a clear, strong male voice called out from below, "*Bore da!*" she lost her balance.

For a split second of terror, she wasn't sure which way she'd go . . . but then, despite the heave of her stomach, she hauled herself backward and fell into the tower.

When she recovered, she leaned out the window again—this time not nearly as far, with her feet firmly planted on the floor—and looked down at the young man. As near as she could tell from this height, he seemed completely unconcerned that he'd nearly caused her untimely demise.

"*Bore da,*" she replied. Not being a native Welsh speaker, she knew her tongue fumbled around the greeting of "good morning," but it was decipherable enough. Here in south Wales, near the border to England, most people spoke at least a smattering of both languages.

"You must be new here," he called up to her, switching to English. "My name's Glyn."

"Oh, I'm not new," Myfanwy said. "I've been here for years."

Glyn was silent for a moment. "You mean, in Cardiff?"

"No," Myfanwy said. "Here in Castell Coch. My aunt Siwan is cousin to the Marquess of Butte."

The Marquess, whose father had been the founder of modern Cardiff, had never visited the small, charming castle he'd built in the hills above Cardiff, so he allowed Siwan to live there. Myfanwy never understood why he'd built a holiday home pretty much within sight of Cardiff Castle, which he'd also built over the ruins of a Roman fort, and where he lived. Or why he'd spent so much money for William Burges, who'd painted the bright, fanciful medievalesque interior of Cardiff Castle, to also decorate Castell Coch in the same manner.

Myfanwy's own room was a blaze of bright blues, rich reds, vibrant greens, and glimmering golds. Stars seemed to gleam with a life of their own in the deep blue of the ceiling between the crimson arches. There were birds, butterflies, vines, pomegranates, and all manner of allegorical creatures painted on, well, just about every surface that could be painted.

"How very odd that we've never met," Glyn said. "I've had more than one meeting with your aunt here."

"I don't get out much," Myfanwy said, suddenly nervous. "It's probably best you don't tell Siwan that I talked to you."

Then she ducked back inside, surprised to find herself trembling more than she had when she'd almost toppled out of the window.

A bird twittered at the window.

Myfanwy humphed in annoyance, rolled over, and pulled her pillow over her head. What bird in its right mind was singing now? And why did it have to be so close to her bed?

The pillow didn't help. Finally, with a groan, Myfanwy sat up, lit a candle, and headed to the window to close the shutters.

Before she could, the bird flew into the room. But it wasn't really a bird.

Fully awake now, Myfanwy stepped back, her mouth open as she watched the sinuous, pale blue creature dart forward and float in front of her.

To her further astonishment, she heard it somehow *speak*.

"*Myfanwy of Castell Coch,*" she heard in her mind, "*If you can understand me, please indicate so.*"

Myfanwy jerkily nodded her head.

"*It is very important that Glyn speak with you. It is best that no one else knows. Is there a way you can let him in? Or have you a rope?*"

Myfanwy peered out the window. Below, she saw the flame of a lamp, barely illuminating a person she guessed was Glyn.

Her door was barred from the outside, so she couldn't sneak down and unlatch the front gate. She didn't have a rope—and really, could anyone climb that high? She shuddered at the thought.

As she pondered the dilemma, she also questioned whether she should do anything at all. Her maid, Rhian, said men were trouble. But she often said it with a grin and a twinkle in her eye.

Glyn said it was important. He'd come back to see her. Nobody saw her, spoke to her, except Siwan and Rhian and the cook and the stable hand.

Rhian slept in a room nearby—if Myfanwy shouted, Rhian would come.

Myfanwy suspected that Rhian also wouldn't give her away if she discovered Glyn in Myfanwy's room. Rhian held a fierce dislike for Siwan but stayed, she swore to Myfanwy, for Myfanwy's sake. •

The thing that tipped Myfanwy's decision in Glyn's favor was the thing hovering in the air before her.

It was, if she correctly remembered, a sylph—an Air Elemental.

Which meant Glyn was a Magician or possibly even a Master of Air.

Myfanwy hadn't met any magic users other than Siwan; hadn't learned magic from anyone but Siwan or from the books Siwan provided her. Her thirst for knowledge and her curiosity about the Element of Air practically made the choice for her.

The sylph had said no one else should know, so she couldn't ask Rhian to open the front door for Glyn.

So what to do about the lack of rope?

She paced the room, staring at everything. The bed sheets would work, but she might not be able to get the knots out afterwards.

Then her eyes alighted on the trunk, painted with a unicorn-in-the-forest scene, which held her shorn hanks of hair, each one nearly as tall as she.

"Tell him to wait," she told the sylph, who darted away, leaping joyously out the window before plummeting out of sight in a way that made Myfanwy's stomach lurch.

Myfanwy swiftly found her embroidery kit and sewed the braids together into one long strip. At the window, she affixed one end to the shutter latch and carefully lowered the makeshift rope down.

She nearly wept when she saw that it wasn't long enough, the end dangling out of Glyn's reach.

But then Glyn stepped back, took a running leap . . . and seemed to float upward, as if lifted by something Myfanwy couldn't see. Even as he climbed her hair, hand over hand, he went faster than she would have thought possible.

After he clambered through the window—it almost wasn't wide enough for his shoulders—he explained how he'd done it.

He explained many things that night, and on subsequent nights.

He was indeed an Air Master, and was able to manipulate the air and wind. He couldn't *fly* per se, but he'd gathered an air current to boost him up so he could reach her rope of hair, and used it to make him a little more buoyant on his journey up.

He'd guessed that she was a Magician, so he'd sent

the sylph to see if she was able to perceive it. Even though it wasn't an Elemental of her talent, her affinity for magic made it visible to her—and she couldn't control it, other than asking it to do what Glyn himself wanted.

"I suspected you had talent when we first met—but when I asked my colleagues, none had ever heard of you. Have you always been kept in the tower?" His face was grave.

Myfanwy nodded. "I'm not allowed anywhere in the castle or the grounds without supervision," she said.

"Do you know what your aunt is?" he asked cautiously.

"She's a Fire Master," Myfanwy said promptly. "I have an affinity for Water, though. She's training me—which seems silly because Fire and Water don't mix."

He blinked. He had the loveliest blue eyes, Myfanwy thought, and a strong chin with a cleft in it, and a ready smile. Now, though, he looked puzzled.

"Do you know why she's training you?"

"She needs help with her cousin's canals."

Wales was riddled with veins of coal; indeed, coal mining was its biggest industry. To transport the coal, there were trains—which were expensive to maintain—and canals.

Siwan (Myfanwy explained to Glyn) wanted Myfanwy strong enough to assist with the upkeep of the canals.

"If the Water Elementals are happy, then the canals will run smoothly," Myfanwy finished. Her brow furrowed. "Except she won't let me communicate with any of them yet. I don't think that's very fair."

"It's not fair," Glyn agreed, "and it's certainly not the

best way to train you. There's a great deal Siwan hasn't told you, or taught you." He shook his head. "You're correct: Your training should properly come from a Water Master. The fact that she's kept you away from the Council . . . I don't understand it."

"Does that mean she can't train me—or that you can't, either?" Myfanwy was crestfallen.

"We can both teach you the fundamentals," Glyn said. "Basic communication with Elementals works the same for all Elemental Masters. But to show you exactly how, a Water Master would make more sense."

Myfanwy felt an uncomfortable twist in her stomach. "But Siwan says she'll begin training me soon to control the Water Elementals."

Glyn shook his head again. "You don't control them, Myfanwy. You learn to work with them. They'll do your bidding if they respect you, if you've befriended them. The only people who try to control them are those who practice the dark arts."

Myfanwy bit her lip. "Perhaps I misunderstood, then."

Glyn hesitated for a long moment. Finally, he seemed to make a decision.

"I don't think you did misunderstand," he said. "The Council has had questions about Siwan's use of magic. They asked me to keep an eye on her in my spare time—"

"Spare time?"

He explained that he worked for the mining companies, purifying the air in the mines from the poisonous gases that collected underground. All the Marquess knew was that Glyn went down to test the mines; he thought Glyn's tests always showed the air was clean.

"Do you think . . ." Glyn paused thoughtfully. "Do

you think you would be willing to find more out about her plans?"

Myfanwy pondered this. "If you'll teach me," she said finally, firmly. For knowledge, she would take the chance. And the words he said had rung true for her. Siwan wasn't really her aunt, and although she hadn't been outright cruel, Myfanwy had always felt uncomfortable around her; had always suspected, deep down, that something wasn't right.

And so Myfanwy's life changed. During the day she was taught by Siwan, and at night, Glyn came and taught her his own methods. Soon she learned to control water—move it, mold it—thanks in part to Rhian's assistance, as the maid brought bowls of water for her to work with, and once snuck both Myfanwy and Glyn down to the kitchen so Myfanwy could work with an entire tub of water.

She also learned to work with the undines and minor nymphs, although the naiads and river-horses were beyond her reach. Water Elementals could appear anywhere there was a place of their Element for them to manifest in. Even a bathing tub of water wasn't big enough for a river-horse.

When Siwan finally decreed it was time for Myfanwy to work with the Water Elementals, Myfanwy had already established a rapport with them, and they knew how to act when Myfanwy "commanded" them.

She didn't dare whisper a thank you out loud to them, but she hoped they could hear her thoughts—for the magic Siwan urged her to use felt oily and dark, and left a bitter taste in her mouth.

Then came the day when she heard the heels of Siwan's boots tap-tapping up the wooden stairs, echoing in the round tower, and then Siwan opened the door and said, "I think it's time we go to the river."

Myfanwy nearly squeaked with excitement, but she managed to stifle it. Siwan frowned upon anything that wasn't proper and ladylike.

Siwan herself was proper—and properly imposing. She was tall for a woman, and austerely thin, with white hair braided tightly around her head. Her eyes might have been blue, but they glimmered with the flames of her talent. She rarely smiled, and when she did, it never seemed quite . . . pleasant.

The afternoon was overcast, a brief respite in the rain showers that had lasted for weeks and would no doubt continue (Myfanwy had some sense of the weather when it came to rain, and wondered if that was something else she was scheduled to learn). Despite the gloom beneath the trees and the muddy path, Myfanwy savored the rare outing. Plus she could barely contain her elation. Finally!

"We'll start first with an undine," Siwan said. "Command it to your presence; bind it to your will."

Myfanwy reached out with her power and her thoughts, requesting an undine's presence. Her heart fluttered when she saw the surface of the slow-moving river ripple, then churn, followed by a sleek, laughing, finned woman undulating out of the water.

She winked at Myfanwy, clearly apprised of the situation.

Myfanwy told it to do what Siwan told her to tell it, and it did, and then finally Siwan said, "Now. The river-horse."

The churning was more pronounced this time, a roiling white foam, and then it leaped out of the water, suddenly *there*, drops of water spattering over Myfanwy (though not over Siwan, who had wisely stood farther back).

The river-horse was magnificent and terrifying. Myfanwy had ridden normal horses, but this was more beautiful and more powerful and potentially more dangerous. His front end was that of a horse, but his hindquarters ended in a large flat tail.

The undines and naiads and nymphs seemed to have had a network through which they had all been apprised of Myfanwy's secret trials.

The river-horse was another matter. Did it know? Would it resist when she outwardly, as a performance for Siwan, tried to bind it—or would it drag her down to her death?

"My cousins have told me much about you, Water Magician," it said in a voice just for her, one Siwan couldn't hear. *"You will always be safe with me, so long as you respect us all."*

Myfanwy held her back straight, not succumbing to the desire to wilt from relief. She did everything Siwan told her to do, and the river-horse—with perhaps a small sense of amusement, it was hard to tell—performed as she bade it.

The connection she found with it was exhilarating, and she felt humbled.

She couldn't wait to tell Glyn. But first, that evening, she dined with Siwan in the banqueting hall with its huge arched window and massive fireplace over which was painted St. Lucius.

Siwan expressed her rare pleasure at Myfanwy's accomplishments, and it was an opportunity, Myfanwy realized, to ask Siwan about her plans.

"When will I be able to work with the canals, do you think?" she asked. "Will I be of use to our cousin, the Marquess?"

Perhaps it was Siwan's belief in Myfanwy's control of the Water Elements, that Myfanwy showed an affinity for the darker magics—or perhaps it was Siwan's rare indulgence in a glass of wine—that loosened her tongue.

"Our cousin!" she scoffed. "He hasn't a fraction of the business sense of his father. He's far more interested in religion and architecture—" and here she waved a hand at the Gothic grandeur of Castell Coch "—this place, and his own home. Coal is the future of our country, Myfanwy, and he will lose it all, as surely as if he crumbled it in his hand and let it sift through his fingers."

She leaned forward, a spark of flame flickering on her own fingertips in her passion. "The mines need a strong hand to guide them, and the canals are the way to do that. If we can do this, Myfanwy, then we will be rich and powerful beyond our wildest dreams."

Myfanwy was certain of several things. One was that the riches and power were well within Siwan's wildest dreams. And the other was that those riches and power wouldn't be shared with herself. She was a tool, and she would be used, and when she was no longer useful, she would be discarded . . . or worse.

She squared her shoulders. She would tell Glyn that night. She would tell him of her triumph and of Siwan's plans, and beg him to take her away with him, wherever that might be. Away from the tower, away from Siwan.

It was time to live her life.

The rain—her very Element—had other plans.

The storms had started up again during supper, and

as Myfanwy stared out her window at the water sheeting down, she knew Glyn wouldn't visit her tonight.

So with Rhian's help she prepared for bed, although she lay awake, her mind racing and her body tingling with the memory of the river-horse, the knowledge of Siwan's plans, and her ready desire to be away from this place, this beautiful fantasy castle that was her prison.

Thus she was awake when the sylph came.

The sinuous, pale blue creature seemed ragged in the lamplight, as if the rain had torn bits of it away. Air and Water weren't in opposition, but they couldn't exactly coexist, either.

Its mere presence was an omen. Myfanwy shot to her feet. "Glyn—"

The sylph wasted no time with pleasantries. "*The mine is flooding. Glyn needs your help. You must come.*"

She saw in her mind's eye which mine the sylph meant. She was grateful for that, because she could get nothing further from the sylph. It dipped and darted through the air, agitated, unwilling to leave through the rain but unhappy to be trapped, just as she was.

Myfanwy swiftly drew on the set of men's clothes Glyn had brought her. Boning and bustles and over-skirts meant restricted movement, and these garments were for an emergency—which was now.

In the time since she had met Glyn, her hair had grown to the floor again, and Siwan had just yesterday sheared off the braid. Myfanwy had placed it in the trunk herself, not wanting Siwan to see how the other braids were tied together into a rope.

Now, Myfanwy feverishly sewed the newest extension to the golden rope . . . praying it would be long enough.

As she had so many times before, she affixed one end to the window latch, and threw the rest out the window. It tumbled down into the sodden darkness.

She couldn't see how close to the ground it came.

She couldn't even see the ground, although she knew, from the many hours and days she'd gazed from the window, just how far below it lay.

And it terrified her.

Panic flooded her as she gripped the wooden frame. A glance over her shoulder confirmed that the sylph was gone—whether it had fled or dissipated, she didn't know.

All she knew was the ringing in her ears, the shaking of her limbs, and the knowledge of what she had to do: the thing she feared the most.

But she would do it, for Glyn.

It took every ounce of strength she had to lift one leg and straddle the sill. Her stomach lurched and roiled, and dizziness threatened to consume her, but she battled it back. It was hard to breathe, but she sucked in what air she could, girded her loins, and twisted her body as she slid her other foot out the window.

She was slimmer than Glyn, thankfully, and the narrow space didn't confine her. She poised, half-in and half-out, her booted toes clutching for purchase on the sandstone bricks.

Now or never. All or nothing. She slid backward, out into the darkness and the rain.

She couldn't see the ground, and yet that didn't ease her fear. Instead, she focused on one moment at a time, one movement at a time: grip the braid, slide one foot and then the other down, lower her body, and repeat.

She trembled, not just from the fear but from the strain. Her arms and hands ached. But letting go was far more terrifying than anything, and she crept lower, and lower still.

Until she reached the end of the braid.

Myfanwy felt beneath her with one foot, but the ground didn't meet her. She looked down. There was no light; she couldn't see if she was inches from the grass, or feet, or yards, or more. She hung there, her mind a blank, no hint what to do.

She realized that in a few moments, her straining arms would give way; her fingers would no longer be able to grasp.

She didn't want the choice to be taken away from her. She released both feet from where they touched the wall, stretched down as far as she could—and let go.

And fell.

She would have screamed, but she swallowed the sound.

Then, something caught her. Not an abrupt stop, but a slowing down, an easing of speed, something cradling her.

Her feet touched the ground.

Then her knees, and hands, and she didn't care that her trousers were getting soaked, just that she was on solid earth again.

Hurry, said the sylph—the same one, or another, or many?—and then it was gone.

She stumbled toward the river, blinded by the rain and darkness, using her Water-magic instinct to guide her in the right direction. She toppled down the bank, skidding in the mud.

For the second time that day, she called into her presence the river-horse.

She might have a terror of heights, but she had no

fear of water, despite the fact that she hadn't a clue how to swim. (You couldn't learn to swim when you'd never been in a body of water larger than a bathing tub.)

Most importantly, she trusted the river-horse to keep her safe.

"Hold tight," it told her, *"and don't give in to panic when we go below. You'll not drown."*

Still, when they plunged beneath the surface, she tensed. It wasn't natural for a person to be below the depths, and not only was the water icy cold, but it was dark—oh, so dark.

She didn't know whether her talent for Water made her able to breathe within it, or whether the river-horse (or a sylph?) had created an air bubble around her. She knew only that when she couldn't hold her breath a second longer, when her burning lungs forced her to gasp, she didn't choke on water.

She buried her face in the river-horse's watery mane, and kept in her mind the vision of the mine the sylph had given her, sharing it with the river-horse.

At some point they left the Taff, joined a canal; she wasn't sure how. All she knew was that eventually she was deposited, half-frozen and shivering so hard she thought she'd come apart, on the bank near the entrance to the mine.

There were a few men with lamps near the entrance to the main shaft. They didn't notice as she crept close to them, intent as they were.

"—can't lower the cage, it just ends up in water—"

"—must be a flood—"

"—told them not to dig that canal so close to the mine—"

"—that woman insisted—"

Myfanwy dropped to her knees and pressed her hands against the ground. Although she had no rapport with Earth Elementals—indeed, they were the opposite of Air, not compatible with—she asked only for passage, for a route below.

Perhaps because the ground was so sodden from rain, or perhaps because the gnomes were sympathetic to her plight, she found herself able to connect with and visualize the scene below.

The men were right: The canal had been dug too close to the end of a tunnel, and while it hadn't completely collapsed through, it had started to seep through, aided by the rain soaking the ground, and now bigger holes had appeared and the water ran faster, sluicing and slipping its way down the tunnel, rising, rising . . .

Myfanwy could move water—in small quantities, and for short distances. She couldn't shove all this water back the way it came, back through the holes, back against the wall of the canal.

Although she tried, she couldn't even shove it all the way back past the shaft where the cage hung, high above. She could get some of it past, but the pressure from the other end fought her. More water was flowing in, too strong for her to resist.

If she didn't hurry, it would fill the area where the men—where Glyn—were trapped.

If she didn't figure out a solution, they would drown.

In her mind's eye, she called up the plans for this mine. Siwan had insisted she study the plans for all the mines in Glamorgan, along with the existing canals, the railways, the rivers.

Just before the shaft, there was another tunnel.

The encroaching water had bypassed it, however, because it ran uphill.

She might not be able to push the water back far, but if she could push it back to that junction, and then divert it . . .

Myfanwy called to all the undines and naiads and nymphs, to the river-horses if they could come, and with humility and kindness, asked them for their help. Never commanded, never controlled. Simply requested, if they would be so kind.

And they were. For her, they came.

Their strength lent itself to hers. She imagined she pushed the water back with her hands, with a large scoop, pressing against the weight of it until she moved it, inch by excruciating inch. When she reached the juncture, she erected a barrier, leaving the water no place to go but up in the incline.

Her back and arms and legs trembled from the effort, already weak from her precarious climb down the tower.

"Tell him it's safe," she said to a sylph that hovered under a nearby overhang. *"Tell him to come to the shaft and call for the cage.*

"Tell him to hurry. I can't hold the water back for much longer."

She waited in the darkness, in the night, in the driving rain, all of which seemed to go on forever as she struggled to hold the water to its course. But then, through the hammering of the raindrops, she thought she heard a bell.

Yes!

And then the men atop were shouting and lowering the cage, and the cage was rising, and miners were coming out, and the cage was going down again, and she knew Glyn wouldn't leave until the last miner was saved.

He would be in the last trip of the cage.

She had to hold on until then.

But although she'd been trained, she hadn't been tried, and there was still one more group of men—Glyn among them, she knew—to rise when her control faltered, and the water slipped and started to fill the main tunnel again.

No! she thought. *"No!"* she screamed silently, and then something within her split open, something she didn't understand, but it filled her with light and heat and brought her to tears, and she wept from the joy and the struggle and the pain and exhaustion.

But tears were Water, tears were her Element, and they leached through the soil and into the mine, and like the Elemental creatures who aided her, they gave strength to her barrier against the water. They gave her one last surge of energy to bind the water back, divert its course, let the final cage descend, fill . . . and ascend, rise to the surface.

Then, only then, did she collapse, releasing the water to flow where it may, releasing the Water Elementals from their task with the deepest gratitude she could muster.

"Myfanwy? Myfanwy!"

Glyn was there, cradling her. In the faint illumination of the lamps near the mine entrance, she saw that his beautiful face was streaked with soot and exhaustion.

Saw that the press of the earth had weakened him—Air Magicians didn't thrive well so far down below.

But he was alive, and they were in each other's arms, and that was all that mattered.

Until a moment later when agony consumed her, and she screamed.

"What is it?" Glyn's voice barely penetrated the pain. She felt as if her scalp were aflame, searing and blistering. Even the chilling rain failed to put out the excruciating fire.

Still, she clung to his voice. Dimly she was aware of the river-horse, rising from the canal nearby, and the Water Elementals, fragmented as they were in the raindrops that hammered around her. From them, she was able to choke out what was happening.

"Your hair."

Glyn's words made no sense. Her hair, short as it was now, was plastered to her head. It wasn't on fire, searing her scalp.

"Siwan must have discovered the rope you made. She kept your hair because she could use it to bind you to her. It was her last resort in case you broke free of her. She's burning your hair, Myfanwy."

Her back arched as she writhed in pain. She didn't know how to stop it, how to end it, how to—

Then she felt the Elementals of Water surround her again, nymph and dryad and naiad and river-horse, before they dove into the water and sped toward Castell Coch, and somehow she knew that the sylphs and other Air Elementals did the same.

It was the last thing she knew before she fell, blissfully, unconscious.

*   *   *

"Myfanwy."

She rose out of the depths of sleep, reaching toward the voice she knew.

The voice of the man she'd realized, just before agony struck, that she loved.

She opened her eyes. She didn't recognize the room she was in—a hotel, she guessed, with soft white sheets and the scent of tea in the air.

She reached a hand to her head. It ached, but didn't burn. Her short hair was there, her scalp was unblistered.

Seeking answers, she fell into Glyn's blue eyes.

Siwan's body had been found in the banqueting hall of Castell Coch. She'd been burning something in the massive fireplace when, according to suggested reports, a surge of wind had blown down the chimney and the flames had escaped, consuming her.

But even more odd was the fact that the flames had gone out, that they weren't what had caused her death.

That doctors had determined (and Glyn hinted that the doctors had been members of the Council) Siwan had actually died of drowning, her lungs filled with water.

"Well," Myfanwy said finally, "I suppose I have no home now."

"You can go wherever you wish," Glyn said. "There are people in London who wish to meet you—and who can provide the rest of your training."

"What about Rhian?" She couldn't abandon her maid, not when she'd been so protective and kind.

"She'll accompany you—after all, a lady needs her trusted servant."

"And what about you?" she asked.

He smiled, and her heart thumped. "I think perhaps

you'd need someone to show you around the city, if you'd have me."

Myfanwy smiled. "I would like that."

She would also, she thought, like to meet the river-horses who lived in the Thames.

She would like to get on with her life.

The Phoenix of Mulberry Street

Michele Lang

New York City
November, 1885

The little match girl stood on Mulberry Street between Houston and Bleecker Street, near the Central Office of the Police Headquarters of New York. The sight of her stopped young Fire Mage Jane Emerson in her tracks, on the threshold of the offices of the *Daily Clarion*.

The day was fading, and a cold wind whipped down Broadway, chilling Jane to the marrow. The Central Office rose up behind the shadowed figure across the street, a whited sepulcher of brick and marble. The little girl reminded her of the Biblical plague of hail, the fire inside magically enclosed in ice, striking the land of Egypt and destroying it. She shuddered at the image that rose in her mind: New York City pummeled by an icy storm such as they had just experienced, then immolated by a hidden fire.

The moment passed, and Jane stood on the threshold of the Clarion Building, trembling. She steeled herself against the sight of the girl—she saw the same or worse in the slums of the Tenth Ward every day of her working life. She could not do her work as a reporter for the *Daily Clarion* if she stopped in her path to help every orphan she encountered on the way.

And yet, this little mite . . . something about the child both frightened and compelled her.

Jane tore her gaze away from the girl and directed her steps to the doors of the *Daily Clarion*, where her employer and mentor waited for her report on the crisis at hand.

For the news she had uncovered was indeed a crisis. It threatened all of New York. She barged into Daniel Tappen's corner office without knocking, unafraid of baiting the lion in his very den.

He raised a sardonic eyebrow when he saw who it was who had dared to invade his *sanctum sanctorum*. "Ah, Miss Emerson," he said, his voice dry as vermouth. "I expect you have some news for me this afternoon?"

Jane colored at the flash of his flat, blue eyes, at the amusement playing like a shadow over his thin, patrician's lips. She reminded herself that as his protégée, their relationship was strictly one of mentor and apprentice.

On the surface, in public, to the untrained eye. To the magical one, it was instantly clear that Mr. Tappen and Miss Emerson were linked together by the deepest, most magical ties.

Daniel Tappen, scion of Old New York, had pledged to teach his ward, Jane Emerson, how the other half lived, in the hopes that conditions in the slums could be improved. More than this, as an Air Mage, he had promised his sister to mentor and perhaps even tame the untrained power of the girl's Fire magic. Miss Emerson, latent Fire Master and wielder of a dangerous inferno of magic, was too much for his sister's placid Earth magic to contain and guide.

Their circle of Walden Pond mages had taught Miss Emerson in Boston as best as they could, but Jane's spirited nature and immense promise could not fully flower under the tutelage of Mrs. Polly March, Mage of Earth. Daniel's magic, of Air, had more affinity with Jane's. But their magic was not the same.

Still and all, he had taught her the basis of all magical arts, all that he knew of the lore of binding, shielding, spellcasting, and healing.

But Jane wanted more, chafed under the strictures of her youth, her sex, and the limitations of her teachers. Mr. Tappen had told her that he knew a powerful Fire Master in London, Lord Alderscroft, and he hoped to send Jane across the sea to finish her education under his supervision.

Until then, she had more to learn from the streets of New York than anywhere else.

"I do have news," Jane said. "I think I know who is behind the tenement fires."

Daniel's eyes sparkled. "I trust you have corroborated your sources, Jane?"

"I spoke with some of the ladies of the evening who know the Tenth Ward like the inside of their eyelids. And I spoke with some firemen who were so angry at the fires that they were tempted into . . . impertinence."

Daniel sighed. "You understand that it is you who are playing with fire." They both knew he wasn't speaking in metaphors.

But Jane pressed on with her tale regardless. "Yes, they believe that it is arson. And it is my conclusion that these fires are the manifestation of Fire magic employed for foul ends."

"I fear that is the case as well. But proving the source is another matter."

"My ladies of the night told me that, despite the violence of the blaze at the shirtwaist factory last week, there were no strangers at the scene—nobody at all. Yet the fire was clearly arson, the firemen told me. And the orphanage, just last night . . ."

Jane could no longer keep her voice from shaking in outrage. It was one thing to burn down a business— terrible to put working folk out of their jobs, and dangerous to other buildings standing nearby—but at least a rapacious motive made some earthly sense. But to deliberately set fire to a building filled with innocent children . . . the thought made her seethe with anger.

"I take it the orphanage blaze was arson as well."

"Yes, that is what the firemen said, and they weren't shy about telling me the *modus operandi* was the same in all of these fires. They could not pinpoint the accelerant, no matter how ardently they tried. But it was Fire magic, I am sure! A Fire Mage of some kind has deliberately set these fires, destroyed lives and property, for ends that I can only imagine. Furthermore, I believe our Fire Mage is a financial giant of some kind."

"Be careful now, Miss Emerson," Tappen said. "You know as well as I do how many powerful interests vie for control of this city, even of the poorest precincts that provide political power. If you point your finger, in print, at one of these titans and cry murder, you realize that you are not merely twisting the tiger's tail. The power of the press will not protect you in the end, or me."

"But unless these crimes are exposed to the scrutiny of decent people, what is the point of a free press, sir? We have enough evidence to publish. Please allow me to write up the story, at least."

Daniel sighed. "You don't have enough to go to press,

not enough for a paper that circulates among ordinary people. You may well have uncovered the crimes of a wielder of Fire magic. But unless you can prove with hard, mundane facts what you know only through magical means, we do not have enough to make a story."

Jane could have cracked a tooth in her jaw-clenching frustration. "I understand," she finally said. "You are not putting the kibosh on the story, merely demanding that I further corroborate what we already know. But it is murder, Daniel!"

Two orphans had died in the blaze, despite the children somehow having gotten advance warning before the fire roared through their dwelling. Jane could not bear the thought of standing by and not doing everything she could to stop the carnage before the arsonist struck again.

"Do you even have the name of the arsonist?" Daniel asked, an edge creeping into his voice.

Jane restrained a smile. If she was getting under the skin of her famously even-tempered mentor, she had achieved some kind of topsy-turvy victory, anyway. "I don't have the name. But I have the profile and the motive, and a short list of suspects. This Fire Mage must have some financial interests that are in opposition to the places of business that have burned. And as for the tenements, the orphanage . . . the destruction of these poor people's lives must also benefit the arsonist. In what way, I am not sure. But I propose to find out."

"How?"

It was a simple but frustrating question. "Divination is not one of my gifts. But dear Mr. Tappen, you who move in every level of society from top to bottom, I am hoping that you may know of Sensitives who may divine more than I can with my shoe leather and obnoxious persistence in gathering facts on the ground."

"No, it won't be that easy," Tappen said. "You must prove the wrongdoer's identity if you wish to write about him. And that means uncovering the ordinary evil first, and using that only to make your case. I am sure you understand the need for discretion where magic is concerned. You will have to take down the arsonist with facts, without revealing your own magic, or exposing the magical accelerant used in these attacks."

He returned to the papers littering the top of his enormous desk, and Jane realized with a start that their meeting was at an end.

"I hope I don't vex you to death, Daniel," she said, surprising herself as she said the words. "I don't mean to be a plague upon you. I just cannot stomach any more of these attacks!"

"Nonsense, Miss Emerson. I admire your passion for justice and your ideals. I merely fear that life in this great city will prove a great disappointment to you if you cannot learn to live with the darkness as well as the light."

Jane left Tappan's office in a storm of frustration and doubt. She agreed with every word he had said, and yet she had hoped that somehow they could have found a way to publish the story. She quickened her pace as the shadows lengthened along the alleyways and gutters by the Mulberry bend. It would do no good to prowl such cruel streets after dark.

But when she saw the waif still standing on Mulberry Street near the Central Office, holding her boxes of matches between her blue little fingers, Jane made the mistake of looking at her face. With growing horror she realized those weren't tears shining on the girl's drawn cheeks.

But the glaze of ice.

Jane ran to the little girl, touched her shoulders, and a terrific shock blasted through her gloves and up her arms. It was as if she were Benjamin Franklin, discovering electricity anew on a Tenth Ward street corner on a fading day in November.

With an effort, Jane removed her fingers from the girl, so that she could think again. The poor girl was frozen, and in imminent danger. Jane rubbed her fingers together, took a deep breath, and accepted the surge of energy she had received into her body.

The surge fed her magic, strengthened her physically. She steeled herself for another jolt, and touched the girl's arms again, rubbed the cold little fingers. This time the energy stayed with the girl, and she stirred under Jane's fingers with a tiny groan.

"My dear child," Jane said. "You are nearly frozen through. Come with me."

The girl shuddered again, but met Jane's gaze. Her fingers tightened over the girl's, and she sent the energy back into the girl's body as gently as she could. She didn't want to frighten the child with an overt show of magic, but the girl's condition was too grave for Jane to hesitate.

She was rewarded for her efforts with a flush of pink into the girl's features, her frozen little fingers. "Let's go, now," she said. "Can you tell me your name, dear?"

The girl blinked hard, as if she only now heard Jane's voice. "Rose," she whispered through chapped lips. Her voice was a slight chuff of wind in a desolate arctic waste.

Jane removed her fur ruff and wrapped it twice around the girl's shoulders. "You are coming home with me, and no mistake," she said, hoping her voice carried a note of authority she did not feel. "A warm bath and some brandy, and you should be right as rain. And then we can find your people again, get you home."

"Home," the girl whispered, longing in her voice. "No home for me."

Jane was shaking now, not with the cold but with both grief and anger. The Tenth Ward was a scandal and a shame, even without the prospect of deliberate arson. Little children like Rose lived in the streets all over New York, and one orphanage more or less was not enough to house them all.

But as God was her witness, this child would not freeze to death as more prosperous citizens like Jane herself walked by, rendering her suffering invisible. Jane would never look away again.

Jane hailed a carriage, and was lucky enough to find one near the police station before the light failed altogether. But when she arrived at the apartments for young ladies where she lived, north of Gramercy Park on Lexington Avenue, her landlady, kindly soul as she was, still almost refused the little girl entry.

"My apologies, Miz Emerson, but those Five Points orphans are all pickpockets or worse! Regular Fagin's army they are, begging your pardon. I can't allow such a creature up here, into the rooms. What if she nicked something?"

Jane summoned up her best manners and her magic, too. She understood Miss Annelise's point, certainly. But there was something about this poor girl, something that broke Jane's heart wide open. Somehow, she had to convince her landlady that Rose posed a threat to no one.

"I'll watch over her, every minute," Jane said. And

ever so subtly, she sent the Fire into her words, investing them with a spark of persuasion that her unguarded, open-hearted landlady could hardly resist.

Miss Annelise shook her head, then laughed. "My goodness, your guardian in Boston did well to send you here. Always into some mischief or other. But always to the good. Well, let her in, give her some warm vittles and a hot bath. But she can't stay here! These apartments are only for young ladies of breeding."

Jane smiled sweetly, nodding her thanks, knowing that this was as much of a victory as she could expect to win.

The clawed tub upstairs was so enormous that Rose all but disappeared into the warm, sudsy bath that Jane drew for her. Jane gently undressed her and lowered her into the water, and after a moment of panic, the girl relaxed into the bath with an audible sigh.

Jane hoarded her questions like jewels, knowing the time for asking them would come. After she got Rose wrapped into a big, plush towel, she rubbed her long hair until it was only slightly damp, and then she carried her into her private bedroom.

"How do you feel now, Rose?"

"Better. Not so cold, finally."

Jane smiled at that, and searched her wardrobe for some article of clothing that could decently cover Rose without overwhelming the girl's tiny frame. After rummaging for a while, she found a silk chemise that could serve as a dressing gown until she could find the child some suitable clothes to wear.

Dressed in the shirt that came down to her knees, and wrapped in a wool afghan that Polly had crocheted, Rose looked like an entirely different girl. Her hair was black as jet, slicked against her angular skull; her eyes were almost amber. The warmth had returned to her cheeks and her limbs, and Jane was relieved to find that all evidence of hypothermia had gone, and that she would not need a doctor until morning.

Dear little thing. Jane's heart warmed to the girl, and when she looked into her eyes again, the oddest feeling stole over her. It was as if she knew this child, knew her better than Daniel Tappen, her guardian Polly—better even than she knew herself.

Rose looked back at her, her gaze steady, all her shyness gone. She whispered something exotic and foreign under her breath, in a language that Jane could not identify. The shadows from the flames dancing in the hearth flickered over Rose's face.

And then the moment was gone. Two people, a young woman and a waif of the slums, sat together on a bed in an elegant boarding house for young ladies, in New York City in 1885. They had emerged from eternity and re-entered ordinary time once more.

"Where is your mother, dear?" Jane asked. She asked the question as gently as she could, because she had no mother herself, and she knew how much the question itself, simple as it was, could hurt.

Rose shrugged and sighed, those brilliant amber eyes now downcast. "I don't know," she said simply. "I was a foundling. I lived at the orphanage, the one what was on Rivington Street."

The one that had burned.

"Oh," was all that Jane could think to say. The police had told her they had taken all the orphans to safe shelter, but apparently they had missed at least one. After a moment, Jane swallowed back the huge lump in her throat and composed herself.

"The police, they worked for the dragon anyway," the girl whispered, as if she had read Jane's thoughts.

"The dragon?"

"Yah, the dragon. You know who I mean."

Her words, barely spoken above a whisper, set a chill deep into Jane's flesh. "Tell me, Rose. Please."

"Everyone what dies feeds the dragon's power. She's terrible powerful now, miss. Enough to grab the whole city for her hoard."

Jane couldn't believe her ears. This little urchin held a world of secrets inside of her, and she knew the identity of the arsonist that Jane had hunted from one end of Gotham to the other in vain. "Do you know her name, Rose? Tell me!"

Rose solemnly gazed back at her, the amber eyes unblinking. "Her name is Imogen Stewart. I read her name in the fire what ate me up, and gave me life."

Jane gasped for air at Rose's revelation. Not just of the identity of the arsonist, but of what Rose had experienced in the blaze.

"What are you?" Jane asked. It was her voice now that was hoarse and cracked.

Rose smiled, and looked into Jane's eyes again. "A girl."

"You are not only a girl." Jane reached for her, clasped her bony little fingers in hers.

And as soon as they touched, that electric warmth poured through Jane again, as if her kindness to the girl had replenished the flow. Jane's heart leaped with wonder and delight.

Rose was a girl, in her mortal guise . . .

But when Jane looked upon Rose with her Inner gaze, with her magically trained discernment, she was overcome by her true, magnificent aspect.

The brilliant, iridescent feathers stretching past the long, elegant neck. The piercing eyes, the sharp and dangerous talons.

Risen from the ashes of the orphanage on Rivington Street.

Jane had heard the name of the lady robber baron before, Imogen Stewart. Miss Stewart, the arsonist, had made a terrible—perhaps a fatal—mistake.

"Phoenix," Jane whispered in wonder. "It is an honor."

"I was looking for you," Rose replied. "Your magic called to me. Why do you not unleash it?"

Imogen Stewart's Fifth Avenue mansion rose far from the squalid streets where creatures of the night, filthy immigrants, and pathetic paupers eked out a wretched existence.

Imogen was made for better.

True, she had arrived in Castle Gardens as an immigrant herself, long ago, in a different life, a Scottish lass in search of the father who had abandoned their family for a new world of luxury.

She never found him. She suspected her father James had experienced the American Dream as nothing more than a snare and a nightmare, and that he had died somewhere in the gutter. He was too fond of pleasure, dreaming of Easy Street, good times, nothing more.

The American Dream was real. But it demanded human sacrifice.

Imogen had lived on her wiles—and her magic. The Fire magic, untamed, that had killed her own mother by accident, only grew more hungry and insistent across the great ocean separating her from her native land.

Elementals had crossed that great gulf as well. So when Imogen summoned dragons and compelled them to do her bidding, she knew then that she could conquer the streets, make them, like the dragons, hers.

She did not reckon on the corrupting effects of treasure. As the years flew away on their massive wings, slow at first but then faster, and faster still, Imogen added to her wealth, created an empire.

But her riches were never enough. The more she amassed, the greater the hunger for more. Imperceptibly, from moment to moment, from conquest to conquest, Imogen Stewart, lady robber baroness and denizen of the highest New York society, became possessed by the lust of her dragon.

At first, she only burned factories and workshops to gain a financial advantage over her commercial rivals. But once she discovered the power contained in the lives that she immolated, Imogen burned the tenements and the sweatshops to harvest the richest treasure of all.

Souls.

For souls fueled her power, made her all but invincible. The city itself was a pearl trapped in her talons. She was on the verge of destroying the mightiest of the Wall Street titans, Gould, the reclusive, all-powerful financier.

She had planned the burning of the orphanage for some time. Such a plunder of young, tender, untarnished souls would have fueled her destructive power beyond all redemption. But for the first time, her arson did not unfold as she had planned.

Instead of dying in the fire, the orphans had somehow escaped the flames. The two that had died, died instantly, without pain, their souls escaping her before she could trap them. And one of the others . . .

One of those miserable little wretches . . .

Had not run from the flames, but chose to burn. Danced in the inferno.

Stole Imogen's own power.

Imogen sensed a great Fire magic had risen in opposition to hers. The snow and ice that had come in the previous day's storm had blunted that raw power, contained it.

But New York City was now in thaw.

Imogen planned to strike her enemies dead, fast, before another magical master could trace the trail of souls up Fifth Avenue to her mansion's oaken door and marble threshold.

And if fire wouldn't do the job, she would not hesitate to resort to ice.

Morning found Jane Emerson unable to sleep, watching the young phoenix slumbering in her bed. She could hardly breathe for awe. This little child, curled beneath her covers, was in fact the newest incarnation of an ancient being, destined to burn and rise, and rise again.

Her appearance heralded the dawn of a new age. Such creatures, so rare, never appeared at random. Jane's heart pounded at the thought of it, and when she caught her reflection in the looking glass on the far wall, her lips were trembling.

Rose had appeared to *her*.

The visitation of a phoenix was not only a precious gift, but a clarion call to arms. The phoenix had sought her out, attracted by her latent powers.

Jane had been imperfectly schooled by mages of lesser inherent power, and invested in different Elements. Could she claim her fire magic now without getting burned?

Jane honestly did not know. Tappen's words from the day before rang in her ears. "... *Twisting the tiger's tail ... You mustn't use your magic ...*"

Jane feared the rogue mage had already discovered Rose's identity, and hers—she had done little to hide while hunting the identity of the arsonist who was devastating the city. She had little time to seek protection for Rose before the rogue Fire Mage hunted them down.

She knew no higher ordinary power in New York than the Mayor's, despite the corruption of city politics and the immense wealth wielded by the robber barons and titans of Wall Street. William R. Grace, the new mayor, was a philanthropist and a reformer, determined to rid the metropolis of the corruption choking the city's politics and commerce.

Daniel Tappen was a friend and supporter of Mayor Grace. Jane would take Rose to the Mayor's office, make sure he knew the identity of the arsonist and that Jane was ready to expose her. And then at least Rose would be protected from the dragon's wrath.

Miss Annelise, bless her heart, had regretted her harsh judgment of the night before, and brought Rose a full set of pretty clothes to wear. Decently arrayed, Rose and Jane dined hastily upon Miss Annelise's famed breakfast, and then slipped away to face the coming storm.

Jane planned to meet Daniel Tappen at City Hall, after sending a messenger along. Both as a newspaperman and as a mage, Rose's appearance would surely dazzle him, too.

Miss Annelise insisted on a hired carriage for the little one, and so they traveled in solitary splendor to City Hall. The morning sparkled with clear, abundant sunlight, so different from the day before. Though it was still

mid-November, the inviting breezes and warm tempera-
tures falsely promised that spring was right around the
corner.

The icy slush had melted away beneath the carriage's
rapidly turning wheels, and the sun reached down from
the heavens and embraced Jane in warmth. She and
Rose alighted from the cab and paid the fare.

They stood hand in hand on Chatham Street near the
entrance to the East River Bridge, stretching across the
banks of the river all the way to Brooklyn. "Your for-
tunes have changed," Jane said. "I believe your news will
make the front page of the *Clarion*. But not a word
printed until you are safe."

That was the last thing that she said before the ordinary world was ripped apart.

In the next instant, a wall of fire rose up on either side
of the East River Bridge, vibrating the heavy cables like
the strings of an enormous harp. Rose and Jane ran up
the stairs to the promenade to see what was happening.

The few shopgirls and clerks strolling along the
bridge's promenade fled in terror, screaming. But once
the ordinary folk passed through the wall of magical fire
engulfing the bridge, they rubbed their eyes and shook
their heads in confusion. The leaping flames surrounding Jane and Rose evidently wiped the minds of regular
New Yorkers clean.

An enormous black dragon swooped out of the clear,
sapphire-blue sky, its webbed black wings blotting out
the morning sun. It alighted atop one of the massive
towers of granite rising high above the river, its claws
clutching at each of the two archways. And the fire rose
on either side, like an infernal rainbow reaching up from
the banks of the East River.

The dragon turned its heavy, obsidian head and gazed upon Jane, a smile revealing cruel teeth and a plume of steam, rising from its nostrils like exhaust from a factory smokestack.

After her initial shock, Jane realized she must not run away. A Water Mage could have perhaps found shelter in the waters of the river below, or called upon Elemental powers hostile to the dragon's fire. But Jane could only prevail here in a battle, Fire against Fire.

Daniel Tappen, Polly March, the streets of the city itself, all had taught Jane everything they knew. But the key to defeating Imogen Stewart and her dragon Elemental was hidden deep within Jane's own heart.

Jane was ready to fight, even to die, to protect the miracle of the young phoenix who stood beside her. As she squared her shoulders to face the dragon, Jane embraced the power she had feared to wield. For Rose's sake, she would find the power within to claim the mantle of Fire Master.

Quickly, Jane wove her shields, though the day was so clear and serene she could not call Fire energy out from thunderclouds. The Elevated was not far from City Hall, but before she could go about the business of drawing energy from the great machines that ran along the track, Jane felt small fingers slipping into her own.

Rose.

The energy poured into her, a cascade of pure power. Jane wove her shields around them both, braided them into a ribbon of light surrounding them. She considered a sending to Daniel, but she did not have time—and besides, the dragon's appearance and her magical gathering of power would attract the attention of every mage in the city.

The dragon leered down at her, licking its lips as it watched her work. Jane smelled the acrid sulfur of the foul creature's breath, watched the sinuous coils wrapped against the top of the bridge's granite tower.

"Give me the child," the dragon crooned.

Jane whispered the last iota of strength into her shields before replying. "Of course not," she said. Her fingers squeezed Rose's, to show her that she would protect her, and the tips of the girl's fingers sent burning heat through Jane's kid leather gloves.

"Surrender!" the fire serpent hissed, and its wings beat against the sky, whitecaps scudding in the dragon's wake all along the surface of the East River.

Jane gulped, but she stood her ground. "I'd rather die."

The dragon laughed, and its talons scraped against the granite, scoring it with deep, parallel scratches. Its wings beat the air even harder, and it rose into the sky, preparing a lungful of fire to blast through Jane's perfectly competent yet unspectacular shields.

Rose's fingers slipped out of Jane's hand and before Jane could register the fact, a rush of wind pressed against her with a fearsome roar and all but knocked her off her feet.

For a moment, Jane forgot Imogen Stewart, her imminent battle with the dragon, even the fact that the city still stood outside the twin walls of fire enclosing them. For Rose shot into the air, her wings iridescent fire of green and indigo and brilliant scarlet.

She screamed into the sky, a breathtakingly beautiful and lonely cry, and the phoenix lunged for the dragon's head with her talons. The dragon flew backward with a roar of belching flame, but it could not escape Rose's attack. The terrible talons slashed at the dragon's neck, at the beady, orange eyes. Her left leg connected with the dragon's face, and a talon pierced through the dragon's eye and entered the cold brain enclosed within that black fire.

With a scream, the dragon fell out of the sky, dragging the phoenix down with it. Only at the last moment did Rose disentangle her talons from the dragon's face, before it smashed into the water, launching an enormous wave onto the shores of the river, and sending the ferries and schooners moored at the seaport into a wild instant storm. A plume of steam rose up from the dragon's body before it sank beneath the surging waves.

Before Jane could cry out or augment Rose's flight with her magic, Rose stood next to her again, back in the form of a little girl. Rose looked exactly as she had a few minutes before, except her left hand was scorched and covered in blood.

Jane clasped that hand anyway, and drew Rose close. "Bless you child, you saved my life," she whispered.

"I'm only returning the favor, but look out," Rose replied, and Jane turned to see Imogen Stewart herself standing atop the gigantic granite tower where her dragon had perched only a minute before.

"How dare you," she bellowed. "Vicious, murderous girl! I will drink your blood before conquering the city."

"What you conquer, you destroy," Jane called up into the sky. The prim, proper figure of Imogen Stewart cut a hole into the blue behind her. "Come down, submit yourself to the justice of your fellow mages," Jane said. "You need not die."

"No untrained child is going to murder me!" Imogen shrieked back.

Without warning, Imogen blasted Jane's shields. They

held, barely, and Jane whispered her power back into them, reweaving them where they had frayed under Imogen's magical assault.

But Jane could not carry the day solely through defense. She stood tall and stretched her arms out from her sides. Rose flew up behind her, her wings catching the sunlight and sending multicolored streaks of light into the sky all around them.

Jane drank in the energy the phoenix so freely generated, and crafted a spell of binding. It was not a customary spell of Fire Mages, who preferred blasting and electrifying with their Fire power. But Daniel had taught her the intricate spells of Air, and the very oxygen in the air around them fed Jane's spell, augmented it.

The Air magic, coupled with Fire, caught the rogue mage off guard. Imogen thrashed, fighting the purple and orange streaks of light that surrounded her, ate up her own shields to feed Jane's spell.

And right behind her, Jane heard Daniel Tappen's dry, imperturbable voice: "Brilliant spellcraft, Jane, better than mine. I've never seen Fire and Air woven together so artfully. Truly, the work of a Master."

Jane wanted to give full credit to the phoenix, or even to Daniel himself, but she was too winded to resist his praise. Jane had never done magical battle before, and she was making up for it now.

"Thank you," she gasped.

Daniel stepped forward. "Miss Stewart," Daniel called into the sky, "your crimes have been exposed. The authorities intend to prosecute you to the fullest extent of the law. Surrender now if you wish to seek clemency."

"No one can stop me, much less that magicless milquetoast Grace! Go to hell, all of you." The rogue mage stared defiantly back at them, as the phoenix swooped over the bridge, screaming its desolate cry.

Imogen Stewart struggled against the bonds that Jane had looped around her shoulders, and it became clear to them all that she could work no magic, not under the constraints placed by Jane's spell.

"The story will run in the evening edition," Daniel said. "You are ruined, unless you surrender now."

"None of you can stop me, never!" And with a terrible wrench, Imogen yanked herself free.

But instead of assailing them, Imogen Stewart hurled herself off the bridge into the East River, hundreds of feet below. Her body hit the water with a hideous crash, and the currents sucked her under.

A horrible way for a Fire Mage to die, by drowning, but Imogen Stewart would never burn a child again. And if Imogen hadn't ended her own life, Jane had stood ready to embrace the darkness and murder the rogue mage herself.

Rose shot back to where Jane stood and resumed her human form. For a long moment, the three of them stood, staring at the place where Imogen Stewart had met her death.

"Are you really running the story? How will you manage?" Jane asked Daniel, her voice shaking.

"I suppose we'll have to tell it slant," Daniel said, his voice dry and sardonic as ever. "The headline will read: *City Rises from Ashes of Arsonist Empire, Is Reborn.*"

Jane glanced at her beautiful phoenix and smiled. "And I'm just the girl to write that story," she said.

Air of Mystery

Jody Lynn Nye

Aurelia Degard inclined her slender body ever so slightly toward Mme. Noisette and rotated the empty cut-crystal flacon held delicately between her pliant fingertips. The older woman, in spite of her corset and bustle, could not help but match her angle, so appealing was the sparkle of the leaded glass.

"But of course I can prepare the lavender toilet lotion for you as M. Rupier does, Madame," Aurelia said, her gentle voice holding no touch of reproof. She turned the glittering bottle so that the warmth of her hands under the small electric lamp would cause soothing aromas to arise from the drop of vetiver on her skin. She knew, as her master did, that there would be some protests against his absence in the Levant, so she had prepared a scent that calmed the senses and relaxed anxieties. Though subtle among the multiple sweet odors that permeated the shop, it still pervaded. It worked on her as well as on the privileged clientele. "He has taught me well. I have his recipe book, which lists not only the formula, but also the alterations you have requested over time. Are there any special requirements that you have for this replenishment?"

Aurelia tilted her conservatively coiffed head of

smooth, dark hair slightly to show deference, but not unctuous servitude. This was, after all, Le Parfumier Rupier, the finest purveyor of scents and perfumes in all of Paris, perhaps of France, and therefore of the world. It held its place proudly on the Rue du Faubourg St. Honore, just off the Champs Elysees in the 8th Arrondissement, that most exclusive of shopping precincts.

Mollified, Mme. Noisette placed a purple-deerskin-gloved fingertip to her plump cheek and looked around the shop as she considered. Much was there to please the onlooker. The warm, rosewood paneling of the walls made a charming, cozy setting for the Tiffany glass lamps in the dragonfly pattern, brilliant with greens and blues with a daring hint of red at the eyes. The counters were also of rosewood to the level of Aurelia's waist, where the display cases began. Those, polished to mirror brightness, picked up colored lights from the lamps. Underfoot, the soft silk carpets from Turkey and Persia glowed with subtle color, a blended perfume for the eyes.

"If you would add a trifle less of the chamomile oil, that would suit me. The scent seemed a little heavy the last time. You did not formulate it then, did you?"

Aurelia looked concerned. The expression brought a V-shaped line to her smooth, narrow forehead, and lowered her dark brows over her bright, hazel eyes. She consulted the large chestnut-colored, leather-bound ledger that lay upon the counter between them. The rasp as she turned each crisp page was like a whisper that hinted at deep, intriguing secrets.

"Alas, no, Madame," she said. "That would have been in February, just before the feast of St. Valentine, would it not? It is certain that M. Rupier created your lotion with his own hands. He will be desolated to know that you were displeased with it."

"Hmmph!" Madame snorted. "It was not so bad, I admit. But he will not return in time to mix this one for me?"

Aurelia folded her hands together on top of the ledger's cover.

"I regret, but no. It will cause him much pain to have missed a chance to serve you, such respect he has for you and your custom! His trip has only just begun. I have received a telegraph message from him that he has reached the kasbahs of Morocco. He will travel all the way across the north of Africa before he turns his feet back toward Paris. Perhaps not until June, or even the celebration of the republic in July."

Madame waved a hand.

"That is far too long. Very well, I have no choice but to trust you. My footman will call for the bottle in five days."

Aurelia drew herself up. Her slender back went stiff with pride. "He may come for it in three, Madame. That will be sufficient time to compile it to your chosen formula. I will give my personal and immediate attention."

Her emphatic reply surprised a nod of approval from Mme. Noisette.

"That will be satisfactory. Good day, Mlle. Degard."

Aurelia accompanied her to the heavy, carved door with the twinkling leaded panels cut into it. The apprentice clerk, a stocky boy of twelve with unruly red hair, ran to open it for the client. The trio of tiny silver bells hanging from a curved bronze Art Nouveau bracket shaped like a fairy at the top chimed farewell. He bowed deeply.

"Good day, Madame."

Aurelia turned away as the door closed. She would have brushed her hand in weariness across her forehead, but she needed to get the vetiver serum off her skin. It was a powerful preparation. M. Rupier rarely used it, and only in the presence of very important new clients. His personality was enough to cow his usual patrons. Aurelia did not consider herself to be impressive. In fact, she often went unnoticed by the very customers who fawned upon her master. She felt that she needed the serum to deal with Mme. Noisette.

Aurelia preferred not to attract much attention. Her plain black silk dress and modest kidskin shoes were meant to be self-effacing. Her features, while not considered plain, were, as her mother kindly put it, an acquired taste. Her hazel eyes were large and liquid enough. Her lips were perhaps a trifle thin for the current style of beauty, and her cheekbones too sharp to attract a gentleman's kiss. Her nose drew attention, not because it was large or red, but of an unusual shape, with an upward-tilted tip. Her brothers called it a pig nose, but truly, it did not bear any real resemblance to a snout. But, like the unlovely pig's, Aurelia's nose was remarkably sensitive. Luckily, everything in the shop smelled delightful to her.

"That was good," Alfonse said. "She bought, and she did not complain overmuch. Will you tell M. Rupier how well you did?"

"No," Aurelia said, with a smile for the boy. "Not until she has received it and not returned it with a curt note. Then I will crow about the success."

Alfonse nodded.

"That is a good idea. But you will make the potion

well. M. Rupier would not have trusted you with the entire shop if he did not expect you to. He would just have closed it, as he used to do before you came."

Aurelia frowned.

"Didn't he have an apprentice then?"

"Oh, yes, Robert, but M. Rupier didn't trust him as he does you," Alfonse said, with a dismissive wave of his hand. "Or Jean-Pierre, or Louise, or Darnelle. None of them have the magic. . . ."

"Stop!" Aurelia said. She covered her ears in mock horror. "I hope when it is my turn to depart, you won't tell tales about me to the next trainee!"

Alfonse smirked, his cherubic cheeks rounding.

"There will be no other trainee. You will be *parfumiere* after M. Rupier retires. I can tell. He has been looking for one such as you."

Aurelia liked the sound of that. *Parfumiere*.

She loved her job. The skills at mixing scents to achieve the desired results—such heavenly results—was a profession that she had barely dared contemplate. When she had been small, she assembled nosegays from gardens of the surrounding houses to create a mix of perfumes pleasing to the senses, so remarkably delicious that her friends and her mother's friends called upon her for almost any occasion that required a fragrant atmosphere. It was as if she could paint a picture with scents instead of colors like her more talented friends. She could tell just what little ingredient was needed to make the sought-after mood complete.

When she reached sixteen the previous December, a kindly guest at her father's home said he had seen a discreet notice for an assistant in M. Rupier's shop, and suggested she apply for the position. She could not be-

lieve how God had smiled upon her when M. Rupier
had taken her on.

During her interview in his luxurious and expensively
scented office, it had been as if the famous man did not
look directly at her once. He sat in his deep, chestnut
leather chair, upright like a cat, which he greatly resembled, with his narrow black mustaches waxed to points
like whiskers, and his green eyes watchful in his high-
cheekboned face. Even his glossy black hair was combed
back over his somewhat flat skull like the fur on a cat's
head. His hands were not like paws, though his fingers
ended in spatulate tips.

He had assigned her to mix the essential oils on the
table in proportions that would evaporate in the correct
order and at the correct rate. He had watched her hands
as she combined drops of the precious oils and extracts
with pure spirit, then sniffed each vial and tested each
preparation on his own wrists without meeting her eyes.
Until the end, when he came around the desk, took her
hand in his and bowed over it. His cat-green eyes seemed
to sparkle.

"Remarkable, mademoiselle. You have the job. Please
be prepared to start on the Monday of the new moon."

Over the past few months, she had progressed rapidly.
M. Rupier told her that she had excellent natural instincts
for what fragrances would be best as top, heart, and base
notes in perfumes and what would work best with what.
All she would need was technique, which he drilled into
her. He exclaimed over her triumphs and detailed carefully when she erred. Her finest day was when he accepted one of her own formulations to sell in the shop,
and she had the pleasure of seeing a customer buy it.

She thought of M. Rupier as a second father, and

trusted him utterly, but clearly he had secrets that he was not yet ready to share with her. She often thought that she saw things in the workroom behind the shop, among the ranks of retorts and distillation equipment that she could not explain, dancing crystal lights and liquid color. The room was indeed full of mirrors and bright glass, prisms and reflections, as though he sought to extend the effects of his potions even farther by dint of light.

He also had a private room he slipped into now and again, when something special was called for. Tactfully, Aurelia never mentioned it. If he wanted her to know what was in the small room, he would tell her. She knew the combination to the safe, which contained not only the money but some of the most precious ingredients. Some of them were poisonous, and could only be used in combination with others to denature their toxins, others were used as catalysts to cause the blooming of other potions. All of it smelled sweet and wholesome to Aurelia. She had favorites, of course, and unfavorites, those that she did not like, but she never shirked to check everything. Every Sunday, she prayed in the Cathedral de Sainte-Chapelle under the glory of its fifteen colored-glass windows, and gave thanks for such a brilliant opportunity to do what she loved.

Customers did not notice her, but she did not mind it. Her ambitions were small: to open a shop one day in a less fashionable part of Paris, or perhaps Lyon or Nice, and supply a select clientele. She, too, would go on exotic journeys like her employer, to find the best ingredients. Perhaps one day she would marry, a handsome man who came in with his sister to buy a present for their mother.

She returned to earth with a thump. Alfonse was regarding her with a surprisingly adult expression, almost one of indulgence.

"But what of you?" she asked, regretting her selfish fantasies. "Do you not wish to become a *parfumier*? You have been here longer than I."

He smiled.

"I do not have the nose, as you do. It is your magic. I am content to be a guardian. That is my nature."

She regarded him with puzzlement. Always to watch the doors of another, never to be the master of his own establishment? How curious that was.

Aurelia did not have time to ponder the oddity of Alfonse. The jingling of the door announced the arrival of another customer. Automatically, her eyes went to the large clock standing on a shelf high on the wall. This visitor took advantage of them. The shop hours went to five in the evening, and it lacked only six minutes until then. Still, it was not Aurelia's place to correct the manners of her betters. She straightened her back and applied her best smile as Alfonse brought the newcomer to her counter.

Since the fantasy had only just evaporated from her imagination, she eyed the gentleman as if he could be a prospective lover and husband. He stood a good foot taller than her petite height of five feet one inch. Aurelia tilted her head back against her lace collar to meet his eyes. Those were blue, but not the sea-blue of the Gauls—rather a gray that seemed diluted from India ink almost to colorlessness. His blond hair was, alas, from a bottle, not from nature. His skin—well, he wore cosmetics. Not an unfamiliar conceit among the fashionable gentlemen of Paris, particularly if one had been so unfortunate as to suffer the pox as a child, or catastrophic acne in adolescence. Otherwise, she found him quite handsome, though it seemed almost to her as if he wore a mask. His face was not his face, so to speak. He also wore a heavy *eau de cologne*, and not a becoming one. When he came closer, she became aware that he stank. The cologne was to hide his personal odor. The combination was nauseating, to be honest. She opened her mouth to offer some advice to him as to better scents to try, but he stopped her from speaking with a sharp look in his very pale blue eyes. A masterful man, then, and one aware of his rank. Perhaps he would not like a shop assistant for a wife.

"Your employer is on the premises, mademoiselle?" he inquired. His tenor voice had music in it. *Most appealing*, Aurelia thought.

"No, sir. He is away. May I serve? I am Mlle. Degard, M. Rupier's assistant *parfumiere*."

"I hope you may. You are experienced at formulations and potions?"

"Perfumes, lotions, eaux de toilettes, creams, powders, and sachets," Aurelia said promptly.

"I want a present for my dear friend," he said. The *chere amie* was politeness, Aurelia knew. His lover, then. "Something special. You may have noticed that I wear a perfume of my own."

"I . . . admit that I did, sir."

Her lowered eyes evinced a bitter laugh from him.

"It is because, well, to put it indelicately, I do not have a good smell of my own, and I want her to breathe in only good airs while I am with her."

"I can advise you," she said, eagerly. "I know many scents that can mask one's personal aroma. Most discreetly, of course."

He shook his head, almost sadly.

"Nothing has ever helped me," he said, his hands turned palm up. *Well, what can one do?* they seemed to ask.

"How may I serve, then?"

He removed a kidskin billfold from his inside breast pocket and extracted a slip of paper.

"I have consulted an expert, who has analyzed my . . . situation. These ingredients will mask my natural scent and also give my dear friend much pleasure. If you can concoct a perfume using them, then I can give her a gift that will make me the perfect beau, one whom she will want to keep near her all her life."

It was then Aurelia noticed that the gentleman's gloves were a trifle worn around the percussion side of the palm and under the fingertips. Not as new as they looked. And the coat, though of a fashionable color, was not of the most fashionable cut.

Aurelia examined the list he proffered her, and frowned over some of the items.

"It can be done, sir, but I fear that it will be a most expensive preparation, if you require *all* of these ingredients. The musk alone is several livres per gill."

His breath seemed to catch. She looked up at those ice-colored eyes. The pupils swelled for a moment, immersing the iris in black, then shrank again to a normal size. He smiled.

"All, if you please. I wish to win her heart for my own, mine alone. She has many admirers, as one might guess. At present I stand out, but not in a good way."

A rich lady, then, Aurelia guessed, since he did not mention her beauty. His *chere amie* was one whose financial gifts he hoped to realize, not just the favors of her person. The situation was not an uncommon one at all. There were as many impecunious gentlemen in Paris as there were destitute young ladies. She did not turn her nose up at them, knowing her own good fortune.

"I will do my best," she promised. "Has she a favorite flower or spice that I may use as the middle note for this gift? It is not a musical term," she explained as he looked puzzled. "It is the scent noticed, after the top note, which is usually something light and bright. This is the scent that will last the longest, giving her the most pleasure. The others listed here will work underneath it like servants, making all well behind the scenes."

"Ah, I understand," he said. "Tuberoses. She is partial to those. Any of the fragrant roses. I have brought her armloads for her pleasure. And she has asked for lilies."

"I see," she said. No doubt Madame wanted very strongly scented flowers to counteract the stench that pervaded this man's person. "Will you give me a week, sir? I wish to consult several of my employer's books for the best way to achieve the goal you require."

"But it is a surprise," he said, bringing his gloved finger to his lips. "No one outside this room must know of the gift."

Aurelia nodded grandly.

"Your consultation and purchase are confidential. It is the policy of M. Rupier, *Parfumier*, never to discuss the business of our clientele."

"Promise!"

"I promise," Aurelia said, with a puzzled frown. He took her hand and shook it firmly. The wave of unpleasant smell surrounded her, almost attaining a physical presence. She gasped. He could not help but notice her reaction, but kept his eyes fixed on hers.

"It is agreed, then. I go. Until we meet again, seven days from now."

"Until we meet again. Oh, sir, may I have a name to put in M. Rupier's ledger?"

He looked at her through those long, blond eyelashes. It was a wicked glance, and she saw how he could have attracted a wealthy patroness.

"Call me M. Casanova."

Aurelia felt her cheeks flush with hot red blood. He bowed to her and departed. The jingling of the doorbells sent a tingle up her spine.

"You should have asked for a partial payment," Alfonse said, when the sound had stopped. Aurelia's mouth fell open in dismay.

"Oh, you are right! But such a disconcerting man," she said. "So handsome, and yet . . ."

"I did not like him," Alfonse said, locking the door and turning the sign over to show that the shop was now "*Ferme*" instead of "*Ouvert*."

"Well, would you? You are not fond of men."

"I would not like him even if I did. He is a *poseur*. What is on the outside is not on the inside. How he smells, and that is very bad, speaks of his true nature to me. Did you like him?"

"Ah, but that is not our business," she said, with a sigh as she looked toward the closed door. "We create perfumes, airs of grace. He is a customer, and I will make up the gift for his lady friend. If she chooses to send him on his way, it will not be because she is displeased with a perfume from M. Rupier."

Aurelia laid the list on the table in the workroom and began to accumulate the ingredients. She read through the

great herbals and M. Poucher's manuals, and compared
them with the items in the inventory book. The mix of ingredients that M. Casanova wished combined would be
dreadful and heavy by itself, but since it was meant to mask
a very unpleasant human body odor, it had to be strong. At
her order, Alfonse retrieved most of the items, but the rare
musk was not to be found. She opened the safe. The rest of
the musks were there beside the rose and jasmine attars,
but not the one she needed. She threw up her hands.

"It must be in his small room."

Alfonse regarded her with an air of astonishment.

"You can see the door?"

"Why, yes, of course! I have even seen beyond the
threshold, though I have never gone inside."

Alfonse smiled.

"You are the right apprentice," he said. "You must be
a magician. No one else can see it."

Aurelia clicked her tongue impatiently. The door was
a door, like any other. She opened it and went in.

What she had glimpsed over M. Rupier's shoulder
did not have the impact of stepping inside. The small
room looked like a drawing by M. Aubrey Beardsley. Silvery tracings on the walls and carpet seemed to frame
her in an Art Nouveau forest. On one wall were shelved
many books. Where some were tied with ribbons, others
had chains around them. One, curiously, was immersed
in an enormous jar of water. Bubbles rose from between
its pages. The rest of the walls were filled with shelves of
stoppered flasks and bottles, some sealed with wax, others with leather or wood or other materials she could
not identify. The bottles themselves were made of cut
glass, rock crystal, wood of every color including blue
and green, beeswax and bakelite.

She had to hunt for the musk. M. Rupier had it tucked into a drawer at the side of the enormous desk. The jar was exquisitely beautiful. It had been cut from a piece of quartz that had veins of color running through it like ribbons or a folded rainbow, like pieces in the shop windows of the cristalleries Saint-Louis and Baccarat, but those were made of glass. Aurelia knew this was a natural piece. It must have been worth a fortune, but the musk inside was far more valuable. M. Rupier always cautioned her that enough to fill the tiny arc underneath her little fingernail would be twenty livres. This recipe called for almost that much. And rightly, too; it smelled wonderful.

She opened the jar to breathe the heady aroma.

A puff of blue steam whooshed out of the container.

In shock, Aurelia dropped the jar. She scrabbled for it, but another hand caught it before it hit the ground, one of translucent blue. A manlike figure arose behind it. Aurelia screamed and raced for the door.

The figure swooped around her and headed her off. She fell to her knees and put her palms together in supplication.

"Oh, dear Mother Marie, protect your child," she prayed, her voice trembling. "Bless me and keep me from demons!"

The figure coalesced into the shape of a preadolescent child, naked, of supernal beauty, more perfect than an alabaster statue.

"Fear me not, Sister," he said. His voice thrilled like a harp glissando. Aurelia covered her face with her hands.

"God, take this apparition away from me, lest it steal my soul!"

The strings of the harp tingled in an unmistakable laugh.

"I am not a threat, magician. What is your will?"

"I am not a magician!" she cried. "I mix perfumes. Oh, spare me, demon!"

"I am not a demon!" he said peevishly. "And you will bring the neighborhood down upon us, or at least Alfonse."

Aurelia looked up from her hands.

"What are you talking about—does he know of you?" The spirit flitted impatiently about her.

"Yes, of course! We are acquainted, though he is dull, like all those of Earth. You, though," he said, flying down to hover before her. His enormous eyes fixed upon hers with a bright expression of curiosity. "You are different. I believe—yes—you are one like me."

"I am not like you! I am a good Christian girl!"

He clicked his tongue, much as she had a moment before.

"You have all the power of the element of Air—but you are untrained. By Mother Nature, what a jape!"

He tittered with laughter. Stung, Aurelia summoned up all her courage.

"What are you?"

"A sylph," he said proudly. "A spirit of Air. I am Hyr. M. Rupier never told you about me?"

"No. And what are you doing in this jar of musk! It costs a fortune!"

"And delicious it is, too," Hyr said, his eyes twinkling.

"You are *eating* it?" she demanded in outrage. "This jar costs more than a year's pay!"

Hyr shook his head. "Not the substance, the scent. I am nourished by such as this. It is my pay for assisting M. Rupier. It is quite marvelous. Breathe it."

"Not now," she said, seizing the jar from Hyr's hands. "I must make up a perfume that uses this."

Hyr twisted his slender body and flew up to circle the electric light on the ceiling.

"But this is marvelous! I shall help you with your spell!"

She found herself growing impatient with this laughing sprite. However magical, he was exasperating!

"I don't know how to do spells!"

"But M. Rupier does. Where is he?"

Aurelia did not want to believe her ears, but her eyes showed her an impossibility, so she had to lend some measure of credence.

"He is a magician? An Air Magician?"

"No, he is a Water Master—how is it you work for him and do not know this?"

Overwhelmed by the strange concepts, not to mention conversing with a spirit, Aurelia burst into tears.

"I don't know any of this! He went away to the Levant and told me nothing!"

Hyr zipped to her side. She felt a gentle breeze touch her cheeks, drying the tears away.

"It is simple, mistress. It is the energies of Air and Water together that make up great perfumes. They incorporate notes from Earth and Fire as well. A good perfume is like a good spell. It calls up gentle powers to create an effect that is magical. Do you not feel that way?"

That Aurelia understood, to her very bones. The concept helped to assuage her terror.

"Oh, I do!"

"Good!" Hyr exclaimed. "Come, then, and I will mix the airs for you so you need not waste your ingredients working out the proportions to use."

Alfonse did not blink at the translucent blue child

hovering beside Aurelia as they emerged from the small office.

"You found the musk, then," he said, with a cheerful smile.

"Yes, I did," Aurelia said crossly, "and this fellow beside! And how long would it have been before the three of you saw fit to explain the witches' coven into which I have wandered?"

"Not long. M. Rupier thought of doing so before he departed, but he realized he would have more to explain and to teach you than time permitted. It was to occur once he returned. But you have surprised his secret. I have sent him a message by way of an Earth Elemental. He should have it by now."

Aurelia frowned.

"How . . . ? I shouldn't even ask. I can only hope my soul is not imperiled by associating with all of you."

"Only if you do evil," Hyr said, blithely, whisking toward the worktable. "Come! I am impatient to smell this new concoction!"

With Alfonse standing by, Aurelia and Hyr went over the ingredients. As he promised, the sylph seemed to be able to draw the aromas together in a small crystal bowl from which Aurelia could inhale the scents. Instead of being invisible, the aromas were wisps of color that danced around like dust devils.

"Put your nose to that, magician-who-isn't," he said. "Not your nose as such, but your sense of balance."

"I don't know what you mean!" Aurelia protested. She sat on the tall, wooden stool with the erect posture of a schoolgirl, her heels hooked through the bottom rung.

"Let me guide you," Hyr said, flitting around her like a housefly. "Feel the scent. It is not substantial to you as it is to me, but you know when they fit together, like a puzzle. Close your eyes. Find the way to make them work in harmony."

Aurelia dipped her head toward the bowl. Aromas warred with one another. It was an unpleasant combination, all too earthy. Too much of the myrrh essence made her choke. It argued with the licorice root, ginger, and calamus oils. She cringed as the cedar and bergamot entered the fray. The musk threatened to overwhelm all the other ingredients. But if she used only a tiny bit of it, and pulled in the flavor of jasmine—yes, jasmine!—for the heart note, she could make a scent that was not only pleasant, but appealing, even serene. The top note must be flowery and a trifle spicy.

"I need a light floral scent," she said, almost to herself, beginning to get down from her perch.

"I will fetch some!" Hyr said, whisking away. Ten small glass bottles floated in the air toward her.

"Thank you," Aurelia said, watching the flight in wonder. "I did not mean to make you do the work."

The Sylph laughed, a tinkly sound like ringing crystal.

"You command me, not the other way around. Now, what do you require?"

Clover—yes, that would be delightful. It was a humble flower, but one could not fault its delicate aroma.

"Clover," she said. At once, the stopper flew off, and a wisp of pinky whiteness rose to join the rest of the tinted airs in the bowl. Yes, that was the last element to make the whole harmonious. She sat back with a sigh of pleasure.

How marvelous to be able to work so effortlessly! It was

a miracle! Shyly, she looked up at Hyr, who let out another of his bright chuckles. She returned to her musing. She would only do good with these wonders, please God.

"This reminds me of something," the sylph said, circling around the bowl like a goldfish. "I can't think of what it is. But it was a very long time ago. And perhaps it wasn't even I who smelled it, but one of my kind."

Aurelia groaned. She was becoming impatient with his breezy memory.

"He forgets a lot of things," Alfonse said, laughing. That is why he cannot be trusted to carry messages."

"He has done good service for us today," Aurelia said. "For us and M. Rupier."

Hyr exploded in a burst of blueness from sheer pleasure. Aurelia smiled indulgently.

Aurelia sat in a cab, straightening her skirt nervously. M. Casanova had not come in himself, for which she was grateful, but he had sent a message with his payment. Would Mlle. Degard kindly deliver the perfume herself to the lady? There was enough money included for a taxi for both the outward and return trips. Aurelia was impressed by his generosity. She could rarely afford to ride in cabs. This one had good springs and a good horse. She clutched on her lap the cranberry-red carton marked in gold with the name 'Rupier,' which contained the perfume bottle.

The flat at which it deposited her had a most fashionable address. This was not a neighborhood where one found courtesans or mistresses, as near the theatres, but people of independent means. If the lady in question had once been the dear friend or wife of a wealthy gentleman, it was she who commanded now.

Aurelia told the cab to wait. The service entrance was much less grand than the white-outlined front door with a uniformed footman on duty. Aurelia walked past a boiler-suited workman and up four flights to the apartment designated as the home of Madame du Charpentier. A maid in a starched white apron and cap over a trim black uniform answered her knock and accepted the package. Aurelia began to descend the stairs. She had not yet reached the door when a cry from above arrested her.

"Mam'selle! Please return! Madame wishes to see you!"

It was most irregular for her to be admitted to the front part of a customer's domicile. Aurelia stood nervously in the center of a room that was more a jewel box for its inhabitant than a mere chamber. Sumptuous silk hangings of warm, beautiful colors depended from ornamental bronze fittings. The furniture had been expensively upholstered in damasks and brocades to match. Madame du Charpentier lounged upon a fainting couch in a satin gown with her small feet in Chinese slippers. She was a lady of a certain age, older than Aurelia's mother, but not as old as *Grandmere*.

Aurelia smelled, or, rather, sensed something wrong in the room. She could not identify the source of the discomfort. The sylph had awakened a new sense in her! She had many questions for M. Rupier when he returned.

"And how may I serve, madame?" she asked.

Mme. du Charpentier appealed to her, blue eyes wide with pleasure and curiosity.

"Mademoiselle, I implore you! It is so nice to get a parcel from M. Rupier, but who gave it to me?"

"Madame, I do not know his name."

"Describe him!" Madame commanded.

Aurelia shook her head. "I regret, Madame, that he swore me to secrecy. No doubt he wishes to tell you himself."

The woman and her maid exchanged glances.

"It is M. le Bovin," the maid said.

"Doris!" the woman exclaimed, rapping her maid on the wrist with her ivory-backed fan. "You should not refer to M. Carnau in that fashion."

"It is true," the maid said, unrepentant. "I will call him M. le Cochon instead. No matter how many gifts he gives you, he smells like a pig, not an ox. And he is a pig!"

"Well, this makes up for it," Madame said, opening the small bottle and inhaling the essence. "Oh, it is heavenly! Tell M. Rupier that it gives me much joy."

Aurelia inclined her upper body.

"I shall, Madame. But I must tell Madame that your admirer gave me the basis of the formulation himself. He wished to please you."

"Of course he did." Madame waved the fan. "He is most persistent. I know a man who has an eye out for opportunity. I do not cast my *sous* as if they were breadcrumbs. If he was not so infernally handsome, I should send him about his business. Still," her expression softened, "if he has such a sensitive soul as to cause you to create such a perfume for me, perhaps I am too hasty to dismiss him. And this will greatly abate the displeasure of his miasma." She took another deep sniff of the bottle.

"That is its intention, Madame," Aurelia said.

Mme. du Charpentier seemed to have forgotten that she was present. She waved her fan.

"Thank you, mademoiselle. You may go."

Aurelia was troubled by the dazed look on Madame's face, but she departed.

Over the following weeks there was much to do. Madame Noisette had spread the word about her lavender lotion, and how it picked up her spirits. Aurelia had many orders from the lady's friends.

"You see, your talents are manifesting themselves," Alfonse said.

"It is chemistry, dolt, not magic," Aurelia corrected him.

"I think you will find that it is both."

While she worked and Hyr darted around her like an insane hummingbird, Alfonse read to them from the newspapers. He adored the society columns, especially the rumors and confidential whispers. Now that they knew their mystery customer's name, Alfonse looked for any reference to M. Carnau.

"It said yesterday that M. Carnau must declare bankruptcy or leave the country," he said, "but today, here is word that he has been rescued from ruin."

"Good for him," Aurelia said, signing to Hyr to add chamomile to the dancing wisps in her mixing bowl.

"In fact, he is getting married!"

"He is? To whom?"

"To 'the delightful Mme. du Charpentier, a widow of means.'" Alfonse held up the paper. A drawing of 'M. Casanova', by a popular artist, depicted him in a local café with Madame at his side looking rapt.

Aurelia put down her vials and frowned at the page. She could not possibly have fallen in love with him. He was too conceited and she was too sensible.

"Hyr?"

The translucent boy child obediently whisked to a stop before her eyes.

"Mistress?"

"That perfume that we made for Madame. Have you recalled why it smelled familiar to you?"

"Which perfume? The one with musk and ginger and bergamot and . . . ?"

"Yes!" Aurelia interrupted him. "Is it a love potion?"

"Oh, no!" Hyr said, floating away from her on his back as if swimming in a river. "It is more of . . . an obedience drug. You may command the wearer to do your will. Well, nearly. What you formulated lacked at least one ingredient."

Aurelia felt herself grow very still.

"And what was that?"

"Oh, it is unpleasant. Cow urine. That is why it is so seldom used any longer. I can't think of the last time it was employed. Was it two hundred years ago in Persia, or three . . . ?"

"He does that to himself," Aurelia realized. The dreadful smell was deliberate. He caused her to surround herself with scented things. "Can he persuade her to give him money?"

Hyr waved his hands expansively.

"Anything! Speak, and it is done."

"Could he persuade her to marry him? Could he command her to make over her entire fortune to him?"

"Naturally. But the potion wears off quickly if it is not renewed, and especially if the commander is no longer close. Pheromones, the natural perfumes of the body, are part of it. It is most specific. She would only take instructions from the one."

He couldn't have added them to the perfume. The pheromones must have been present in the room already, no doubt in one of the other gifts the maid said he had brought.

"If it wears off, she would come to her senses," Alfonse said.

"Not if she died," Aurelia said.

"What?" Alfonse asked.

"Hyr," Aurelia asked, seriously, "could he tell her to . . . to die?"

Hyr was untroubled by the notion.

"Oh, yes. It is a powerful potion. It would be easy. All he would have to do is tell her that her heart must stop beating. And it would."

A horrible picture suddenly rose before her eyes. Aurelia laid down her pipettes.

"He is marrying her for money. Surely someone, perhaps her grown children, already suspects this terrible man of fortune-hunting. But if she dies after the marriage, her money will pass to him. My father is a man of law. I have heard many such cases discussed over the dining table. A court suit would take a long time. A marriage, only minutes."

"That is horrible!" Alfonse declared. "What can we do?"

The stink was the clue. The terrible smell was one of the things that had been missing from the completed potion—for it was a potion, not a perfume. It was evil magic, against the will of God. The Holy Bible did not say that a witch must not live, but rather that a poisoner must die. And M. Carnau was poisoning this poor woman, but through her pores and her nose, not her lips. She had fallen into his power. He had done it deliberately. Why else the strange list of ingredients? Why else the secrecy? He had made Le Parfumier Rupier complicit in a future crime!

"We must create a counteragent," Aurelia said, firmly. "I must recreate the potion in its entirety, and find a way to undo its works. We have little time. Hyr! Help me!"

"At once, mistress!"

Hyr began to send vials and bottles flying her way. Alfonse went out, locking the door behind him.

Aurelia assembled from memory the elements of the perfume in the crystal bowl. She still liked her formulation. If it had not such dire associations, she would be pleased with herself!

Alfonse returned suddenly, holding a covered crockery jar at arm's length. He handed it to Hyr, who made a terrible face. The contents made Aurelia's eyes water.

"It is pig," Alfonse said. "Do not ask how I got it."

Aurelia smiled at him.

"I won't."

Moaning about the stench, Hyr added a yellow wisp of pig's urine to the luscious mixture in the bowl. As soon as he did, Aurelia felt a strong sense of compulsion coming from it.

She closed her eyes and concentrated. It was a strange thing, but she understood how every element went together. She felt her way through the sweet and sour. The bitter, dry notes of the myrrh should have made it feel sacred, but it was overpowered by the hot, fierce stench of the pig's excretion. Her eyes stung. The sylph's favorite musk was last, its heady, rich aroma tickled her nose, but she felt it go deeply into her mind.

"Come back, mistress!" Hyr shouted. She felt a wind buffet her backward. She coughed, reassembling her wits. She sniffed. The sylph smiled at her. He gestured to the bowl. The wisps had vanished.

"I have cleared the air, mistress."

"Thank you," Aurelia said, sighing. "Magic is indeed a gift."

"Is there an answer?" Alfonse asked. "Can you counteract the poison?"

"Indeed there is," Aurelia said. Her thoughts had tiptoed among the scents and odors at her command, and come up with the right scent. "And it is so simple, as simple as a key slipping into a lock. This is a sin. It is only appropriate that trinity flowers should heal it. Hyr, let us begin."

The sylph flitted around the workroom lamp with joy.

"Command me, mistress! This is fun!"

Alfonse delivered the box to the home of Madame du Charpentier. It was a gift from Parfumier Rupier, the enclosed note said, in honor of her upcoming marriage. The young guardian returned to the shop.

"Are you certain that this will undo the evil?" he asked Aurelia. "Must I cast additional protections upon the premises?"

"I think not yet," she said. "Wait and see."

And they did. The very next day's paper contained an interesting note in the gossip column.

"The engagement between Mme. du Charpentier and M. Carnau had been called off, definitely and for good," Alfonse read, relishing each word. "The gentleman has departed from Paris."

Aurelia could not help but be relieved.

"Now the poor lady will never have to smell that stench again. She can enjoy the perfume in peace."

"What if M. Casanova learns that the gift was from us? He may seek revenge!"

Aurelia showed him the small vial that hung around her neck on the same chain as her silver cross. Its value was greater than a month's pay, but M. Rupier would undoubtedly forgive the debt—since he had left her without explanations of the many secrets hidden in the shop.

"If he comes here, I shall give him a taste of his own medicine," she said. "I will compel him to turn himself in to the Gendarmerie. That will teach him to pollute the element of Air."

A Flower Grows
in Whitechapel

Gail Sanders
and Michael Z. Williamson

Isabelle Helen Harton, Headmistress of the Harton
School for Expatriate Children, was in her office when
Karamjit knocked discreetly.

He said, "There is a child at the entrance, Memsa'b.
The guardians want to speak to you."

She knew by his tone and phrasing that these were
not the usual nursemaids or concerned parents that normally came to the doors of her school.

She closed her book, stood and said, "Thank you, Karamjit. I'll be right there." She rose from her chair and
walked downstairs.

When she opened the door to the chill, damp, February air, she gasped and stared. There was indeed a child,
but the guardians holding her hands so carefully were
Elementals.

It wasn't uncommon for waifs to be dropped off at
police stations, orphanages, or churches.

It was quite rare for one to be brought to the front
door of the Harton School by Earth and Air Elementals.
In fact, it had never happened before.

Gathering up her astonishment and sitting on it hard, speaking with at least the appearance of aplomb, she politely asked, "May I help you?" Protocol must be adhered to when dealing with Elementals or unexpected things could happen.

"She is pursued. She is in danger. She is alone." The breathy syllables could barely be heard above the noises on the street. The sylph's feet did not touch the ground and she did not leave a shadow, of course, but she gripped the hand of the little girl with desperation all too visible, despite the sylph's transparency.

"What pursues? What is the danger?" Isabelle's astonishment was giving way quickly to alarm.

"We know not. All we know is that it has consumed her parents, and reaches out for her. Will you take her into your charge? Knowing that there is danger?" This was remarkably formal for a normally flighty satyr. This was also alarming to Isabelle and she hesitated, knowing that the request was both a geas and a binding. Looking at the confused and frightened eyes of the small girl, she knew that she could not turn her away.

"I will take her into my charge and protect her to the extent that I am able."

"It is well," both Elementals said in unison, before disappearing, one sinking into the ground and one fading into the air.

The girl collapsed onto the frosty front step, as if only the Elementals had been keeping her going.

The child appeared to be far too small for the neat little room. Her dark hair spread over the pillow as she restlessly shifted, but she did not awaken. She had a faint Chinese cast, but was clearly mostly European.

What am I going to do with you, little one? Isabelle wondered as she kept watch from an overstuffed armchair. She had no idea what the guardianship of the Elementals could mean and the prospect of danger was not new, yet she was used to having at least some information from which direction that danger might come. She also knew that she couldn't have left the little one to her fate. She sighed deeply and then reached up to caress the hand that had appeared on her shoulder.

"Who do we have here?" Frederick Harton, Isabelle's soft-footed husband, said in his quietly concerned voice.

"I don't know, but potentially a very great problem." Isabelle gestured over to the clothing that was laid out on the other small bed in the room. Neatly laid out was a skirt with petticoats, as English as would fit in any middle to upper-class neighborhood, but next to them was a blue silk tunic of distinctly Asian design. The fabric was a bit worse for wear, with a couple of ragged tears.

She ran her fingers over the rich fabric. "It's a *cheong sam*. They're Chinese, and this quality of material is only worn by higher-class diplomats or their families. I encountered a few Chinese merchants in India and they didn't wear anything this fine. The Chinese are very structured, with strict laws on what each level can wear. Why would a European girl child be wearing something that only a Chinese diplomat would be allowed to wear?"

He offered a reassuring squeeze but no comment.

She continued, "We won't know anything until she awakens. She was also wearing a red silk pouch around her neck. I left that alone. Even in her sleep, she became very agitated when I touched it."

"Does she have a name?"

"Mei-Hua," she replied. "Which is also a puzzle. She's clearly English, and her accent places her to Cheshire. Yet she offered a Chinese name in excellent Mandarin."

"Headmistress?"

If her office hadn't been so quiet, Isabelle never would have heard the hesitant question.

"Yes, Mei?" She tried to project reassurance. The little thing was so self-effacing that she almost blended into the walls, even after being here for a month. She had no problems with the other children per se; it was almost as if they didn't know she existed. Everyone in the school was surprised when she spoke, as if by her speaking she had become real to them again.

"Agansing said I was to talk to you, please? About the garden?" Mei-Hua bowed deferentially and kept her eyes low, avoiding eye contact with Isabelle.

"What about the garden, child?" Isabelle had to work hard to keep a sigh out of her tone. To a woman used to cheeky Londoner children, this politeness seemed both extreme and worrisome. Combine it with Mei-Hua's knack of remaining unnoticed, and it spoke of unseen damage from whatever she could not remember—either in what happened to Mei's parents or how she came to the school.

"Agansing said that no one really has time to take care of it. So may I, please? And may I have a pot and soil for a plant in my room?" Mei waited, her slender body seeming tense and anxious.

"That sounds like an excellent idea. Tell Agansing I gave you permission, and if you need anything for the garden, he can help you with it."

"Thank you, Headmistress." Mei bowed again and closed the door behind her.

Perhaps with a useful activity she will come out of that shell. With that thought Isabelle turned back to reviewing her students' progress.

Isabelle stared, and searched her memory. Yes, just a few days ago, this plant had been dry, sallow, wilted and near death. She'd noted the contrast to those around it.

Now, though, it was vibrant with color, flush with growth and taller than its neighbors, which also seemed to stand more proudly. The bloom atop it was perfectly picture-book symmetrical, and seemed to glow violet with a lip-red sheen underneath. It was beautiful.

"How did this happen?" she asked the girl.

Mei-Hua shrugged slightly and mumbled, "It was tired. I helped it."

"You most certainly did!" she replied, but the girl had turned shyly away and offered nothing else.

Within days every flower in season bloomed huge and bright, even those that barely budded in April. The stalks straightened, the leaves filled out. All the herbs in the garden behind the kitchen sprouted thick and healthy, and the food gained an extra little zest.

Two weeks later, Isabelle happened to pass Mei-Hua's room whilst on an errand. The girl was just coming out on her way to breakfast. Behind her, near the window, the pot she'd asked for sprouted a huge white peony.

It was impossible for such a blossom to bloom so quickly. Or was it? Clearly it had. Clearly also, Mei-Hua had a talent for flowers.

The girl took her classes, quietly, and had no trouble with grammar, arithmetic, or history. When not busy with schooling or chores, she spent most of her time out in the garden, caressing and talking to the various plants, all of which responded with straight, robust growth. The plant in her room remained in brilliant bloom, new flowers replacing the old.

Lord Alderscroft's carriage was familiar, but its arrival unexpected. It drew up in front of the school, and he debarked in a hurry. He reached the door as Karamjit opened it in surprise.

"Good day. I must speak to Frederick and Isabelle at their earliest convenience," he said as Karamjit took his cane and hat.

In minutes he was seated in the drawing room, and hot, fragrant tea was placed on a table between them.

Isabelle gave a nod that indicated Karamjit was to leave them alone. This was clearly something under the rose.

Frederick remarked, "So, David, what brings you to our little corner of Whitechapel? It's hardly your usual haunt." He poured three cups of tea with splashes of milk and delicate sprinkles of sugar.

Alderscroft accepted his cup with a nod and spoke directly to the point.

"I bring tragic news. You have heard that the King has been fatigued of late. It has reached a crisis. Yesterday he collapsed unconscious, and is now bedridden. They aren't sure if he's in a coma, or has suffered an aneurysm or something similar."

Isabelle widened her eyes. "There was no mention in the morning news, nor have I heard anything from the stands."

"No, it is all word of mouth, to keep it from the tabloids."

Her stomach fluttered.

"Oh, dear. They have no diagnosis?"

Over a sip, Alderscroft said, "Not yet. Officially, he is taking a few days' rest at Marlborough House and responding to a personal matter. You see, the reason I came to you is that I don't think that the doctors are going to find anything. I think that the reason for his collapse has something to do with magic—but not my sort of magic, not Elemental magic. After his collapse, my contact at the palace was able to get me into his rooms. They were awash with, something . . . I could almost feel myself going under, slowing down. But I could not *find* anything."

"And so you've come to us for help?" Isabelle's scepticism caused David Alderscroft to flinch. "Don't tell me you've found something that your 'White Lodge' can't handle?"

"Actually, I was hoping that Sarah and Nan could have a look. I can get us into the Royal Residence, into the King's rooms."

She flared her nostrils and tensed as she placed her teacup down gently, but with haste. "No! Absolutely not. David, you know how I feel using the children that way. Sarah Jane Lyon-White and Nan are still children, and I will not put them into danger."

"Love, I think we must," Fredrick quietly interrupted her angry reflex with a hand on her wrist. She leaned back into her chair as he continued, "Will we be with them, Alderscroft?"

He nodded and placed his own cup down. "Yes, I can promise that much. And I'll have to go along as well. They won't let you in without me."

She unclenched her jaw and accepted the wisdom of the idea.

"Tonight then. I want time to prepare the girls."

They rode in Alderscroft's carriage to the rear of Marlborough House. He stepped out first and spoke at length to a military officer, a captain, probably of the Lifeguards, but in field uniform, not parade. The other men all appeared to be police. Marlborough House was a Royal Residence, but not the Palace. The informal presentation would help disguise the King's presence.

The captain frowned darkly, but acceded after several minutes of talk punctuated with gestures. He stepped inside, and spoke into one of those new-fangled telephone boxes.

With a command and a gesture, the two guards at the door snapped their rifles to port arms and stepped aside. That seemed to be assent to entry.

Isabelle was impressed. Not even two waifs with birds and three obvious foreigners with a less than fashionable schoolmistress caused them to be anything other than impassive statues.

Inside, a young man in a bespoke suit gestured for them to follow him up the stairs. Even the rear servants' staircase was broad and elegant.

Little noise was made and nothing was said. They walked down a long corridor, the children uttering soft gasps at the sights but otherwise silent.

Another guard stood at a double door, its panels book-matched of some highly figured wood. There was an exchange of gestures between their escort and the guard, at which he nodded smartly, opened the door and stepped aside.

Within was a private chamber, richly appointed and

smelling of tobacco. A doctor sat beside a huge, soft bed. Nestled in the deep comforters was His Royal Majesty, Edward VII, clearly sick.

His eyes were closed and sunken, his cheeks hollow. Even his proud beard looked scraggly and weak. Looking up at this remarkable group of people, the doctor approached Lord Alderscroft and obviously started to make a fuss.

Words were exchanged, the doctor wide-eyed with raised eyebrows. He looked at the unusual party and then back at Alderscroft, opening his mouth to protest. Then somehow, with the addition of but a few more low words, the doctor quietly gathered his bag and let himself out. Isabelle's cynical mind suspected a method other than sweet reason had been used to get the doctor to at least temporarily quit the scene.

"He won't be gone long," Lord Alderscroft commented, rejoining the rest of the group.

At once, Gray whistled low. *"Bad. Something here."* The parrot fluffed up her feathers and then spread her wings over Sarah's shoulders.

Even the humans could feel it. There was an aura of despair. It was if they were standing on the edge of a cliff, staring down mesmerized at the rocks below, just waiting for the pull of gravity . . .

Neville quorked loudly, startling everyone. The raven on Nan's shoulder had his feathers ruffled as well, and looked as if he wanted to bite something, if he could spot it. Even with the warning Alderscroft had given them, they had almost been drawn in themselves.

Sarah looked up at Gray and then over at Nan. It was obvious neither of them wanted to get closer to that feeling, but Isabelle knew it was the only way.

With a polite tug at her sleeve, Karamjit said, "Memsa'b, we need light. We need light to pierce the darkness around the King."

Isabelle's voice began a chant that the girls probably found a bit familiar. Sarah would have heard that chant before, when the girls had been trapped in a house haunted by something worse than any ghost. Nan reached out her hand and clasped Sarah's before joining her voice to the chant. The other members of the party joined in. Slowly a glow surrounded the two girls and they walked forward, approaching the pillared bed.

As the girls stood by the bed, time drew out endlessly. Sarah and Gray appeared to be conversing with . . . nothing . . . or rather, with something that wasn't there.

The darkness got heavier and the two girls retreated.

Nan blurted in a forceful whisper, "Let's get outta 'ere. 'Tain't safe. Back to the school." Even though she was a child, no one felt the slightest inclination to argue with her.

They made a hasty retreat, and Isabelle felt safer the farther they moved from the King's bedside. When they reached the stairs, she was merely unnerved. By the time they entered the carriage, she felt adequate.

"Not a word until we are at the school," she cautioned.

When they arrived back home, Nan and Sarah seemed comfortable and secure enough.

"I think that we could all use a cup of tea. Agansing, could you please bring it to the parlor?" Isabelle briskly took charge and chivvied everyone in that direction.

Sarah said, "Please, but . . ."

"Yes? Go ahead, young lady."

Sarah hesitated only a moment.

"Memsa'b, before I tell you what I found out, we need Mei-Hua. She has to be here." Her solemn tone lent her a maturity out of place for such a young girl.

Mystified, Isabelle went and found Mei in her room, talking to her White Peony in a soft melodious voice, in Mandarin. Startled, the girl looked up as Isabelle entered the room.

"Mei, we have a situation that may involve you. Please come with me."

Mei simply bowed and followed the headmistress. She did not seem at all surprised. She followed to the parlor and took the worn chair in the corner.

Finally, with all of them gathered, Sarah spoke nervously. "The King is possessed. They seek his life force. That is why the doctors find no malady. It is almost as if his dreams hold him captive and out of his body. The longer this goes on, the weaker he will become, until the King dies."

"Who does?" Isabelle asked. "Who controls his dreams?"

Sarah shrugged in agitation. "I do not know. Only that he is held."

It was entirely possible the doctors couldn't determine his condition because of limits in their art. However, Sarah had been accurate in her spiritual sojourns before. Isabelle was inclined to believe her. She did have one question, though.

"How do you know this, Sarah?"

"Mei's parents told me."

Mei-Hua gasped.

"What do you mean my parents told you? My parents are dead and gone, I saw them die," Mei-Hua whimpered. "I saw them die," she repeated.

Isabelle was glad that Mei's memory was returning, but she was afraid that the shock could be too much. She leaned over and took the girl's hand in comfort.

"Please wait just a moment, Mei," she said gently. After a few moments of sobs and deep breaths, Mei-Hua nodded, and she explained, "Sarah can sometimes talk to the departed."

Turning back, she asked, "Is that what happened, Sarah?" She gave a pleading look, wanting the girl to be gentle.

Sarah nodded around her tea.

"Yes, Memsa'b. Mei's mother was a gardener, and Mei's father was a foreign minister. They learned of a plot against the King because of England's actions in Hong Kong."

"By whom?"

"They said it was some enemy of the Emperor Zuan-tong."

Mei-Hua said, "*Xuāntǒng*." She looked a bit more alert.

Frederick asked, "Could it be the last gasp of the Boxers?"

Fully attentive, Mei asked Sarah, "Did they mention *guizi*?"

Sarah nodded and said, "Yes, I heard exactly that."

"It means 'demon,'" Mei said. "It's what the Righteous Harmony Society, the Boxers, call foreigners."

Isabelle asked, "Mei, were your parents working on a treaty with the Emperor?"

Mei shifted in the chair and looked uncomfortable.

"Well, it wouldn't be with the Emperor, no one sees him, but with Royal Ministers. But I don't know."

Isabelle tabled that for now, and turned back to Sarah. "What then?" she asked.

Sarah said, "There was a spirit attack in China. Mei's parents had come up with a counter to it. Then the spirits moved here."

Isabelle said, "If they couldn't succeed against the Emperor, then the King would be the next choice."

"Yes."

Mei said, "So, that's why we came back." She looked very unhappy, but sat erect and strong.

Isabelle said, "Then your parents were attacked—" she didn't say 'killed' "—in London, before they could tell of it. Once Mei was under the protections of the school, they couldn't find her. So, they've been at the side of the King, hoping against hope that Mei would find them."

"What is this plot? Who's doing the plotting?" asked Frederick.

"They didn't know. They were only able to find that it involved getting at the King through his dreams."

"And the counter?"

"It's my White Peony." Mei looked terrified and elated at the same time. "The one in my room. It's from the plant my mother bred. It's like no other in the world. Its scent will protect the King from the dreams. We were coming to England to present it to the King when my parents died. Now I remember why they're dead." A tear crept down Mei's face. "Now I remember who they were."

Isabelle leaned over and carefully held the girl. Between the spirit attack and the shock of it, her memory had blocked it all until now. Its return would be painful, too.

After some discussion, they formed a new party, much smaller this time; Isabelle and Lord Alderscroft escorted

Mei-Hua to the House. She carried her White Peony in a beautifully painted pot.

With due ceremony, Aldercroft's carriage was let into the courtyard. They debarked and entered through the main foyer, in daylight this time.

The doorman and guards let them through, and their suited escort showed them to the front private stairs. Alderscroft said something, and there was another brief argument, but their guide bowed briefly and departed.

As the three of them climbed the narrow stairs, Mei-Hua slowed, and then stopped.

"I remember this place." Her whisper was so quiet that Isabelle almost couldn't hear it.

With increasing concern, Isabelle knelt down and looked at Mei.

"How do you remember it? You haven't been here."

Mei couldn't answer her. Her eyes were wide and she was caught up in memories, trembling so hard she could barely retain her grip on the flowerpot.

"We were here," she said. "It was on these stairs."

The fear in her eyes caused Isabelle to glance up at Alderscroft. His expression was one of mild annoyance at the delay, but behind him Isabelle noticed a gathering darkness.

"David! Shields, now!"

Alderscroft reacted at once to her commanding tone, and raised the shields of a Fire Master, shields of ethereal Fire. Through their swirling flames they saw the darkness strike at them and rebound, and strike again. It resembled a swarm of insects in its glittering darkness, but with no actual discernible forms. Eventually, after long minutes, it drew back and waited, just beyond reach of Alderscroft's shields, leaving them in a black stairwell that sucked up all the light that entered it. It even felt dank.

With the initial attack rebuffed, Isabelle felt Mei still trembling.

"Mei, what else do you remember?"

The girl stared vacantly, gasping in whimpers. She knelt and hugged the flowerpot.

Isabelle gave her just a slight shake. "Mei, we need to know now. What else do you remember?"

Finally Mei focused on Isabelle.

"They were only able to protect me, to get me out. I ran and I ran and I didn't stop running. They died to protect me." Tears rolled unnoticed down her cheeks.

Remembering the Elementals that brought Mei to her, Isabelle turned and said, "David, they were Earth and Air. Are your shields still holding?"

He nodded. "Yes, but we need to start moving. This is going to get noticed. We need a guide through the darkness."

"Will a Warrior of the Light do?" she asked, though it wasn't really a question. Firmly, she added, "Mei, take my hand. This time you are not running."

Isabelle's appearance changed with each step of the staircase. She began to glow with a light that pierced through the darkness and lit the way forward. Her stature grew and her aspect became that of an ancient Greek huntress, wearing a short, chemise-like garment that would have scandalized proper society. At least, it would have done so until they had seen her face, then they would have been terrified. Step by hard-won step, the trio climbed the sweeping stairs, Isabelle coaxing Mei-Hua along while Alderscroft reinforced his rebounding shields. When they had reached the top, the darkness gathered itself up for one final blow. Sensing the increase in tension, Alderscroft changed tactics; instead of blocking the onslaught, his flames engulfed the glittering bits of darkness. The flames roared up as they fed and then muted back down on his command. The hallway stretched in both directions, silent. Any staff had vacated the area from either spirit influence or in fear of the ethereal battle in progress.

"Mei, which door?" Isabelle wanted her to lead as much as possible, to keep her attention focused so she wouldn't have time to be scared.

"I think . . . that one, Headmistress." Mei indicated with a tilt of her head, as one hand gripped Isabelle's tightly, and the other clutched the peony's pot.

"Are you ready, David?"

He nodded and said, "Let me go first. I'm still shielded." It was also clear he was straining to maintain those wards.

Alderscroft opened the door to the King's chamber. The wave of despair was visible coming out of the room, but it never reached them. As it neared, it simply dissipated and became the illusion it really was. The White Peony worked. Seeing no more visible threat, Alderscroft thinned his shields until they were unnoticeable.

The trio approached the King's bedside. The attendant doctor looked as if he were coming out of a long sleep in the chair where he had been sitting watch. Already the gloom was lessening, the light through the gauzy drapes brightening.

Mei-Hua approached the bed, carefully cleared small items from a bedside table and placed her White Peony as close to the King as possible. She fluffed it gently with her hands, delicately wafted air over it, and whispered soothing encouragement. The plant seemed to stand tall and fan itself out.

As the fragrance permeated the room, the King's color began to improve, and the remaining dimness retreated in ebbing waves.

Isabelle and Mei stood close to each other, but back from the bed, holding hands and waiting. Alderscroft continued to be on guard, scanning the room for any new threat.

Finally, the King's eyelashes fluttered and opened.

As the last traces of gloom vanished, Mei-Hua's eyes widened, tears continued to run down her checks unnoticed, yet she stood straighter. They all stood straighter, as if the gloom had been pressing down on them physically as well as mentally.

There was a long pause, while the King stared at her, and she said nothing, only stared back. Finally she gathered her courage and released Isabelle's hand.

Bowing deeply, she said, "Your Majesty, I bring greetings from my honorable departed parents, Special Envoys and Ministers Plenary to the Emperor of China, Henry Walsingham and An-Hua Walsingham, to His Royal Majesty Edward the Seventh, of the United Kingdom of Great Britain and Ireland and of the British Dominions beyond the Seas. May I present this flower on their behalf, in hopes that it will keep you well."

The King stirred, seeming most fatigued, but raised a hand. She extended hers for him to take, and curtsied.

Finally, he uttered, "Our thanks to your parents for their service, and my personal thanks to you." His voice was gravelly and strained, but his smile was clear.

Isabelle sighed. Needs displaced desires, but change, even for the better, was always a complication. She had finally accepted David's invitation to move to the estate he offered.

The country would be both healthier and safer for the children than London's often thick air. Also, she was concerned about Mei. Since the King had recovered, Isabelle was afraid that the unknown plotters would make another attempt at either him, or Mei-Hua. The King had Alderscroft's White Lodge to keep an eye on him, but Mei was Isabelle's responsibility, one she took seriously. At least Lord Alderscroft's offer of his estate out of London as a new home for the school would give them some distance.

His Majesty did have inquiries as to the cause of the attack. It should be possible to determine the opposition, but it would take agents and ships and long weeks at least. In the meantime, they knew the threat existed.

The girl continued to improve. His Majesty and His Majesty's chief gardener had many conversations with Mei on the properties and history of her White Peony, for His Majesty had developed a personal interest in the flower. For now, though . . .

"Come, Mei, it's time to go." Isabelle firmly took Mei's hand. Mei was wearing her gift from His Majesty; He had arranged a *cheong sam*, in a shining white to match the Peony she had given him, brocaded in broad patterns.

"Where are we going, Headmistress?" Mei-Hua looked around avidly. There was still a shadow lurking in the corners of her eyes, but Isabelle was relieved to know that she was on the mend.

"We're going back to the school to finish packing. I'm sorry we can't remain longer, but you can visit again."

"Thank you, Headmistress," the girl said, beaming.

Isabelle took a final look around the Kew Gardens. The sculpted hedges made neat, geometric shapes around the controlled riots of colorful flowerbeds. But Mei-Hua's attention was focused on a new exhibit, the result of her work with the Royal Gardener. It had taken many hours in the greenhouses and beds, and had only been made possible by Mei's talent with plants. It was an exhibition on the White Peony, now named after Mei's parents: the HuaWang-Walsingham Peony.

Mei-Hua Walsingham bent over the wide expanse of beautifully blooming White Peonies, inhaled their fragrance, and smiled.

"I am ready," she said.

Tha Thu Ann
(Scots Gaelic for "There You Are")
Tanya Huff

"Dr. Harris! Brian! Over here!"

Ealasaid Harris tightened her grip on her father's arm and directed his attention to the man trying to get his attention at the end of the pier. She felt muscles relax as he raised his other arm to wave.

Short and stout with bristling, blond muttonchops, Dr. Evans was the physical opposite of her tall, thin father, although they shared a certain indefinable similarity. Most would assume that those similarities came from their shared profession, but Ellie knew it was as much their shared Earth Mastery as their medical degrees.

Her father actually staggered under the enthusiasm of Dr. Harris' greeting and Ellie braced herself as he turned to her. But he only smiled and said, "So you're Ealasaid." Even after eighteen years in Nova Scotia, he still had enough of Edinburgh in his voice that he didn't mangle her name. "You have the look of your mother about you. The shape of your face." His smile broadened. "Your hair."

Ellie only just stopped herself from rolling her eyes. At seventeen, she was old enough to control her reac-

tions but her hair, thick and red and curling, was the
bane of her existence. Twisted into a knot and secured
under a straw hat before leaving the ship, she could already feel escaped tendrils brushing against her ears
and neck. On the other hand, it was one of the two things
that identified her as her mother's daughter and, of the
two, gave her significantly less trouble. Not that the Captain's six-year-old daughter had been trouble; tied to the
moment of her mother's death by her father's grief,
she'd been more than willing to move on. The trouble
had come when Ellie's father found her on the aft-castle,
comforting Captain Wooler as he sobbed.

And from her father refusing to believe.

"The dead are dead, Ellie. You have to stop this . . ."
He'd had to breathe deeply for a moment before he could
continue. *"I can't . . . Doctor's wives die young."* His expression had held equal parts guilt and pain. *"Just, don't."*

So she didn't talk to him about seeing the dead. But
that didn't stop her from seeing them. Or doing what she
could to help them move on. Or hating the new distance
that had grown over the last four years between herself
and her father.

" —impression of Halifax, Miss Harris?"

Too late she realized Dr. Evans had been speaking to
her for some time. "It's very different from Edinburgh,"
she said, hoping he hadn't noticed she'd missed all but
the last five words.

He smiled, apparently unaware, and gestured at the
city, roads rising up from the docks to the Citadel on the
hill. "Well, it's a lot younger. The whole country's only
four years old although there's been a British garrison
here in Halifax for over a hundred and thirty years." His
smile broadened. "Keeping an eye on the French, you

know." Bushy brows drew in and his smile faded. "But our work, yours and mine, Brian, would be easier without that garrison or all these sailors in and out, let me tell you. Never mind though, we soldier on, as it were. Nothing we can do about drink and . . ." A glance at Ellie, a reminder of his audience, and the final word remained unsaid. "I have a cab waiting," he continued, "The shipping office has your address, the porters will send your trunks on so there's no need for you to linger in this miasma of dying fish and warm tar. I found you a house."

For a moment, everything stopped. The noises of people pouring onto and off of ships, the screaming of gulls, the slap of the water against the pier. Everything. In a moment of perfect silence, Ellie's father said, "You found us a house. With a garden?"

"With a garden." Dr. Evan's smile softened and he clasped the other man's arm. "It's on the south edge of the city with land enough to make your own. My own house isn't far and—"

A shrill whistle cut him off and, over Dr. Evan's shoulder, Ellie could see the waiting cabbie make what could only be a very rude gesture. He grinned and touched his cap when he saw Ellie watching.

The area immediately around the docks looked both poor and rough, but with her wide experience, for she'd seen the docks in Glasgow when they boarded and in Ireland from the ship, Ellie knew that was only to be expected. The streets were narrow, the buildings three- or four-story red-brick tenements, dark with coal smoke. The accents she could hear were mostly Irish. The children were thin and grubby, and the women were . . .

Cheeks flushed, Ellie turned her attention back to the inside of the cab. It was one thing to know such women existed and another entirely to observe them at work in the middle of the afternoon.

". . . you and I at the hospital and the youngest son of Lord Burroughs—and when I say youngest, the man's fifty if he's a day—who has orchards in the valley." Dr. Evans was saying quietly, his voice barely carrying over the sound of the wheels against the cobblestones. "Four ship captains that I know of are Water Masters—they sail out of Halifax although they're seldom in port at the same time—and there's another, a retired captain, in Annapolis Royal. His late wife was an Earth Master. I've heard there's a Fire Master in the garrison though I've not met him, and an Air Master in Chester. Rumor has it she hasn't left the house since her husband's ship went down last spring. There may be more, I don't know; we're an independent lot here in the new world."

"The discards of the old world. Looking for new lives because the old lives have failed us." Ellie's father sighed. "Or we've failed them."

Dr. Evan's ginger brows dipped in. "That's a little harsh, Brian."

"Would you have emigrated if your family had accepted Caroline? Would I, had I still had Ellie's mother, and not merely the memory of her haunting my every step? Do the sailors and the soldiers Her Majesty sends make homes here? No. We are the flotsam and jetsam of the British Empire, Conrad, and of as much importance in the councils of the Queen."

"We are men of power—" Dr. Evans began.

Ellie's father raised a hand. She frowned at how pale it had become. "Men of power we may be, but you were cast off by your family for the love of a woman without power, and I am broken by the loss of a woman I'd have given up power for."

"Papa—" Ellie began but he turned his hand toward her, silencing her before she was entirely certain of what she'd been about to say.

The house Dr. Evans had found for them was small and square, its two stories clad in wide boards painted a soft, butter yellow—the paint colors of the shore moved inland a mile or two. Set back from the road behind an evergreen with almost fanlike branches, the house had a center door, with a window to each side and two small windows on the second floor. There was a new house maybe fifty feet to the left, and an older one more than twice that distance to the right. Ellie could see what was probably a small stable at the end of the drive and, more importantly, beyond that nothing but grass and trees and unfamiliar weeds.

"You own right back to the next road," Dr. Evans smiled broadly at them both. "It's a bit of a jungle, but I thought you'd rather sort it out yourself."

Ellie didn't know what her father saw when he stared back into the land that was his to guard—well, not specifically anyway—but his expression suggested he saw *something* and she, in turn, saw the tension drain out of him. She started to follow when he headed for the back of the house but Dr. Harris touched her arm and stopped her.

"Let him go," the Earth Master told her quietly. "It's hard for a man like your father to spend so much time at sea, with no earth under his feet at all." When Ellie nodded her understanding, he asked, "How is he, in general? Does he still blame himself for your mother's death?"

"Yes." There was so much more she could say to that, and perhaps if she came to know Dr. Harris a little better, she might. For now though, that single word would have to suffice.

The next morning, Ellie watched her father hurry down the front path, pause and look toward the rear of the house, then be tugged into the buggy by Dr. Harris. She couldn't hear what was said between them, but she thought he looked better as they drove away. Although he didn't look happy. He hadn't looked *happy* for the last four years.

Back in the house, Ellie headed for the kitchen, sliding sideways around the two trunks in the hall to borrow an apron until her own could be unpacked.

"Mrs. Dixon, may I . . ." She stopped, uncertain.

The two men at the table stood.

"Miss Ealasaid, this is my husband, William, and my son, James." Mrs. Dixon set the pitcher of water down on the counter by the pump. "They're here to carry the trunks upstairs before James begins work in the garden. Your father left detailed instructions," she added, when Ellie opened her mouth. "And you two might as well get started; Miss Ealasaid's room is at the front of the house and Dr. Harris' is at the back. Don't mix the trunks or you'll be moving them again!"

The old man nodded as he passed, the younger, James, who couldn't have been more than fifteen or sixteen, shot her a sideways look, and she thought he might have blushed when she smiled but his skin was too dark to be sure.

"Is there anything you needed, Miss Ealasaid?" Mrs Dixon watched her, carefully as though they were strangers, which Ellie allowed they were, having only met briefly the day before and then this morning as the cook/housekeeper served breakfast.

"Could I borrow an apron, please? Just until mine are unpacked."

"Of course, Miss Ealasaid."

She tried not to stare as Mrs. Dixon crossed the kitchen to where three identical white aprons hung, but she'd never been so close to an African before. She'd never had a chance to speak to any of the few who lived in Edinburgh, and while there'd been more working on the docks in both Glasgow and Halifax, they were men, stevedores, and she *couldn't* have spoken to them. Yesterday, before going into the house, Dr. Harris had asked if they minded.

"Comes highly recommended, used to keep house for Colonel Briant before the regiment got sent home. And just keep house," he'd added, color high on his cheeks. *"But if you have a problem . . ."*

"You and I have done enough surgeries to know skin color has nothing to do with what makes up a person," her father had snorted. *"If she can do the job for what I can pay her, I don't care if she's green."*

Mrs. Dixon had beautiful, rich brown skin, more like black tea than like coffee. Her palms were paler, her hair curlier than Ellie's own although better behaved, and her eyes so dark Ellie couldn't see the pupil. More importantly, though, her eyes were kind as she handed Ellie the apron and said, "Strange new world for you, isn't it Miss Ealasaid. Never mind though, it'll look more familiar when your bits are out and about. I had your other trunk moved to the sitting room first thing."

With the painting of the Highlands up over the sideboard and silver stag-head candlestick holders and her grandmother's embroidered runner on it, the sitting room had begun to look . . . not more like home, exactly, but a little less strange. Ellie had just set her mother's china shepherdess on the morning room mantle when she heard voices. A quick look out the front window showed an older woman and three—no, two—girls bustling up the path toward the door.

Mrs. Evans was as round as her husband, pleasant enough, but it wasn't immediately apparent why Dr. Evans had abandoned family and homeland for her. Both sixteen-year-old Anna and fourteen-year-old Katherine had her dark coloring. It didn't take Ellie long to realize that only she could see the third girl standing like Anna's shadow.

". . . and settled you with some Gaelic monstrosity of name. Still, Ellie's pretty isn't it?" Smoothing her skirts, Mrs. Evans examined the parlor. "It's not a pretty room. It needs a woman's touch, doesn't it? How lucky your father is to have you. Well, at least until you find a husband of your own."

All three girls giggled, even if only two could be heard. The third girl raised her left hand to her mouth as Anna raised her right.

"Did you see the paper this morning, Ellie?" Katherine demanded. "Isn't it horrible?" When Ellie admitted she hadn't seen the most recent paper, although she'd seen a stack of old ones piled in the kitchen, the younger girl was quick to tell the story of graves disturbed and bodies taken. "It happened first about a month ago and it keeps happening! Papa says it's like Edinburgh!"

Ellie frowned.

"With the body snatching and then the murders and then they hanged them!" Katherine expanded.

"Do you mean Burke and Hare? That was . . ." She did the ciphering in her head. ". . . forty-two years ago."

"There's no new evil in the world," Mrs. Evans declared before Katherine could speak. "But we're not here to discuss such horrible things. We're here to ask you if you would like to accompany us into the city. The Halifax Garrison Artillery Band plays every Tuesday morning in the Public Gardens."

"Sometimes officers come to hear the band," Anna broke in. "From the Fort. The 78th Highlanders are there now, and there's a luncheon after, put on by the Woman's Temperance League for a small donation."

"It's a pleasant way to meet eligible young men," Mrs. Evans agreed placidly.

Ellie did not want to meet an eligible young man. She'd only just begun a new life, and had no intention of beginning another. She should politely decline the invitation and continue unpacking. But while her father wanted—needed—land, she missed the bustle of the city. Besides, she glanced at the nearly translucent girl sitting beside Anna on the settee, there was Anna's shade to consider. "I'll need to change . . ."

All three girls clapped their hands and Mrs. Evans beamed. "We can wait."

Used to the gardens of Edinburgh, the Public Gardens appeared to Ellie to be either very new or gardening in this new world was a little chaotic. The band was no better, or no worse for that matter, than any of a hundred military bands Ellie had heard. Anna looped her arm through Ellie's and, with the blessing of her mother, who kept a tight grip on Katherine, the two—three—of them wandered closer to the junior officers of the 78th.

"They look like they're clustered together for protection," Anna giggled.

Ignoring the giggle, Ellie thought the observation sound. While she personally had no interest in any of the young men, most of the music lovers in the gardens appeared to be young women of a marriageable age and their mothers. She wondered if the senior officers had ordered them to attend as a kind of penance.

"Look, Ellie! There's one with hair as red as yours. I wonder what his name is?"

Ellie wondered if there was any way of finding out if Anna had lost a twin. The shade seemed perfectly happy with its existence. It didn't seem lost. Actually, it . . . she seemed as interested in the red-haired officer as Anna was.

"Oh, Ellie! He's seen us. He's coming this way!"

Lieutenant Harry Marshall seemed captivated by Miss Anna Evans and both Anna and her shade were entirely captivated by him. Ellie'd never seen a shade blush before. Although the lieutenant politely tried to include Ellie in the conversation—his accent so redolent of the Lothians she felt homesick—she soon found herself on the sidelines, and not even the shade noticed as she slipped away.

Camp Hill Cemetery, the cemetery the bodies had been taken from, was to the west of the gardens, across Summer Street. Katherine had happily filled in the details on the horse-tram on the way into the city. Ellie had hoped to be able to wander among the graves. There were always shades in cemeteries, some new and lost and needing only a gentle push, some there so long they thought they were where they belonged, some . . . well, there was a tomb in Gray Friars locked so as to keep *something* in. Unfortunately, the gates were closed and men in dark jackets moved in and around the gravestones.

"You're a terrible chaperone."

It was the slender, dark-haired friend of Lieutenant Marshall, smiling down at her from entirely too close. His eyes were a surprisingly pale hazel with flecks of gold in among the brown and green, his nose looked as though it had been broken at least once, and a small scar puckered the bottom of his chin. Suddenly realizing she'd been staring up at him for an embarrassing length of time, she started and said, "I'm a what?"

"A terrible chaperone," he repeated smiling. His bottom teeth were slightly crooked and he had dimples. Two dimples. She had no idea why that suddenly mattered. "You've abandoned your friend to the company of an incorrigible flirt. I thought I'd best retrieve you before any permanent damage was done."

"Done?"

"To her reputation. Unless," he added, as Ellie glanced through the cemetery's closed gates, "you'd rather remain here in hope of seeing something ghoulish."

Ellie knew that if she could only talk to the witnesses, she could help stop this before body-snatching escalated to murder as it had back home. Unfortunately, she couldn't speak to the dead with so many people around. *Be careful who you share your gift with*, her mother's shade had told her. *Be cautious. Be your father's daughter in this, not mine.* "There's no reason to stay," she sighed, and turned her attention back to the young officer. "We might as well rejoin my friend."

His smile broadened as he placed a hand over his

heart. "I am truly touched by your enthusiasm for my company."

Ellie stared at him for a long moment, saw his lips twitch, and burst out laughing. It was unladylike, and she should have tried to stop herself, but when he laughed with her, she didn't bother. They gathered a few disapproving stares, whether at the laughter or because they were laughing outside a cemetery where crimes had been committed and solemn horror was the expected reaction—but Ellie didn't care and when he tucked her hand in his elbow and lead her back into the gardens, she allowed it. "Do you have a name?"

"Do you?"

"I asked you first."

His lips twitched again. "Captain Alistair Williams at your service, ma'am."

"Aren't you young to be a captain?"

"I'm very good at what I do." After a moment, he added, "And you are?"

She was distracted by the hard curve of muscle under her hand. "Sorry. Ealasaid Harris."

"A Gaelic Elizabeth."

"You know Gaelic?"

His free hand gestured at his uniform. "I'm in a Highland regiment."

"But you're English."

"My maternal grandfather is the McGillivray."

"Ah." The McGillivrays were a powerful family in Scotland. Her father had once scoffed at how they were breeding for powers and, through careful marriages, had ensured the family included Masters in all four elements.

"My mother disgraced her family by marrying the

second son of a minor English Baron. Fortunately, my grandmother convinced my grandfather to forgive her."

Captain Williams must be a power, then. If she'd inherited her father's ability instead of her mother's, she'd know, but there was no way to ask. And no time, even had there been a way, for they were back with Anna, her lieutenant smiling at her every giggle. Mrs. Evans and Katherine soon joined them, the band played *Scotland the Brave*, the luncheon tent opened for business, and Captain Williams stayed at her side until all the officers had to quit the park for the Citadel.

"Did the captain ask if he could call on you?" Anna demanded, her shade looking equally starry-eyed about the promises Lieutenant Marshall had made.

"No."

"No? Oh, my poor Ellie. Are you crushed?"

"Why would I be crushed? I only just met him."

Both Anna and her shade stared at her as though she were crazy, but Ellie watched the clapboard houses go by outside the horse-tram and thought she might like this new world, this new life after all.

It was dark by the time her father came home, but he went immediately to the back garden and sat, leaning against an old apple tree. It seemed his first day in their new life hadn't been as pleasant as hers. Ellie stood in the doorway, the kitchen dark behind her, and wished she could help.

Then she heard him speaking softly and, though she couldn't hear it, she knew he was answered. This bit of land in a new country had welcomed a Master, and it would provide the comfort he needed. She was happy for him, she truly was. Tied to the university and the hospital, the shared wildernesses of Edinburgh had only barely been enough, but she did wish she didn't remind him so much of the love he'd lost that he sometimes forgot the love he still had.

It rained the next day and the day after that. Confined to the house, Ellie unpacked, went over the household requirements with Mrs. Dixon, read the newspaper her father had arranged to have delivered, and waited for the rain to stop.

It was still raining on the third day, but no one talked about the weather. Another grave had been disturbed, another body snatched; this one taken from the Old Burying Ground, not from the Camp Hill Cemetery.

"Old Burying Ground's been closed for over thirty years," Mrs Dixon pointed out as they sat together at the kitchen table snapping yellow beans. "Won't be pulling much of anything that resembles a body out of any grave there."

Mrs. Dixon had been more willing to allow her to help than their old housekeeper ever had. Less insistent she act like a lady, doctor's daughter that she was. Ellie hoped that in this new land she could change what that meant. Discards of Britain, her father had called them. Why should the discarded have to follow the old rules?

When her father came home late that night, she was in the sitting room reading *East Lynne*—they'd had gaslights in Edinburgh, and there were gaslights in Halifax proper, but she suspected it would be some time before they made it out as far as Inglis Street. Lamp in hand, she hurried out to the hall to greet him and realized he wasn't alone.

"Dr. Evans. Good evening. Mrs. Dixon has left cold

chicken for your supper, Papa, but I'm sure there's plenty for two."

Her father sighed and set his umbrella aside. "We've eaten, but if you could manage a pot of tea . . ."

"I can." She'd warned Mrs. Dixon, and the housekeeper had left the coals in the stove's smaller firebox banked. The water in the kettle would still be warm and easy enough for her to bring to a boil.

"If she can make tea, she's a damned sight more useful than my girls," Dr. Evans muttered as she opened the door at the end of the hall that led to the kitchen.

As it closed, she heard her father sigh, "She's had to be."

With any luck Dr. Evans presence would keep him from falling into the despair he often gave himself over to when reminded of her mother, but Ellie hurried with the tea anyway. Balancing the pot, two of the mugs her father preferred over cups, a small pitcher of milk, and the sugar on a tray she pushed her way back through the door and paused at the sound of voices from her father's office, the sound carrying clearly through the stovepipes that heated the hall in the winter.

"—almost rather go back to worrying about having our anatomy license revoked." Dr. Evans sounded unsettled.

"You're sure they could have taken nothing but bones?"

"Positive. Heather DeChampes has been dead for almost a hundred years. They might have gotten a bit of jewelry, but . . ."

"They're not after jewelry."

"No."

"You're sure she was a virgin?"

Dr. Evans snorted. "From what I hear, when she died they tried to make her a saint."

"And one of the other four was a newborn infant. Necromancy then, it's the only answer."

"The council . . ."

"If we put a letter on a ship with a Water *and* Air Master, they might get an answer back to us in a month. If they bother at all. The next dark of the moon is in two days, and if our grave robbers are willing to dig in this weather, then I'll bet money that's what they're aiming for."

"So what do we do?"

"Strengthen our own protections. See that our families are safe. Be ready to help pick up the pieces." Ellie heard her father sigh. "I can't see what else there is to do. We haven't enough information, and there's no way to get more."

They fell silent when she entered with the tea, and her father wished her a good night so pointedly she knew she'd been dismissed.

"I've never actually been to the Old Burying Grounds," she heard Dr. Evans say as she started up the stairs. "There may be dryads . . ."

There *may* be dryads.

There *would* be shades, and they saw everything. She could get the information her father needed and prove she could speak with the dead, finally convincing him that he had no responsibility in her mother's death.

Her father spent the next morning in his office. Considering what she'd heard the night before, she assumed he was layering shields around the property. She had to assume because he hadn't shared what he was doing. Her mother had come from a family with Elemental ties, although she herself had none, and Ellie's parents had never kept what her father could do from her. She knew he'd hoped she would inherit his power.

Instead . . .

"I told him what you said. Exactly like you wanted me to. He doesn't believe I can see you, Mama!"

"It's because he's a physician, mo cridhe. For him, death is a failure, and it hurts him to look beyond the end. You must be patient with him. Now, you must help me move on, as I've show you . . ."

He emerged in time to eat before going into the city. Ellie was restless, pushing the food around her plate, but he was still too caught up in his own head to notice. Mrs. Dixon looked between them as she set down the bowls of fruit and cream, clearly aware something was wrong.

The moment her father left for the hospital, Ellie ran to her room to change.

She expected questions when she told the housekeeper she was heading into town but Mrs. Dixon merely nodded and asked if she wanted supper ready at the regular time.

The Old Burying Ground was close enough to the Halifax Medical College for Ellie to be grateful it wasn't a day her father was there teaching. There were barricades up around the disturbed grave, but the gate itself remained open. Surrounded by trees, the cemetery was an oasis in the midst of brick and stone and macadam and carters and soldiers and sailors.

Ellie slipped through the gates. With no new dead, there were no wisps of smoke or shimmers of light and she paused, unsure of how to go on. Then she heard the laughter. Hair raising on the back of her neck, she followed the edged sound away from the violated grave toward a dark jumble of cracked stone under a tangle of trees and vines. The name on the broken stone was Arietty Brown, the date of death the thirteenth of September, 1811.

It was cold at the grave. Ellie rubbed her arms and took a deep breath, heart pounding. This was the first shade she'd gone looking for, the first who hadn't come looking for her. *"Don't fear the dead,* her mother's shade had said. *"They need your help."*

"I know you're there, Arietty Brown."

The laughter grew louder.

"And I know you saw what happened."

"What's a lovely young thing doing all alone here?" Cradling a half-empty bottle, the sailor lurched toward her.

Ellie took a step back. Focused on the dead, she hadn't given a thought to the living even though she knew better. Knew what parts of Edinburgh to avoid. Knew not to walk alone out of sight of witnesses.

Had known.

It seemed this new world came with the same rules as the old and, as Mrs. Evans had said, there was no new evil. "My young man is only just out of sight."

The sailor leered. "More fool him."

"If you come any closer, I'll scream."

"I like girls feisty, me."

Time to run. He'd laugh at her fear, but that was all he'd be able to do. She turned, caught her heel on a marker, and felt two cold hands shove her hard enough to tumble her to the ground.

"Oh, yeah, on yer back's the best . . ." The liquor in the bottle began to boil. "Jesus, Mary, and Joseph, what deviltry . . ."

Ellie covered her eyes as the thick glass exploded. She heard a crack and grunt and the thud of a body hitting the ground.

"Miss Harris! Miss Harris, are you hurt?"

"Captain Williams?" She lowered her arms and stared up at flecks of red disappearing from pale eyes. It took heat to boil liquor. Easy enough ciphering for her father's daughter. "You're the Fire Master."

Concern turned to astonishment so quickly she couldn't prevent a giggle. "Sorry. I don't usually . . ." She sat carefully. The sailor's legs protruded from behind a gravestone, but she could hear his wet breathing so assumed he was fine. Or as fine as she cared about. "Dr. Evans said there was a Fire Master at the garrison."

"And Dr. Evans . . ."

"Is an Earth Master. Like my father."

"I see." He rubbed a tanned hand across his forehead. "And you are?"

"I . . ." Why not? Just because her father didn't believe her. "I speak to the dead. More than speak, really, I help them move on. My mother's shade taught me."

"That explains your fascination with cemeteries."

"It's not a fascination." She paused as he carefully shook broken glass off her skirts, then allowed him to help her up. "Dr. Evans and my father believe the graverobbing means necromancy. If I can find out where and when, they can stop it." They'd said they were merely going to protect their own, but surely if they *knew* . . .

"And they know you're here? Risking yourself?"

Pulling her hat up by the ribbons, she shook her head. "No. My father doesn't believe in my abilities," she continued hurriedly, recognizing his expression as one likely to have her immediately removed from the cemetery.

"People could . . . *will* get hurt if we don't stop this. Arietty Brown has the answers we need. And since she's the reason I fell . . ." Turning back to the grave, Ellie snapped, "She owes me!"

"I owes you nothing!" Responding to the challenge, Arietty Brown appeared. She was dressed in black, middle-aged, dumpy, angry . . . and familiar. When Ellie gasped, Arietty's narrow lips curled into a nasty smirk. "You see it, don't you girl? You're like me, you are. See the dead. Be the dead. No rest for the wicked is there?"

"Is she talking to you?" Captain Williams stood so close she could feel the air warm between them. "What's she saying about the necromancers?"

"The pretty, pretty man wants to know about necromancers. He doesn't care that you know the dead, but he will." Her eyes went black and she glared past Ellie at the captain. "They care. They leave!"

"He's none of your business! Tell me of the necromancers?"

"A newborn babe. An untouched woman. An aged man. The noose's child. One of power. With what they've gathered, they deconsecrate and summon Darkness. Darkness creeps through windows and under doors and steals the breath from young and old and uses death to open the passage."

"Open the passage for what?"

"For a greater Darkness. Darkness whispers to me always. Send me the dead. Send me the dead." She clapped her hands over her ears. "STOP IT!"

The shriek distorted Arietty's face and drove Ellie back against the captain's chest. Before he could react, she straightened and stepped toward the shade. She wondered if the dark shade in Gray Friars had been one

of them as well only even further gone. The edges of
Arietty Brown felt much the same. "It's long past time
you continued your journey." Her voice shook only a
little. "Come."

"To you?" Arietty scoffed.

"Through me." Taking a deep breath, Ellie opened
herself to the light as her mother's shade had taught her.

"No . . ."

"Yes." Ellie took the shade's hand, able to touch her
for just this moment and draw her forward. But she'd
never tried to save a shade so old. Or one who hadn't
been searching for what she offered. She dragged Arietty toward the light one . . . step . . . at . . . a . . .

"They've locked the door," the shade whispered as
the light began to take her. "Only the dead can open it.
You'll fai—"

Done.

Ellie staggered as she released the light and once
again found herself leaning against the captain's chest.
This time, she lingered for a moment, one hand clutching his uniform, her legs shaking.

"Miss Harris . . . Ealasaid? Are you all right?"

"She didn't want to go, but she'd been twisted by un-
happiness and pain and she was already listening to the
Darkness. I couldn't let her stay and become something
to fear."

Ellie felt his chest rise and fall, his breathing matched
to hers. "You opened a gate?"

"I am the gate." His hold on her shoulders changed.
"They care. They leave!" Fingers trembling, she pushed
herself away. "I'm sorry."

"For what? That was amazing." He smiled, and she
couldn't help but return it.

Then she remembered. "Tomorrow is the dark of the moon! I have to tell my father!"

"Tell him what? That it's necromancy? You said he knew. I suspected as much; it was why I was here."

"We know two things more." Ellie poked a strand of hair back into its knot. "One of the bodies taken belonged to a man of power. If we can find out who he was, his shade can help us." She frowned. "But I need his name. He'll need a sense of self to help, and I'll have to return that to him."

Captain Williams frowned as well. "And the second thing we know?"

"That they deconsecrate and summon Darkness."

"Deconsecrate? They must be in a church!" He grabbed her shoulders again, blushed, released her and stepped back. "A church where they have no fear of interruption . . ." He frowned again. "A church without a pastor?"

"Temporarily closed for some reason."

"For repairs!"

"Still consecrated!"

"Can you find it? By tomorrow night?"

"Halifax isn't Edinburgh, Miss Harris. I can find it." He tucked her hand in his arm and led her toward the cemetery gate. "You find out who the man of power is, I'll find the church."

"But Papa—"

"No! Enough, Ealasaid!" He pushed his hand back through his hair. "You're too old to be continuing this fantasy. Your mother's ghost did not come to you to grant me absolution in the matter of her death!"

"This isn't about—"

"Stop it! It isn't enough you're sneaking off to meet young men—"

"Papa!"

"—but you have to bring your mother into it? You will not leave this house tomorrow, Ealasaid." The finger he pointed at her trembled. "You will . . . You look . . ." He closed his eyes and when he opened them again, turned on his heel and headed for the back garden.

"I never mentioned Mama," Ellie whispered as the door slammed behind him. She climbed the stairs to her room and held the lamp close enough to the round mirror over her bureau to see her reflection clearly. She knew she looked like her mother. Even Dr. Evans had seen it. The shape of her face. Her hair. Her eyes. Her father's heartbreak. That was all he saw when he looked at her.

When she tried to speak to him the next morning, he cut her off, told her again she was to stay in the house, and left. Ellie stared at the closed door for a long moment, stamped her foot because she was far too old to throw things, then headed for the kitchen and the pile of old newspapers.

It turned out there were multiple newspapers in Halifax, not merely the one her father subscribed to, and the previous occupants of their house had kept all of them. Ellie moved them to the sitting room and settled down to read. By noon when Mrs. Dixon brought luncheon in, the papers were spread out around her over the floor and the furniture like a flock of gulls. The housekeeper raised a brow, but said nothing.

By two, Ellie had the newspapers stacked again, and was pacing the length of the room. A cup of tea at three barely calmed her, and, at four fifteen, when she heard a buggy stop out front, she ran for the door.

"We're a body short," she said, pulling Captain Williams into the house. "Four bodies from Camp Hill Cemetery and one from the Old Burying Ground, but the last taken from Camp Hill was sixteen-year-old Maria Campbell and today's newspaper says they found her body down by the water. I think she was supposed to be untouched but wasn't and that's why they went for DeChampes. Dr. Evans said she was a saint. And the noose's child was an accident. It really was a child, caught up in a loop at the rope works. Archie Tern was ninety-three but, unless he was also the man of power . . ."

"We're a body short," Captain Williams repeated.

"That," said a quiet voice from the other end of the hall, "is because what happens in colored cemeteries never gets reported in white newspapers."

They turned together, Ellie still clutching Captain Williams' arm, to find Mrs. Dixon standing by the kitchen door, drying her hands on her apron.

"My brother-in-law, Tom Byers, he had the shine about him," the housekeeper continued. "He'd talk to the wind and the wind talked back."

"An Air Master," Ellie breathed.

Mrs. Dixon smiled. "Don't know he was a Master of anything, but that's what Colonel Briant said you folks would call him. He was one too, an Air Master." When both Ellie and Captain Williams continued to stare, although Ellie at least had managed to close her mouth, she shook her head. "When this is done, you lot on this side of the water should maybe start talking to each other," she sighed. "Make a new life, stop wallowing in the loss of the old. But here and now, our Tom died two months ago, his body taken from the grave. His was the first."

"Is there a chance they killed him?" Ellie asked. "Once they had a man of power, it would be easy enough to get the others," she explained when the captain turned toward her.

"He was crushed under a slipped load, down on the docks. The net gave way . . ." Mrs. Dixon's voice trailed off. "It was called an accident," she finished at last, but she sounded uncertain.

A convenient accident, Ellie thought as Captain Williams stepped away from her.

"They've set up in a small church on Bedford Row. It was damaged in a fire, and has been sitting empty for almost four years but it's never been deconsecrated."

"A lot of small empty churches in this town," Mrs. Dixon noted. "Folks always trying to save sailors who don't want to be saved."

"But only one with dark wards," the captain pointed out. "Your father and Dr. Evans . . ."

"Don't believe us." *Don't believe me.*

"But then . . ."

"Then we stop it. You and I." She tucked an escaped curl behind her ear. "I deal with the dead, you deal with the living."

He stared at her, biting his lower lip in a way that made him look *much* too young for his rank. Finally he nodded, "All right."

Ellie expected Mrs. Dixon to try and stop them, but all she said was, "Be careful."

"We have to go by Dr. Evans' house," Ellie told him as he helped her into the buggy. "Arietty said they've locked the door, and only the dead can open it. I only know one shade in Halifax not tied to a cemetery."

Anna was thrilled to go for a late afternoon ride, although Ellie possibly lied a little about Lieutenant Marshal being at the end of it. The problem, once she'd slipped away from her mother and sister and was in the buggy, was how to speak to the shade of her dead twin about necromancy and the coming Darkness without terrifying Anna out of her wits. By the time they'd reached Spring Garden Road, with Captain Williams making faces at her over Anna's head, Ellie still hadn't come up with a workable plan. And they were running out of time. She took a deep breath, turned and took Anna's hand, looked past her shoulder at the barely visible shade—three of them on a seat meant for two left little room for a fourth no matter how insubstantial— and said, "One or more necromancers are going to try and open a door to Darkness tonight. The Darkness will feed on death, and a greater Darkness will follow. We have to stop them."

"Ellie, what are you talking about?" Anna's fingers were hot around her wrist.

Ellie ignored her. "We need your help. They've locked the door, and only the dead can open it."

"You're frightening me."

"I'm not talking to you."

"Miss Harris, I don't think—"

"Not now, Captain." Gaze locked with the shade, Ellie opened herself, just a little, to the light.

The shade's eyes widened, and then she disappeared.

"Oh, no." Ellie knew she hadn't opened far enough to make a gate. Barely a peephole! She hadn't meant to drive the shade into hiding, only to make a point. Then she realized that Anna's fingers were icy cold, and it wasn't Anna looking out of Anna's eyes.

"No one . . ." Anna's dead twin sounded excited ". . . has ever asked me for anything."

The chestnut bucked as Captain Williams jerked the reigns. A cabbie swore, a pair of boys pointed and laughed, and Ellie said, "Will you help?"

"Of course."

"Is Miss Evans all right?"

The shade turned Anna's body toward the captain. "I'm Miss Evans. Miss Alice Evans. I don't believe we've been properly introduced, Captain Williams."

"You died."

"As we were born, but I think it's rude to bring that up now, don't you?"

Bedford Row was on the edge of Sailortown, only a few short blocks away from the Old Burying Ground but no longer respectable enough for a decent young woman.

"You're dead," Ellie reminded Alice when she pointed that out.

"Anna isn't."

"Don't worry, Miss Evans . . ." Captain Williams helped her down from the buggy and barely flinched at the temperature of her fingers. ". . . I will do everything in my power to keep you—both of you—and Miss Harris safe."

Alice flushed and giggled.

Only a small wooden cross by the door identified the boarded-up building as a church. Three steps took them from the sidewalk to a small concrete pad. When Ellie reached toward the door, Captain William caught her hand and pulled it back.

"The wards will kill anyone who touches the door.

And I think . . ." He frowned. ". . . I think they're keeping the dead locked in."

"But not out?"

"Why would they?"

"Alice?"

"I think if she passes through the wards, she'll destroy them."

Her father would have *known*, but her father wasn't here.

"I'll come back for Anna," Alice said softly, and stepped forward as Anna collapsed. Captain Williams caught her before she hit the ground.

Ellie's heart leaped into her throat. "Is she . . . ?"

"Unconscious."

"Then you'd better put her down because . . ."

Before Ellie could finish, Alice vanished and, with a smell of rotting meat, the door slammed open.

It was late afternoon, early evening outside on the steps of the church. It was night inside.

Captain Williams spoke a word behind her and six balls of fire sped past, settling into the lamps hanging from the charred ceiling.

"Salamanders," she breathed, reached back for his hand and pulled him with her over the threshold. His fingers tightened around hers as they saw what had been laid out on the ruined altar. The dry bones had to be Heather DeChampes. The rest hadn't been dead long enough to be bone. Ellie gagged, felt the captain's fingers tighten around hers, and said, "I'm not afraid of the dead. It's the smell."

She pulled free of his grip and moved closer. The bodies had been set out at the five points of a broken pentagram. Broken to break the protection it offered.

"They're empty." Anna, no, Alice, glanced at the bodies and shrugged. "There's nothing there. They're just . . ."

"Glowing." Ellie's heart started to pound as five shades began to wrap like spidersilk around the bodies they'd once worn. "Captain?"

"It's not me, I thought it was you."

"It is not the girl who talks to the dead. Nor the Fire Master. Nor . . ." The deep voice paused as if unable to determine what exactly Alice was. ". . . the other. You bring the blood we need to seal the working. We need not wait."

They stepped out of the shadows near the walls, nine men in black robes, faces covered with hoods, in their hands the hooks on poles the stevedores used to guide the nets of cargo over to the docks.

"Ellie!" The rising panic in Alice's voice drew Ellie's gaze back to the altar. The bodies had risen into the air, fully clothed in their shades and writhing in what looked to be pain.

Two shots rang out but before she could turn again, Captain Williams growled, "You deal with the dead. I'll deal with the living."

He was a soldier as well as a Fire Master.

The center of the broken pentagram remained empty. There was still time.

Ellie opened herself to the light and reached for the hand of Heather DeChampes. Their fingers had nearly touched when Alice . . . no, *Anna* screamed and fell forward clutching her stomach, blood spreading like a dark stain under her fingers. When her blood hit the altar, darkness bloomed and the gate to the light slammed shut.

Point of his hook glistening, the necromancer swung again. Ellie ducked, the necromancer stumbled, and Alice shoved him into the Darkness.

He screamed.

Was torn apart.

The Darkness grew.

Teeth clenched, Ellie reached again for Heather DeChampes, but the emerging Darkness had pushed the shades too high above the altar, she couldn't . . . "Tom Byers, Air Master. We need your help."

"Destroy the Darkness."

"What?"

His eyes reminded her of Mrs. Dixon. Kind. But with little tolerance of missishness. "Freeing us won't stop it now. You must draw the Darkness into the light."

She could hear the Darkness whispering to her. *Give me death. Give me death.* "I can't. It's already too strong."

"You must. Do what you do, girl. And do it fast."

She heard Captain Williams cry out in pain. She couldn't help him. She couldn't stop death. But she could send it back where it belonged. Tom Byers held out his hand. Ellie dragged up her skirts, got the toe of one boot up on the altar and jumped.

Strong fingers wrapped around hers.

She opened herself to the light.

It had never been so bright.

The Darkness rolled over her. Through her. It burned. Froze. Hurt. She gritted her teeth and hung on. It was too much. She couldn't . . .

She would!

Then it was gone.

The cry of an infant. The approving chuckle of a very old man. The whoop of a young boy. The sigh of an untouched woman. And a squeeze of her hand and a kiss against her cheek as Tom Byers went into the light.

Clinging to Anna, Alice screamed, drawn to the light with the other shades.

Shades were meant to move on. But Alice was living the life she would have had. Her twin's life at least.

Ellie let the gate close and collapsed to the floor.

Familiar arms closed around her, and she heard Dr. Evans call Anna's name.

Sitting on the edge of her bed, Ellie's father shook his head. "If Mrs. Dixon hadn't sent James for us, the Darkness would have been defeated, but those who called it would have escaped, and Anna and the Captain . . ."

"So it was physicians we needed, not only Earth Masters," Ellie said in the pause.

"You needed to have not done such a foolish, dangerous thing."

Ellie plucked at the quilt, gaze locked on a square of gingham. "You wouldn't listen."

"I know." He tucked a finger under her chin and lifted her head. "I owe you an apology, Ealasaid. I haven't been listening. Not about this, not about your mother. I couldn't, wouldn't believe forgiveness would be that easy. I'm sorry."

There were still circles under his eyes, but the grief and guilt had left them, and a lump rose in Ellie's throat as she saw he'd finally let her mother go. He saw *her*. Granted, he wasn't particularly happy with her at the moment, but the Darkness had been defeated, the necromancers stopped, everyone was alive and . . . "Mrs. Dixon says you should talk, the people of power in the new world."

"Not stay wrapped up in our own hurt pride, discarded from the life we knew." His lips twitched. "Yes, she spoke to me as well. *We* should definitely talk, the people of power in this new world."

"We?"

"We." Her mouth opened as she realized what he meant, and he smiled. "It's time to build a new life." Leaning forward, he brushed a fall of curls back off her face and kissed her forehead. "Past time."

The Collector
Ron Collins

It was just morning, but already heat rose from the road that ran from Summerville on up through Chickamauga. Damned hot for September. Nathaniel breathed it in as he walked into town. He was hungry, but that was no different than ever.

"The President's been shot!"

The runnerboy would have bowled him over as he rounded the corner, but Nathaniel caught him with his good hand. The kid was a scrawny white boy in loose dungarees, his eyes big from the unexpected collision. He waved a four-sheet rag over his head, and carried a pile of papers under his other arm.

"McKinley shot at rally!" he yelled as he slipped away and ran down the street. "Read it for a penny!"

Realization of what the kid was saying finally caught up.

"Is he dead?" Nathaniel called.

"Nah," the boy replied over his shoulder. "Just shot."

Nathaniel gazed after the kid.

William McKinley, the man he and the fellows on Teddy's Hill called King Billy, had been shot. The idea made Nathaniel smile. If he had a penny, he would buy that paper and he would read it with all the grim satisfaction he could muster up.

McKinley promised black folks so much, but he'd done so little. And despite saying he didn't want a war, he still sent the *Maine* to Cuba, and there wasn't no one could tell Nathaniel that King Billy didn't do that on purpose. More than two-hundred-sixty men gone just like that.

And it wasn't just the dead who'd paid for Cuba.

Nathaniel ran a hand over his stump.

He still felt the hand sometimes, and sometimes when he woke up, he would reach out to grab shoes or his hat or something else just to find his arm swinging around, useless as a broomstick. Yes, the image of King Billy lying on a surgeon's board while a sawbones fished around his fat gut for a bullet made Nathaniel smile. Bastard deserved it. But Nathaniel had more pressing problems than wishing ill on William McKinley. His last meal was more than two days gone, and he needed a place to stay before rain came. Crazy Carl down in Summerville told him to come to LaFayette because of a house where he might find a meal if he was willing to work. Work had never bothered Nathaniel any other than it was damned hard to find, even for a man who had served.

Carl said the old woman who lived there was strange. Touched. Had a bit of the magic of some kind. That didn't bother Nathaniel so much, either. He wasn't afraid of no witch, 'less she carried a rifle or wore a hood. Besides, Crazy Carl was more than a bit touched himself. Carl caught the "shine shakes" when he didn't get enough, and he didn't know nothing more about the woman beyond that she was touched, and that things grew crooked on her property. Said he didn't wanna know. Said it was too dangerous to find out, then he shook his head and twitched his hands back and forth. "She ain't right," he said from between blackened teeth. "But she cooks a great meal."

Which was good enough for Nathaniel.

His stomach rumbled.

He had to find that house.

LaFayette had grown up over Cherokee country—a thousand people maybe, and three times that in dogs and horses. It had roads of flat red clay, a schoolhouse, a courtyard, and nothing much of anything else. Men had fought for this ground often, but Nathaniel couldn't see exactly why.

The house was at the edge of town, and had a look that spoke of a lack of men-folk. Untended trees grew from around the back along one side. The grounds were weed-choked, and the wild posies and violets were pitiful, drooping in the heat.

He labored up the porch steps and straightened, putting his hand to the small of his back. The door had been white, but was now peeling to weathered grayness. The floor was bare planks with gaps between the slats. It squeaked as he walked, but at least it was in the shade.

Lot of work to do here, he thought.

The door opened a crack before he could knock.

The old woman peered out. She wore a light-colored shift that was probably just a sheet that had been stitched and quilted. Her hair was a gray wad at the top of her head. She gazed up at him with red-rimmed eyes.

"What do you want?" she said.

"I could dig those flowerbeds for you," he said, nodding at the ground out front. "Make 'em look real pretty."

The door opened further. Her skin was white like bread dough and creased with lines. She looked at him with such intensity that time seemed to stop.

"You got no hand," she said. "How's a man with no hand goin' to work?"

He covered his stump in that reactive motion that made him angry with himself. "That's right, ma'am. Lost it in San Juan. But I can handle a spade and a hoe. I'll do it for dinner and a place to sleep."

She looked at him like she was grading cattle, and once again he felt her gaze pick at him. Something feral rose in defense. Her assessing eyes made him feel naked. They made him see his pa, who'd slaved not more than fifty miles away from here till Sherman burned his swath through Georgia, and who lived free until someone said they caught him stealing a pig and put him up over an oak tree. Made him think of his ma dying of cough when he was maybe five.

His teeth clenched as the woman eyed him.

Nathaniel was a man—a free man of the nation who taught himself to work with wood and to plant corn and to handle a gun true enough that Roosevelt himself wanted him on San Juan Hill. He was a man who'd taken a bullet through the palm and kept fighting and kept fighting and kept fighting until the gangrene rose up and told him different. Now this old woman looked at him to see if he was able to do a dinner's worth of gardening.

"Do the work," she said, her voice shattering his thoughts. "Dinner comes if'n you're worth it."

It was good to work, good to feel sweat rolling over his shoulders and earth on his fingers. The woman's flower-beds were hard-packed from disuse and weeds had grown up a criss-cross of roots, but the rusty red soil turned for him just fine and the work let his mind wander.

He thought about William McKinley and about Cuba.

He remembered thinking about Georgia's red clay as he sat in pain on the black ground of San Juan and the doctor poured rum down his throat and gave him a wooden block to bite down on. He remembered the grain of that wood, remembered marks made by the teeth of men before him, remembered blazing pain and screaming through his clenched jaw for God or his ma or anything else to make it stop. He remembered thinking his hand, with its half-moon nails, looked out of place on the black soil.

Which brought him back round to King Billy and to red soil.

He pursed his lips together as he worked. Each turn of the blade split the ground, and with each split, he listened to the earth breathe.

"Hear it?" Pa had said to him as a boy. "Hear it sing?"

And Nathaniel *had* heard it. He always did hear the rhythm under things, but he never knew anyone else did till his Pa shared that with him. Told him it was their secret. "Ain't no one need to call you on it, hear?" he said. "It's a song special-like for just you'n'me."

That wasn't the only special-like secret he and his Pa had kept. There was the hidden path Pa showed him, a trail that ran down to the creek where a man could hide if the troubles came too hard, and there were the occasional trips to the hooch bar run by Samo. And, of course, there was his name—Gamba, a name his Pa called him one night after one of those hooch runs. The name was special, Pa said. It meant warrior, power, strength. But it also had t'be kept quiet, Pa said, 'cause of the way the folk here feel 'bout names from the past. So that, too, was a special-like secret for just him and his Pa.

Throughout the morning the ground cooed to him

low and strong with a melody he got lost in. It was nearly noontime when it sharpened to a pitch so shrill he had to look up.

Nathaniel squinted against afternoon sunshine to see two men approaching on horses. One wore a star. Both wore sun-beaten hats and mustaches.

"What you doing there, boy?"

"Working the flowerbed, Sheriff."

The sheriff walked his horse toward Nathaniel, pursing parched lips and making a thick sound deep in his throat. He pulled a rifle from its holster and used the barrel to push the brim of his hat up his forehead. Even from this distance Nathaniel smelled whiskey on the lawman's breath.

"Looks like Tilly's got herself a niggerboy to do her up right," the sheriff said to his deputy.

"Half a one, anyhow," came the reply.

The two shared a laugh.

The sheriff lowered his gun to Nathaniel before sliding it back into the holster. "Any trouble, and you and that tree goin' to get acquainted," he said, cocking his head toward an elm at the edge of the woman's property. "Understand?"

Nathaniel's eyes narrowed. "Yes, sir."

And he did understand. Doesn't matter that you volunteered to serve if the man with the star don't change. Doesn't matter none at all. Just like it doesn't matter that King Billy promised to finish the job Abe Lincoln started.

The sheriff nodded and pulled his reins. Both lawmen left, their horses plodding through the Georgia heat.

The woman—she agreed her name was Tilly when Nathaniel asked about it—stared at the flowerbed as if she couldn't see the ground had brought the posies back up and that Nathaniel had shaped it into a bowl that would hold the rain that was surely coming later that night. Her brows rose, and she stared at him with one eye wide. He felt it again, that cutting mark of her gaze that hit someplace deep in his gut.

"Hope you don't mind stew," she finally said.

"No, ma'am. Don't mind that at all."

"Neighbors will squawk if'n I have a negro man sleeping in with me. So you'll get the porch."

He nearly laughed at the image of him and her on a bed together, but he stopped in time.

"It'll keep the rain off," he said.

She looked at Nathaniel. "You split wood with that hand?"

"Yes, ma'am, I can split me some wood."

"Split a cord tomorrow and you can stay another night."

"That's fair."

She served dinner on the porch.

The stew was plentiful and thick, and tasted like it came from the heavens. It had rabbit and chipmunk and some kind of fish that Nathaniel couldn't place. Cabbage and carrots floated in the gravy. He didn't feel her presence here, maybe because they both sat on the porch facing out so they didn't look each other in the eye. Or maybe she had let her guard down, or maybe he was just imagining it all before.

They spoke about the weather and the rain that started rattling on the roof. She asked him about his hand, and he said he left it buried in the ground. He asked about her family and she said they had all died at one time or another, and that she collected things, but fell silent when he asked about what things those might be. He left her silence alone. He understood there were things a person didn't want out in the open.

Crazy Carl was right, though. There was something strange about her, something that gave him the upset stomach. Her stare left him with almost-things running through his mind. Almost images. Almost scents. Almost . . .

He ate three bowls of her stew, though, and sopped each up with the fresh cornbread he'd smelled baking all day.

When he was done, she brought out a flat mattress along with a worn sheet. Though the mattress had long been pounded flat, Nathaniel thought it was like sleeping on a cloud.

He woke to the smell of oatmeal.

He worked all the next day, interrupted by nothing more dangerous than glances cast by children walking from town to the the schoolhouse, and the newspaper runnerboy who brought along news that it seemed King Billy was going to recover. Runnerboy said McKinley was already sitting up and giving people fits from his sickbed.

Cryin' shame.

That night they ate on the porch again. Nathaniel's back ached, but a cord and a half of firewood lay stacked outside the door. He would have done more, but the axe broke, and it took him two hours to make it sturdy again.

The stew was better the second night.

"The root cellar could use some fixin' tomorrow," Tilly said.

Nathaniel looked at the old woman. Maybe it was

just that he was growing easy with her, but she seemed different tonight, calmer, like she had made her mind up over something, that maybe he was gonna be all right.

"Stuff down there needs replacing," she said, gathering his bowl and rubbing it as absently as he might rub his stump. "Things need sorting, old bags carted up."

"Sure," he said, pushing away from the table.

The old woman tottered as she led Nathaniel across the knotted yard to a set of cellar doors barricaded with a sturdy padlock. Clearly no one was gonna steal from Tilly. Whereas the rest of the place was rundown and in disuse, the cellar door's white paint was fresh and spotless. The lock guard was rusted in places, but still held good and solid.

The woman bent to the lock.

The door swung to expose a dark gap in the earth and stairs leading down. A dank smell nearly overpowered him. Nathaniel had lived through war and spent time at a surgeon's ward, but this odor was something beyond description.

"I said it needed cleaning," she explained with a shrug.

Nathaniel felt stillness here. Silence. The low hum of the ground that always filled his head was gone.

"Can't get to the back of the shelves myself no more," she said. "And it's getting too long since its last scouring."

Her head cocked up and she gave him a glance that was held a touch too long. Was she nervous today? Afraid? He looked at Tilly standing in a frock in the middle of a morning yard, and but couldn't for his life place why she should be afraid or worried or anything much else.

"I might start at the back and work my way up," she said.

He nodded and stepped down the stairs.

The cellar was well dug, the walls smooth and sharply cut. The top steps were dry and sturdy, but mold made the last three slippery. Light streamed down to help his eyes adjust. He felt a flash of claustrophobia then, a brief pain that pierced his chest, then released. He shook his head. What was wrong with him? He never minded being in closed places before, kind of liked it, really. But the root cellar gave him the pressures. The walls seemed to bend, straining in like they might squeeze him into nothingness.

He put his hand to the wall. It made him feel better. He moved deeper into the cellar, thinking about the labor gone into it. Slaves? Neighbors? Free Indians? Had Tilly's man dug this before going to fight the war? She was old enough. Could have lost her husband in Atlanta, or Antietam, or anywhere. Had her man fought to keep Nathaniel's pa in chains?

The passageway opened into a chamber.

The air was damp here, cool enough to raise pimples. Light was just enough he could see shelves filled with bulbs and boxes and twisted roots wrapped around like balls of twine or like tentacles of sea monsters he once imagined on the boat to Cuba. Soft mold grew over a bag of something in one corner.

"See all the way back?" the old woman called.

He saw another doorway deeper into the cellar.

"Yes, ma'am," he bellowed. "I'll start there."

Nathaniel stepped to the edge of the darkness, and put his hand to the doorway. A scream came inside his head, a pulse of pain that seemed to start at the base of his palm and stream through every part of his body. He pulled back as if his hand was burnt, but the screaming still echoed. Another shrill voice joined it, then another and another.

He heard the old woman grunt from above. Hinges strained as he turned. The door slammed and the darkness was complete. The *scritch* of lock on brace crawled over his spine. The click of the key was loud as a shotgun blast.

The voices faded to silence.

"No!" he yelled as he ran blindly back to the stairs. He crashed upwards and pounded on the wooden door above, pounding and pounding, but knowing no one could hear him.

This was no root cellar, he realized. This was a crypt.

He saw it clear then. The screaming voices were remnants of other men who had been caught up before him. He felt their spirits as distant vibrations in the soil, and he remembered Crazy Carl's voice when he spoke of the old woman. Why hadn't he listened to him? Why hadn't he followed his instinct?

Nathaniel crashed his shoulder against the door until it bruised. Nothing. He ground his hand into the earthen wall and thought it might give, but it was too strong and would not budge. The sense of sound came back to him though, the music, the beat in the distance that had always been with him. It was far away now, muted as if muffled by the pillow he slept on the past two nights. But it was there and its presence made him feel better, even though he couldn't quite make out its pattern.

As he strained to hear it, though, Nathaniel also realized he could "see" here—only outlines and vague details, but it was vision of sorts and it was coming better with each passing breath. Strange.

He pounded the door above one more time.

"I am a free man!" he yelled. He ran back down the stairs, through the chamber, and into the back room. He threw a moldy bag to the ground, and slime sluiced down in a messy glop. He kicked a shelf and it cracked with splintery echo. "I am a free man!" He hit the walls again and again and again. But as time passed his voice grew less and less firm, his commitment to the idea less and less real.

Finally, he fell back.

Thick air filled his lungs with its morbid stagnation as he sat alone with his defeat. His anger drew down then. Became focused. Became distilled to its purest form, a feeling as powerful and intense as he had ever allowed himself to feel. Calculating and cunning. It sat in the center of his being like a new creature made of only the most needful vengeance. It was bold. It was shrewd. It tasted powerful and sharp . . . and . . . and so bitterly delicious. It rose the hair on his arms and made his skin burn like a cleansing rain—hard, ragged, and clear. It pounded his skull. *I will break you*, it said. *I will destroy you.*

Hatred, he realized. That's what this was.

It was a cool and determined hatred, a hatred he had earned. Hatred they all deserved. Nathaniel would have his revenge. He was done playing by the rules. No more. There were no rules. There was only making things right. And that could happen today or tomorrow or next month or next year or . . . time didn't matter anymore. There was no such thing as rules or time. No such thing as healing. There was only this glorious, glorious thing burning inside him.

He opened his thoughts and felt the presences again,

ghosts and spirits that hovered around him like buzzards on a field.

"Get me out . . . of here," a reedy, almost-not-there voice said. It was a bird-thin man lying in the corner, a frail collection of bones and skin and little else.

Nathaniel's hatred flickered. This was his cellar. What was this man doing in his cage?

"Who are you?"

"Name's . . . Thomas."

He saw the bones then—scatterings of ribs and hips and spines that lay in the corners as if they had been tossed together—a bone salad, Nathaniel thought.

"What are you doing here?" he asked.

"She collects . . ."

"She collects men, yeah, I get it."

"No . . ." Thomas took a thin breath. "She collects . . . magicians."

"I ain't no witch."

"I said . . . *magician*." Thomas tried to move, then gave up. "A witch is . . . another thing."

"I ain't got no magic."

"You must . . . she catches . . . only mag . . . icians."

"Then she made a damned big mistake this time."

His smile relaxed, and Thomas gazed with such pity Nathaniel felt stripped bare.

"Never you mind that, anyway," he said. "I can't get you outta here no more than I can get me outta here."

"Yes, Gamba," Thomas said. "You can."

Nathaniel reacted.

"How'd you know that name?"

"You wear it . . . like a badge." Thomas's paper-thin lips curled in a grin of satisfaction so tight Nathaniel thought it might tear. "At least . . . I can still . . . read that."

Silence grew awkward.

"I . . . can help," Thomas said at last.

"Help what?"

"Call your . . . Elemental."

Nathaniel stared at Thomas, realizing now that his vision here was as good as it might be out in the open. And realizing that this man, Thomas, was crazy as Carl. His eyes had that look about them, too, that piercing clarity he'd seen in other men as they lay dying on red-stained sheets or sweating with the pain of burns, lucid on morphine and smelling of rot and rum and reek.

"Don't . . . let me . . . die here," Thomas said.

"You're the magician," Nathaniel said. "You get us out."

"I am Air . . . my magic . . . doesn't work here . . . but you are Earth . . . do you feel . . . it? . . . I can aid . . . if you will . . . try."

"What do I got to lose?" Nathaniel said.

"Need to . . . do . . . better than . . ." Thomas swallowed again. "That. Must accept . . . need . . . to *be* your magic . . . need to *be* Gamba."

The name felt like a slap this time.

"What do you know about what I ought to be?"

Thomas moved a dismissive finger.

"What do you . . . want? I will get you . . . three tasks . . . three's good to start . . . tell me what . . . you want."

Nathaniel laughed.

What did he want? What did it matter what he wanted? The idea was crazy, the question laughable. He was locked in this root cellar by an insane old woman, and this man wanted him to make wishes like they were butterflies that might spring like gold coins out of the ground. Who was crazier — Carl, the old woman, this dying man, or himself for even bothering to listen?

But Thomas' expression was serious as blood. Nathaniel felt his anger again. He felt both his hands, though he still knew only one was real, felt fear of the old woman and the sheriff and the country he had given that hand for. And he felt the venom of revenge boil in his gut.

"I want out of here," he said in a firm tone. "That's what I want. And I want the woman to pay."

"And?"

He stopped and thought. He knew what else he wanted. It was big. Important. It could change everything.

"I want William McKinley dead."

Could he do that? He was just one man. Could he actually kill King Billy? The idea flowed through him like a river of ice. He could. Yes. He felt it. Someone had to fix things. Might as well be him.

"Oh, no, Gamba . . . that's . . . dangerous magic."

"Don't matter."

"Magic minds . . . itself. Dark magic . . . will eat you up."

Nathaniel said nothing.

"You will . . . lose yourself —"

"How about you quit telling me *what* to do, and start telling me *how* to do it? Else we ain't never getting outta here."

Thomas accepted that.

"Take . . . my hand."

It was so light Nathaniel was afraid it might crumble like ash. He felt a connection at their touch, though. He knew it by the flavor of Thomas's presence — a light taste of mustard.

"Feel . . . the voice . . . inside you? The voice . . . of Earth?"

"Yes," Nathaniel said.

Thomas whispered words Nathaniel could not make out.

"You have . . . great will . . . great anger . . . use them . . . call the voice . . . tell it your . . . need . . . let the voice . . . rise . . . and tell it . . . what it must do."

Through their connection, Nathaniel saw how Thomas matched his anger with the power of the rhythm he'd always had running through his mind. Nathaniel didn't know what to do, but the essence around him— his magic itself—bade him further.

"Call him, Gamba," Thomas said in a voice buoyed by magic. "Call him now. Bring your Elemental here."

Nathaniel had no words, but he opened his mouth and he sang—sang his sadness, sang his need, and most of all, sang his anger. The ground under him rent. Fresh soil rose, and he smelled worms and bugs and roots and limestone and granite. It was a creature, a thing, a mound as thick and dense as the world was itself.

It radiated power.

He felt its presence burn against his mind.

"Get us out of here," Nathaniel commanded through his song.

The Elemental gave a scream of complaint, but it ripped the ceiling away, opening the cellar like a jar and leaving a crater in the yard like an open scar.

The old woman cowered against his cord of wood.

He pointed at her.

"Make her pay for this."

The Elemental plunged what might have been an arm into the ground, and from the soil rose the complete skeletons of ten, fifteen, maybe twenty men. They rose from the cellar floor. They rose from graves dug in the woods around the house. And they rose from patches of ground on the yard. Tilly was an Earth Magician, he realized. Just like him. She had buried these men with her magic, just as she would have buried him. Now her magic turned, and their bones rose to expose her crimes.

People came running from the distance, wanting to know what was happening. A woman screamed and covered her mouth with one hand at the sight of the rising skeletons. The sheriff came on his horse, his rifle flashing from its holster.

Tilly recovered, and spoke to the Earth Elemental.

Nathaniel felt the pull somewhere deep inside.

"No!" he yelled, feeding his anger to the creature. "It's mine!"

He sang a deeper song.

Her flowerbed rose like a red wave and fell down upon her until she was wrapped like a caterpillar in a cocoon. She began to sink, then. Inch by inch she slid deeper into the soil. She cried and screamed and pleaded, but the Elemental had his way, and in a short while the woman and her mound of Georgia clay both disappeared completely, replaced with a silence that seemed to stretch forever.

By light of day, Nathaniel saw how bad off Thomas really was. His skin was gray, his arms no bigger around than a half-dollar. His shirt and pants were torn and half eaten by mold and slime. He gulped air, his jaws working like a fish out of water. His eyes blinked against the sudden Georgia sun.

"Gamba . . ." he whispered.

Nathaniel bent closer.

"Thank . . . you."

"I suggest you be getting away from him, boy." The sheriff stood at the lip of the cellar, rifle dangling from the crook of his arm. "You got some answering to do."

Nathaniel's Elemental made a moan of hunger. He held it in check as he gazed at the sheriff.

"Start talking, or you gonna dangle."

Nathaniel's power surged toward the sheriff, the strength of his will levered by the furious power of his anger. His Elemental was ready. The aura of power was the most incredible thing. He could kill this man. Could crush him. Could throw him over that elm tree he was so fond of.

He could. Yes, he could.

He looked at the Elemental and smiled.

"No, Gamba . . ."

Thomas's grip crushed Nathaniel's hand. He whispered magic. A breeze kicked up, growing to a wind, then a gale. A funnel reached down fast as lightning, ripping the rifle from the sheriff and throwing it into the woods. Wind buffeted the house. The sheriff's horse raced off, as did the rest of the townspeople. The sheriff lost his hat before he ran too.

The gale died as quickly as it began, and Nathaniel was alone with just Thomas and the bones of dead magicians.

"Why did you do that?" Nathaniel said, standing over Thomas. His unsatisfied anger balled in his gut. "I do my own fighting."

Thomas was a husk now. Each word came at immense cost.

"Dark . . . magic . . . you . . . don't . . . understand . . ."

"What's that?" Nathaniel pressed closer.

"Didn't . . . want . . . you . . . to regret."

And Nathaniel saw the truth.

Thomas had seen Nathaniel's intent and stepped in with his hurricane. Damn him. Damn him to hell. What right did Thomas have to protect him? Nathaniel wanted to hit him, but he saw Thomas's eyes carried that lack of fear comes when a man knows he's in his last breaths, and it brought him back to his senses.

He put his hand on Thomas's forehead.

"Promise . . . no . . . dark magic . . . until . . ." Thomas closed his eyes. "Until . . . you know."

"You don't owe me nothing," he said.

"Promise . . . me."

"All right," he said because it felt like the right thing to say. "I promise."

With that Thomas fell limp. A gust of breeze picked at the loose collar of his undershirt. Thomas's death-relaxed face seemed relieved.

"Be Gamba," Thomas had said earlier.

Be true. Be strong.

He felt his pa then. Felt his pa's big hand on his small shoulder. Saw his face. He needed to be as strong as his anger. Strong as his desire. Thomas said he had three commands of his Elemental, and if that was true he had one left. He could tell it to kill William McKinley if he wanted, but while Thomas didn't owe Nathaniel anything, Nathaniel knew the opposite wasn't true.

Nathaniel raised his voice and sang a long melody filled with tones of sadness and glory. Then he looked at the Elemental and pointed to Thomas.

"Take him to the tallest hilltop in Georgia," Nathaniel sang. "Bury him so he's facing the morning sky."

The Elemental groaned, but bent to his will and carried Thomas away on a wave of red soil.

Nathaniel walked the road north, thinking about the world, thinking about his song, thinking about what it meant to be a magician, and thinking about the promise he made to Thomas.

He said he wouldn't mess with the dark magic until he understood it. But he understood dark magic already. He lived it every day. Lived it in Georgia and Alabama, and lived it in San Juan and South Carolina. Lived it when he lost his hand and when he drew stares from white folk he never done no harm to. Dark magic had eaten up his pa and his ma and eaten up Crazy Carl and the men who died on the hill without them even knowing what it was doing. He'd seen it. Oh, yes, he had. Seen it in the sheriff's eyes.

His pa had said things would change.

Said Abe Lincoln had showed everyone the way, and that the world would just have to follow along now. He said Nathaniel just needed to be strong, and the day would come. The name came from that. Gamba. Warrior. Strength. Discipline. Maybe Pa was right. The world *was* different today than when he was just a boy.

Change came too damned slow, though.

He thought long and hard about Thomas' warning.

In the end he came to this: A man's got to do what he thinks is right. What he thinks is fair. And if the magic does rise up and take him, well . . . sometimes a man has to sacrifice something if he's going to make a difference.

King Billy sitting in the office wasn't going to help things no more, and if the runnerboy's reports were right, he was healing up right and proper.

The idea struck him wrong.

Lot of work here, he thought. *Lot of work.*

Somewhere as he walked, Nathaniel found he was singing. And in singing, he found he didn't need Thomas to work his magic. Didn't need no one. His cadence came to match the flow of his stride, and his stride came to match a clock that registered somewhere deep in the earth itself. He thought of the sheriff's gun. He thought of his black brothers and sisters he'd seen beaten and killed. He thought of William McKinley sitting on his recovery bed with a bullet hole in his gut. He saw an image of his own gangrene-blackened hand. Fair's only fair.

He shaped his song into a hard chorus of darkness and disease. He played with it, molded it into a festering, putrid infection. When the pressure built to where he felt it right, he called through the soil. The ground rose up around him to take on the spellwork. Nathaniel sang a picture of King Billy sitting and eating quail eggs and biscuits, sang the command of blackness spreading in the president's gut like the blackness that had taken his own hand. He felt the ground below him rumble, smelled strength in limestone and granite, felt the scrub of sand.

He reached out, then, sending his thought eastward toward Washington.

The headlines came about a week later, when Nathaniel made Nashville. King Billy was dead of his wound. It went septic, they said. Painful in the end. Teddy Roosevelt took office that very day. Nathaniel didn't know if Teddy would be better. Who could tell?

All Nathaniel could say for certain was that he was done drifting. He was strong. He knew wrong when he saw it. And he knew it was time to make a difference.

Queen of the Mountain
Kristin Schwengel

Lasair Connor leaned on the starboard rail of the steamship *Columbia*, letting the hint of a fresh breeze riffle her red hair and flutter her hat ribbons. Despite the way the salty winds and the sun chapped her skin, she had enjoyed the voyages. She admitted to the occasional vague uneasiness when she considered how isolated and tiny their ship was compared to the enormous ocean, but the storms they had encountered had not been severe, and she had never felt truly endangered. Lady Amara, of course, remained securely in her stateroom, as she had on the transatlantic crossing from England to New York.

Lasair glanced up at the rigging, but most of the great sails hung limp, with only a few of the smaller sails puffing out as tiny gusts caught them.

"Still not enough wind to speed us along, sadly."

Lasair managed to convert her startled jump into a tolerably smooth turn to face the newcomer.

"Mr. Ayresbury," she said with a slight nod, providing the minimum deference to emphasize that they were almost equals, despite his obvious wealth and her less obvious lack thereof. Her parents, after all, had been of good if unexalted family. After their fatal carriage accident, she had been raised as ward to another gentleman who had grown up with her father, and she was now respectably employed as companion to Lady Amara. She need not fear Conrad Ayresbury's critical eye.

"Miss Connor," he replied, the tilt of his head equally precise. He, at least, could forgo the necessity of wearing a hat while on the ship, his blond hair tousled by the breeze. "The Captain informs me that we should reach the islands tomorrow, perhaps even tomorrow morning."

"Lady Amara will be delighted to hear that," Lasair replied.

"And even more delighted to be on solid ground?" His lips did not twitch, but she could read the subtle jest in his eyes.

She nodded, not sure what other response could possibly be appropriate, and turned her head back to the bow of the ship, to the featureless blue horizon ahead of them.

"The steamships have certainly made this voyage easier than it would have been even twenty years ago," she said at last, her voice as neutral as she could make it. What was it about him that unnerved her? Why did she see questions in his eyes?

"Indeed. No more need sailors fear a calm day." There was more than a hint of laughter in his voice, although Lasair couldn't imagine why.

The odd silence stretched between them until Lasair gave herself a small mental shake. Whatever he was trying to see in her was no business of hers. "Excuse me," she murmured, and fled to Lady Amara's stateroom without waiting for a reply.

The stateroom was a small suite, surprisingly well-appointed, consisting of Lady Amara's sleeping and dressing chamber, Lasair's own, smaller room, and a shared sitting room between them, which provided the entrance to the center passageway. It was here, near the slatted wall that allowed air to circulate, that Lasair found her mistress.

Leaning back in the broad wing chair, fanning herself in a desultory fashion, Lady Amara Feuerberg looked up as Lasair closed the door.

"There you are, my dear," she murmured. "I wondered how long—" she broke off, her glance turning to an outright stare as Lasair removed her hat. "My dear, your hair! And your cheeks!" She waved toward Lasair's room. "Take a moment to tidy up, and be sure to lotion!" No longer indolent, her voice crackled with energy. Lasair had learned early in her employment that although Lady Amara enjoyed playing the role of a lady filled with *ennui*, it was no more than a pretense.

"Yes, Lady Amara." Lasair ducked a tiny curtsy, ignoring the exasperated head shake at the deference, and moved to her tiny chamber.

The tiny slip of silvered glass on the wall revealed that Lady Amara had been right about her hair. Quite a bit had pulled out of its pins, haloing her reddened face. Taking all of it down and wielding her brush before the slim mirror, Lasair set to reining in the auburn curls. *That was odd*, she thought. There hadn't been that much wind—just brief puffs of air—and yet her hair seemed to have been picked out of its pinnings. Perhaps it had been that wildness in her appearance that had drawn Conrad Ayresbury's quizzical attention. She bit the edge of her lip, not sure why the thought unsettled her.

Gathering all of the long strands, she twisted and

wrapped, tucking the ends to create a neat bundle, a liberal application of pins securing the twist in place at the nape of her neck. She dug through her trunk to retrieve the nearly empty jar of rosewater lotion, dabbing a tiny bit on each cheek before straightening her skirt and rejoining Lady Amara.

"Much better, my dear," the older woman said, scrutinizing Lasair before nodding approvingly. "Now, any news?"

"We should arrive at the Sandwich Islands tomorrow, according to Mr. Ayresbury, who had it from the Captain."

"Thank the good Lord above," Lady Amara sighed. "I shall be so happy to be off this ship and on our own again!" She fanned a little more vigorously.

Lasair glanced up, but Lady Amara did not offer any elaboration regarding her plans for what they would do upon their arrival. She had only been Lady Amara's companion for less than a year, and was not quite certain how the older woman would respond if she inquired further. Even though Lady Amara treated her rather more like a daughter than a companion, she still felt that she knew very little of her employer. In fact, until her guardian, Mr. Rusbourne, had introduced them, she had never even heard him mention Lady Amara before, although they must have known each other a long time for him to place Lasair in her company.

The scenery of the island of O'ahu was astonishing—opulent greens of exotic flora, the air redolent with strange floral scents, the sounds of the harbor and the town punctuated by raucous birdcalls, and the looming mountains above it all. After a few short expeditions

inland, however, Lady Amara had shown little inclination for further exploring, and had established herself
and Lasair in a large suite at one of the finer hotels. She
avoided most social obligations, paying only a single
call to the English ambassador, instead spending her
time seeking out guides and those who could tell her
more about the islands, usually leaving Lasair at the
hotel with only minor tasks to be completed while she
was gone.

About a fortnight after their arrival, Lasair found
herself once again alone in the suite. For the third time
in a quarter hour, she glanced out the sitting room window, but there was no sign of Lady Amara. Restless in
the absence of her normal duties, she began straightening the papers on the tiny writing desk. As she did, she
spotted her own name written in the strong hand of her
guardian.

> *. . . be discreet in your use of Lasair. Others have
> noted the decrease in my own apparent Power since
> she left my company. If you are suddenly seen to
> have significantly greater ability than before, surely
> there will be questions.*

Hearing a noise in the street, Lasair looked up, her guilt
warring with curiosity. A pony cart laden with flowers
and fruit passed by, and all was again silent. Her fingers
tightened on the paper. What was this Power, these abilities Mr. Rusbourne wrote of? And how did it relate to
her?

She glanced over the desk. The two sheets of the letter had been pushed, as if in haste, under another letter,
but not completely covered. Her ears prickling and her

stomach roiling with trepidation, she eased the pages out and began reading.

Esteemed Madam,

    I am pleased that your voyage passed without event. It must have been exceedingly difficult for one of our Nature to spend that much time enclosed, nay, imprisoned, by inimical Water. Suffice it to say that I hope you will find the results you experience at your destination to have been worth such a challenge.

    I must, however, warn you as strongly as I can to be discreet in your use of Lasair. Others have noted the decrease in my own apparent Power since she left my company. If you are suddenly seen to have significantly greater ability than before, surely there will be questions. And it would not be impossible to find our common heritage.

    I doubt that this message will find you before you continue from San Francisco to the Sandwich Islands, but again, I urge caution in acting on your plans. Do not doubt that the White Lodge can find some reach, even across the globe. Though the islands themselves may have been formed by Fire, they are still surrounded by Water.

    Above all, keep the Blood safe.

Your most Dedicated,
Corven Rusbourne

With trembling hands, Lasair shuffled the letter back under the other papers, recreating the untidy pile. The shame she felt over reading Lady Amara's correspondence warred with confusion over the contents. What was this Power that Mr. Rusbourne mentioned? What was the White Lodge? Or the Blood that must be kept safe? And, perhaps most importantly, what use was Lady Amara making of her that required urgings of caution? The role of lady's traveling companion, after all, was a common position, and her duties varied little. She kept Lady Amara company, read to her, and attended to small errands. A breeze through the nearby window brought in the now-familiar floral perfume. This time, however, it was laced with acrid smoke, and she sat down abruptly as memory flooded over her.

A small, dark room, the smell of smoky incense heavy around her . . . a voice—Lady Amara's?—or Mr. Rusbourne's?—chanting in a strange language . . . the image of a stained piece of fabric, then a piercing headache and black silence.

Lasair blinked, her breathing rapid as she came back to her surroundings. The breeze must have shifted, for the air was now fresh and clear, with a bracing hint of the salty ocean coming from the harbor. She took deep breaths to calm herself before studying the strange memory. It must have been a true recollection—no imagined event could have felt so real. And why would she ever have imagined herself bound—but she now realized that she had been, as surely as if ties had been closed over her wrists—in a dark room with such strange sounds and smells? She could more easily believe the whole event to have been a nightmare, except that it was the middle of the afternoon, and she had been wide-awake.

A greeting called out by the hotel doorman disturbed

her, and Lasair realized Lady Amara had returned. She bent down, thankful that she had collapsed onto the window seat, and pulled her knitting from the small basket tucked nearby. She bent her head over the needles, winding the thread through her fingers and placing the needle's point into the next stitch of the lace pattern just as the door opened and Lady Amara swept into the room.

"Finally, all is settled," she said, lowering herself onto the small sofa. "I have secured a boat, lodgings on the greater island, and a guide and horses so that we may explore all of the mountains there."

"When do we depart?" Thankfully, Lasair managed to keep any trace of the distress she still felt from that strange memory out of her voice. An expedition to the big island had been Lady Amara's single goal since they had landed in Honolulu. She had many times expressed her desire to see the active volcanoes, the "living, growing" mountains.

"The day after tomorrow. I could not secure an earlier time for us and still make arrangements for our accommodations. I have no desire to make a rough camp for any more days than I would need to!"

She laughed, and Lasair smiled back, relieved that Lady Amara had detected no alteration in her demeanor.

The small steamer left the harbor quite early, and Lady Amara professed to be barely awake, even as she anxiously stood at the rail as close to the bow as she could manage, studying the big island as they approached.

Lasair was disconcerted to find Mr. Ayresbury also among those headed to Hawai'i. As they boarded the little ship, he smiled a greeting to her. "I have spent some days studying the plants of O'ahu, and thought this an opportune time to visit the greater island to see if they grow differently there."

"A student of Mr. Darwin?" Lasair kept her tone neutral. In some circles, to use Charles Darwin's name was something akin to blasphemy.

The expression in Mr. Ayresbury's eyes was questioning, as usual. "I have read some of his theories, and found them intriguing. It is, in fact, the main reason I traveled to the United States, and then here. Do you have an interest in botany?"

"Not in particular," Lasair replied, glancing at where Lady Amara stood. "But Lady Amara's tastes in reading are wide-ranging."

"Indeed," was all that Mr. Ayresbury offered, before Lady Amara turned to join them.

When they met their native guide the following morning, Lasair was unprepared for the torrent of foreign speech that greeted her. Perplexed, she turned to Lady Amara, who seemed just as confused. It was a moment before the man-of-all-work at the tiny cabin smoothed out his own wrinkled brow and spoke.

"You will forgive, my lady, but some of the inland people still cling to the old superstitions, as this one does." Disapproval tinged his voice as he gestured at the guide, who had fallen silent and now stood with his head bent in Lasair's direction. "He appears to believe that the young lady is a living incarnation of the goddess Pele, whom the superstitious still treat as the ruler of the volcanoes." Lady Amara raised an eyebrow at him, and he shrugged. "I believe it is the hair, my lady. Pele is often described as having hair of fire."

Lady Amara burst into laughter as Lasair raised a hand to her head, making sure that her bright red hair was still neatly coiffed. A passing breeze had teased a few strands to float loose about her face, but otherwise the knot at the base of her skull remained secure.

"Well, if he will not provide us the service we require, we must look to engage someone else." Lady Amara's expression hardened, making the guide drop his head farther.

"If Pele wishes to observe her own mountain as a stranger, Hana'kahi will guide her," he muttered, his accent thick. "Hana'kahi will serve in whatever the Lady of Fire commands."

"Then it's settled," Lady Amara murmured, laughter returning to her voice as she mounted her horse.

The first sight of the active volcano and the blazing lava flow came as a revelation to Lasair. She had admired the steep mountains of the western United States, and had found the peaks of O'ahu attractive. But when she saw the flaming, molten earth jetting out of the blackness of the surrounding mountain, she was awestruck by its fierce beauty. She felt a pull deep within her, a desire to get nearer to the liquid fire. Glancing at Lady Amara, she saw the same fascinated yearning on the older woman's face, mingled with something like anticipation.

"Will we get to the flow today?" Lady Amara asked their guide, who nodded.

"If the Lady wishes, our camp could be made near to it," Hana'kahi said. "There would be safe places upon the rocky ridge, like the bank of a river."

"That will be perfect," Lady Amara said, and Lasair gave a tiny nod when the guide looked at her for approval. Only then did he turn and continue up the narrow, leaf-grown pathway.

As evening approached, they neared the edge of the lava flow. Hana'kahi had said the volcano had been more active of late, the river of fire flowing farther than usual down the mountain, and that even the Princesses had come to pray—Princess Ruth to Pele, Princess Liliuo'kalani to the Virgin Mary—that the lava would slow and the town of Hilo be spared.

It was in a sheltered clearing here, with the hissing and popping of the liquid earth in their ears, that the three of them made their tiny camp, with Hana'kahi sleeping on a mat outside Lady Amara and Lasair's tent.

Lasair was wakened by a sense of pressure, a squeezing through her whole body. Moving numbly, obeying an unheard but felt command, she rose and left the tent. She was able to turn her head enough to look at Hana'kahi's mat, and saw the lifeless body of the guide with his throat slit, his blood thick and black on his simple tunic. Unable to resist the summons, she continued walking forward, through the forest edge to the rim of rock that hedged the lava flow down the mountainside.

Lady Amara stood near the edge of the rocky outcropping, wearing an ornate robe Lasair could not recall ever seeing among her wardrobe, but yet it seemed familiar to her. Small candles were set in a circle on the stones, and by their flickering light and the glow of the volcanic flow, Lasair saw strange symbols and patterns chalked on the rock around Lady Amara. The older woman gestured, and Lasair's feet propelled her toward a second circle of chalked symbols.

Once she reached its center, Lady Amara flicked her fingers, and another ring of small candles flared into life surrounding Lasair. The young woman felt herself at once frozen tightly into place, her body pinned motionless as Lady Amara began to chant, in the same strange language that Lasair recalled from the flash of memory in the hotel on O'ahu.

The lava advanced more rapidly now, bubbling with greater energy, its level rising higher against the edge of the rock they stood upon. Imprisoned by whatever Lady Amara had done, Lasair attempted to shuffle back from the edge, but the soles of her feet stood fast while the liquid earth flowed by, little more than an arm's-length from her bare toes. Looking at the lava, Lasair realized that her fear was not of the molten river. It was of Lady Amara, who had stopped chanting and now reached her hands out along the flow toward the peak of the mountain, greedy anticipation lighting her face. Her expression was one of deep hunger, tinged with a hint of madness.

Suddenly, a tiny breeze like gentle fingers lifted Lasair's hair, teasing it out of its nighttime braid, swirling the skirts of her sleeping chemise and night robe and dancing around to tug at Lady Amara's heavy robe. She had a sense of laughter—where could that come from, for her ears were filled with the hissing of the flowing lava and the echo of Lady Amara's chanting?—as a bit of fabric was pulled free from a hidden pocket in the embroidered robe the older woman wore, floating toward Lasair. As the smoke swirled around them, she saw flickers outlining a shape in the air, a feathery woman-figure holding the white square out to her.

Whatever force held her captive had eased a tiny bit.

Although it was still an effort to move, Lasair could reach forward to grasp the piece of fabric—a handkerchief, she now saw, stained with three dark patches—from the wispy fingers of the transparent woman-figure. As she touched it, her fingertips closed over those rust-brown spots, and more memories and sensation stunned her.

—*Herself, as a child, held down by Mr. Rusbourne as he pierced her finger, dripping three drops of blood onto the handkerchief, and watching as he chanted, unable to move, feeling a tug from somewhere deep inside her as he conjured . . . something. Then, exhaustion and blackness . . .*

Flashes of similar events filled her mind, along with a deep, instinctive understanding. Corven Rusbourne had shaped the magic, and Lady Amara had taken it over, and they had both drained her, used her. A part of her, the part of her that had been "awake" for the last twelve years, struggled to align this revelation with what she thought she knew. The rest of her, newly roused by the return to her hand of those stolen drops of blood, burned with unfettered fury.

They had stolen her Mastery. It was she, not they, who should hold the Power of Fire. Their power was little more than common magicians. Barely aware of what she did, she reached with her mind into the crimson lava, felt its roiling heat deep within her soul. The handkerchief in her fingertips flared into flame and vanished in a wisp of smoke, and Lasair opened her eyes. The candles around her blazed high, their wax melting into rivulets which obliterated the chalk symbols that penned her.

Lady Amara looked at her, only now aware that something was deeply wrong, as the spell bond Corven

Rusbourne had formed and given to her was burned out by the heat of Lasair's wakened power. She raised her hands to start a new conjuring, summoning her bound Elementals to the edge of the volcanic flow, turning them toward Lasair.

Anger, rage, burning resentment rippled through the young woman. "You should not have brought me here, Amara Feuerberg," Lasair said, her voice crackling with heat. "You reach too far, and now you shall learn your limits." Again, that small part of her trying to make sense of this was astonished—*where is this dry voice coming from?*

Not knowing what she was doing, acting out of instinct, Lasair "reached" for the fires of the volcano again, seeking power, and was met by a flood of fiery strength that vibrated through her entire body. Lizards of flame— salamanders—separated themselves from the lava, swarming up to battle with Lady Amara's own.

Power filled her, flame and fury pulsing through her veins, lava instead of blood, as she advanced toward Lady Amara, her salamanders shredding the older woman's until they fled. Without Lasair's Mastery strengthening her, Lady Amara was unable to control the Elementals, to force their obedience, and soon she stood alone, ringed by Lasair's salamanders.

Lasair stopped, drawing herself up to her full height, taller than she had ever stood. Flickers of fear filled Lady Amara's eyes, as a grim smile spread over her former companion's face.

"You should not have come here. You should not have disturbed me." That strange, hot, crackling voice rang out as she *reached* one more time into the depths of the volcano for the source of her power, to send a flood of lava cascading over this one who thought to bind and control her.

"Lasair, stop!" A man's voice, barely heard over the roar of the fire in her blood.

She tilted her head to the side—who was Lasair? Who was this mere man who dared interrupt her?

A drift of smoke floated in front of her, shaping itself again into a translucent female figure—a sylph, she now recognized. And she also saw that the sylph was frightened—of her? But Fire and Air were natural allies. How could a creature of Air be afraid of one of Fire? The question caught her attention, distracting her briefly from her fury, and then again that voice broke into her thoughts.

"Lasair, look at me!"

With effort, she dragged her eyes from the sylph, from the fear-frozen figure of Lady Amara surrounded by salamanders, from the lava lapping at the edge of the rocky outcropping, and turned her head.

Conrad Ayresbury stood at the edge of the forest, sylphs dancing in a shield around him. *Air Master*, some part of her noted. With measured steps, he walked forward until he stood in front of her, his hazel eyes never leaving her green ones, his sylphs weaving between them.

"Lasair," he said, "remember yourself."

Another flood of rage, but this time Lasair realized that it was not her anger. Something within her tried to raise her arms, to conjure and command the salamanders, but Lasair held herself still, her eyes locked with Conrad Ayresbury's.

"I do not know how to get out," she said, this time in her own voice, but even as she spoke the words she knew the answer. As Corven Rusbourne and Amara

Feuerberg had taken her power for their own by controlling those few drops of her blood, now she needed to master her blood for herself. Her eyes unfocused a little, and she felt the blood roaring in her ears, her pulse a drumbeat, the fire deep within. But now she could see that there were two fires—her own and also another one, that one full of chaos and power. Drop by drop, heartbeat by heartbeat, breath by breath, she separated the two, each exhalation pushing the foreign fire out of her blood until Lasair stood exhausted, but completely herself once more.

Her eyes refocused, and she saw the figure of a woman of pure flame standing, almost floating, on the surface of the lava in front of her.

"Pele-honua-mea," she murmured, bowing her head as she spoke the ancient spirit's most sacred name.

"You have managed to push me back, yet now *you bow? You have greater power than you think, little one— although even so, you could not stop me from taking anything I truly wanted."* Now filled with laughter, all traces of fury vanished, that dry, crackling voice rang in Lasair's head. From the startled expression on Conrad's face, he heard the words too. As did Lady Amara, who shrank within herself, her elaborate robe suddenly too large for her body.

The glowing figure of Pele turned to face Lady Amara. *"You have disturbed me, roused me for nothing more than your own greedy pleasure,"* she said, her voice filling once again with anger. *"You have sought to control me, to use me as you used the little one. I. Will. Not. Be. Used."* With each of her last words, the river of lava moved closer to the cowering figure of Lady Amara. Even the salamanders Lasair had called moved away from the fury of the goddess. Several of them slipped to her side, weaving around her in much the same way the sylphs still danced around Conrad.

"It is past time for me to draw back to the depths of my home, but I shall not go alone." The liquid flame welled up as Pele spoke, flooding over the rock ledge where Lady Amara stood and sweeping her under in a swirl of molten earth.

Pele turned her attention back to Lasair, and Conrad Ayresbury reached out, grasping her hand. Her fingers tightened around his as the goddess moved over the lava toward them.

"Fear not, Air Master. The little one is done with being controlled." Again, dry laughter replaced fury, and the figure turned to cast a glance down the mountain. *"Do not fear for the people. I will take the heat of the lava with me, and they shall be spared."*

With that, the red-gold form of the goddess melted like wax, rippling down until she too disappeared into the river of lava, which lessened almost at once, its rapid flow slowing back to its usual rate, darkening at the edges as it cooled to solidity.

Lasair looked down at her hand, still clasped in Conrad's. Sylphs and salamanders twined about them both as she turned her eyes to meet his.

"Well, Air Master, no wonder you found the idea of being becalmed at sea so amusing."

Conrad stared at her a moment, then laughed before bringing her hand to his lips.

"Indeed, Fire Master."

"How did you know I was . . ." Her voice trailed off as she realized that she didn't know precisely what she was asking.

"The sylphs, actually," he replied. "They were drawn to you—surely you noticed how they teased your hair?—and then I realized that your name meant 'flame.' I had earlier received a message from another Air Master that there were questions being asked in London about Lady Amara's power, and it seemed that there must be more beneath the surface of what I could observe. So I followed the two of you."

Lasair was silent, considering everything that had happened, and all that she now remembered.

"But it is late," he continued, "and long past time we were headed home."

Lasair nodded, knowing that he did not mean the cottages where they were staying, but *home*. The flickering light of Pele's fires revealed that his eyes still held questions for her, but now she felt only a heady anticipation of the answers . . .

. . . And of entire new worlds now opening before her.

I Have Heard
the Mermaids Singing

Mercedes Lackey

"Miriam," said the tall, dark man in the plain, dark suit as he touched his hat to the prim young lady in an equally plain traveling dress without a hint of crinoline or bustle. They stood in front of the Gray Gull tea room in the small fishing town of Solace, Maine, positioning themselves just past the door. It seemed they must have come here for the express purpose of meeting.

"Jacob," the young lady acknowledged. Her bonnet and dress were nearly the same pale gray as the wisps of fog that drifted just above the cobblestones of the street, and it was almost impossible to tell the color of her hair beneath the veil wrapped around her head under the hat. It might have been dark brown. "Well, you called, and now I'm here. Your call was not very illuminating, however. I believe I am due an explanation. And a cup of tea, at the very least. And repayment for my travels."

To say that Jacob Harsetter's "call" had not been very illuminating was a drastic understatement. In fact, the only thing that the little brownie had been able to tell Miriam Tayler was *Jacob needs you. Gray Gull tearoom, three in the afternoon, September twelfth.*

She had received the message on September the tenth. The journey from Boston by rail and then coach had been moderately uncomfortable, but at least Jacob had left a more mundane letter for her at the coaching inn. It stated that the meeting was still to take place, but that he had arranged for her lodging and meals at the inn. She was somewhat mollified to find the room to be of the first quality *and* that she would not be required to share it with any other gentlewomen.

But only somewhat mollified. Jacob Harsetter might be a man of means, but she was a lady of a certain age with a slender purse and no prospects of marrying a larger one. She eked out her income making quite exquisite hats and gloves, and an absence of any length from her shop would have a deleterious effect, and the drain of an unexpected trip was most unwelcome. Had the summons come from anyone else, she likely would have ignored it, or sent the brownie back with a sharp rebuke.

But Jacob Harsetter was an Earth Master, and her father's old friend, and she would—this once—give him the benefit of the doubt.

"You are indeed owed an explanation, Miriam," he said. "And more than a cup of tea. Here." He pressed a small leather purse into her hand. "This will reimburse you for the cost of your journey. I chose this meeting place rather than the coaching inn because the dear lady who is the proprietress is as deaf as a post, and her clients are so remarkably self-centered that nothing registers with them unless it pertains to their wants and needs. We shall be virtually invisible."

Miriam gave a graceful little nod of her head and permitted Jacob to hold the door open for her. Once inside, they were ushered to the most inferior table in the very small room, one in the far rear corner, which was dark, a little cramped, and offered neither a good view of the street outside nor a good view of the other tables. These were mostly already occupied by ladies of the sort who bought Miriam's hats and gloves—ladies who were gowned in what passed in so small and remote a town as the height of fashion, but which was a good two years behind Boston, three behind the nation's capital, and four behind London. But, since every *other* lady here was gowned in the same way, they likely were as contented as their kind could ever be. They gave her the briefest of glances, dismissing her as someone absolutely beneath them because of her gown, never knowing that the cage-crinolines they sported were already considered laughable in London, and—well, who knew what they thought she was? Probably not as lowly as a mill girl, since what mill girl would have the wherewithal to spend on a tearoom meal, and what respectable man would *take* a mill girl to a tearoom? But, well, some sort of highly unfashionable bluestocking, surely. She smiled a little to herself.

The rest of the ladies stirred their cream into their tea, poured for each other, and feasted on little, sugary cakes while whispering among themselves, pretending to ignore what was going on at the other tables while at the same time stretching an ear to try to catch it.

Miriam ordered cucumber sandwiches and green tea. She would rather have had the hearty ham-and-cheese that Jacob got, but a lady wasn't permitted anything so . . . satisfying. Jacob, however, surreptitiously and gallantly divided the ham and cucumber between them, averring that he *liked* cucumber, but a man couldn't be seen ordering it. This might have been a lie, or it might not. Since he was the one inconveniencing *her,* Miriam was inclined to allow him to suffer.

"I'll not beat about the bush, Jacob. Why so infernally vague?" she asked, before devouring one of the cucumber triangles in a few neat bites.

"Because I have little or nothing to tell you," Jacob admitted ruefully. In deference to his masculinity, he had been permitted coffee, and he stared down into the cup a moment. "We are experiencing . . . troubles. Of an aquatic nature, so far as I can tell."

She lifted an eyebrow. "Troubles?"

"A fisherman's net was put into the water, and taken up a half hour later cut to ribbons. Another has had his lobster pots smashed—but only his, and not the ones of his brother, who fishes the same ground. A well went dry. A cellar flooded." Jacob shrugged. "It could be a Water Mage. It could be bad luck. It could be both, or neither. I just have a feeling. . . ."

Miriam's eyebrow remained in the elevated state. "Feeling?"

He clasped the coffee cup as if he was deriving steadiness from it. "I'm an Earth Master. You know we are the most stolid of the Elemental Masters. We mostly hear from nothing but our own Elementals. But . . . in the distance, and in the night, I have heard the mermaids singing, each to each. I do not think that they will sing for me. But you—yes. That is your gift, and your nature."

Miriam nodded. Although she was only an Air Mage, and not a Master, her peculiar gift was that she could see and hear all of the Elementals of all four Elements. And she was particularly adept at getting them to confide in her. Perhaps because they knew she did not have the power to coerce them.

If the Elementals could be gotten to talk of what was at the bottom of these troubles, they would, indeed, speak to her.

"Why did the song of the mermaids trouble you, Jacob?" she asked, quietly.

He looked up from his coffee, and his eyes were grieving. "Because," he said, "Their song was pain."

Miriam had let the landlord of the George's Head know that she would be remaining for an indefinite time. He indicated that Jacob had been prepared for this, and that he himself was not averse to having his best chamber occupied . . . so long as . . .

The discreet cough was her cue to smile. "Mister Harsetter was my father's dear friend and schoolmate," she said truthfully. "And my godfather. I have not seen him since my father's death, and being concerned that I was prospering, he asked if I would come for a visit. Unfortunately, with all his children, and now his wife's mother come to live with them . . ." she spread her hands wide, showing her own elegant gloves to advantage. The innkeeper, sensitive to such nuances as expensive gloves, which generally indicated money coming in his direction, nodded. And at the word "godfather," his face had cleared.

"Ah, I see. No room at the inn, so to speak." He chuckled at his own wit, and she dutifully did the same. "Will you be dining in your room, or in the common room, Miss?"

"I shall be breakfasting and dining in my room, if it is no trouble, and taking luncheon with Jacob and his wife," she replied. "Should they choose to also invite me for dinner, I shall have word sent to you."

"Very good, miss," the innkeeper said happily, secure in the knowledge that she was a *proper* lady who was not intending to expose her charms to the men drinking in the bar and the common room. When he took his leave of her, promising a fine roast chicken for dinner, she gladly closed the door of the sitting room behind him, took off her bonnet and gloves, and opened the window. Being only a mage and not a Master, she did not expend her meager store of energies in calling sylphs. But the sylphs were curious little creatures . . . and without a doubt, a few of her own particular favorites had followed her. They would be making friends among the locals, and should be coming to her at any moment.

And so they did.

The poor innkeeper would likely have turned purple and perished on the spot if he had been able to see them. They were mostly clad, if one could call it that, in ribbons and transparent scarves and their own hair. Some had feathered wings, some the wings of moths and butterflies. All were female. Nowhere had Miriam ever seen an explanation of why sylphs and naiads and dryads and nereids and so many of the other Elementals were exclusively female—nor had she ever heard an explanation given of how they reproduced themselves. She recognized three of them as her own particular friends, insofar as a human could ever be friends with an Elemental, particularly Air Elementals, which were not only butterfly-pretty, but had far more hair than wit. The flock of them flitted around the room, plucking at the drapes of the bed, peering into the fire, examining themselves raptly in the mirror.

It was a little like having an invasion of winged monkeys, though prettier, quieter, and less destructive by far.

When they finally exhausted the novelty of having free reign in a human's rooms, they settled about her — and by "settled," only two of them actually dropped to the floor. Several perched on the beams overhead, and the rest hovered. This, evidently, was not tiring for them, as she had seen sylphs hover for hours at a time.

She pitched her voice low, to prevent anyone who might be passing from hearing her "talking to herself." She was not yet old enough to be considered pleasantly eccentric for such foibles. "My friend the Earth Master asked me here because there are troubles," she said, coming straight to the point. "What is whispered on the wind?"

The sylphs looked at one another, and finally the one she called Luna spoke up.

"There is nothing on the wind, and nothing troubles the Air, Lady," the little thing with the great green wings of the Luna Moth said.

One of the strangers up on the beams fluttered her wings impatiently. "There are troubles out to sea, to sea, but they do not come to shore," she said, with a shrug that said without words that nothing that happened on the sea was of any importance to *her*.

"But do you know what the troubles are?" Miriam persisted.

Again, the impatient shrug. "We do not fly so far. Ask the mermaids who sing of pain, or the zephyr or even the boreals of the North Wind. Maybe they know. We only hear the echo of the song, deep in the night, and it is no trouble of ours."

The sylphs could be remarkably selfish — and short-sighted. Well, Miriam had expected this. As much as she enjoyed the sight, the company, and the antics of these creatures of her Element, they were not very reliable.

Nevertheless, they deserved their reward. She went to the wardrobe in which she had hung up her gowns and stowed her belongings, and got out a small carpet-bag, much worn, its pattern so faded as to be nearly invisible. She set a small brazier on the table, fetched a single coal from the hearth with tongs, and sprinkled powdered incense on it. The delicious fumes of sandalwood wafted to the ceiling and the sylphs were near-drunk on them, circling the slender stalk of smoke, twirling and twining with it, until the last lingering memory of incense was gone. Then, with a flutter of wings for thanks, they flitted out the window again. Miriam closed it against the chill and the fog that was already coming in.

She lit candles, for it was already darker here than it would be at the same hour at home, took a cloth-bound book and pen from the bag, and sat down at the little secretary to write. As she had anticipated, since this was a first-class guest room, there was fresh ink in the inkwell and sand in the jar waiting for her use. There was also an uncut goose quill, but she far preferred her delicate glass pen.

She noted everything that Jacob had told her, and the little she had learned from the sylphs. Then she tapped the cool end of the pen against her lips and thought.

Jacob was not inclined to overreact. And he was a *Master*. So why bring her here on what almost seemed like pretense?

Because the mermaids were singing pain.

Now, mermaids were not like naiads and nereids, essentially harmless creatures who could be readily coerced, and easily coaxed, into doing what a Master wanted. Or at least, not all of them were. When one was, like Miriam, a magician and not a Master, knowledge could be as much or more use than sheer strength of power. Miriam had put in a great deal of study, not only of the creatures of her own Element, but, since she could speak with all of them, of the other three as well. It seemed there were many tribes of merfolk out there, and they varied as widely as human tribes. Some were sweet-natured creatures of the warm and calmer waters, easily frightened, and entranced by human men; men only came to harm at their hands because they didn't know that mere mortals couldn't breathe the water that they could; they lured beautiful young men to them with their songs, drew them under to take them home, and drowned them. And being Elementals, mourned them a few days or a week until they forgot them.

Some, however, knew exactly what they were doing.

And some, particularly the mermaids of the North Atlantic, were the cruelest of all. They not only lured men to drown, they shared their natures with the sharks whose tails they wore. They *hunted* men.

Or had. Not so much, anymore. Their ploys only worked when there were no other sounds on the water to drown their songs, and they shared the antipathy to iron and steel that a few other supernatural entities did. Now that men made their boats with iron nails and fittings, had iron gaffes and spears, and often had iron motors in the larger vessels, the mermaids were forced to leave their favorite prey alone.

The question was, then, why were their songs full of pain?

It could simply be that the mass of iron about them had built up to the point that *it* was causing them distress. If that were the case . . . perhaps they could not muster the power to open a path to that half-and-half world of the Elementals where they would be free of it again. This would be at the cost of never being able to hunt a human again, which might be why they had put it off until it was too late, but at this point they would probably be more than willing to go.

It might be one of their kind was trapped. And little as Miriam liked the creatures, it was her duty to free it.

It might be that this was all a ruse; having found that songs of entrancement no longer worked, they might be trying another trick. And it might work on a man, but never on a woman. Miriam would know, and Jacob could administer a rebuke in the form of a Water Master brought over from England if need be.

Or it might be none of these things.

Nevertheless, she made notes in her book; by the time she was at an impasse, one of the inn servants tapped on her door with a tray full of dinner. She put her things away, enjoyed the food and the tolerable canary that came with it, and when she was done, set the tray herself on a stand outside the door for that purpose.

Then she closed the door, threw the window open again, and listened.

But she was too far inland. Or else the mermaids were not singing tonight. As fog drifted in through the window, though she strained her ears, she could hear nothing over the sound of men in the bar and common-room: conversations, a fiddler scraping away, singing. This far from Bangor, customs were still very much what they had been before the war between North and South.

She closed the window again, changed into her night-dress, and got into the enormous bed. The curtained bed frame itself was probably well over a hundred years old;

in fact, it probably dated back to the time the inn had been built. Back then, it would have served as many people as could be crammed into it at night. Whole families, at least. "Decent" people nowadays would shudder at the thought of an entire family in the same bed, but the poor still slept that way. Now, however, furbished with the finest featherbed and goose down pillows, it held pride of place in this best chamber, and was meant for two at the most. Miriam felt like a child in it, and it was tempting to give in to her playful side and wallow in it.

But she had work to do, and Jacob was an early riser.

The chambermaid arriving with her breakfast woke her. "Shall I mend the fire, miss?" the girl asked, as she put down a tray loaded with ham and johnnycake, maple syrup, butter, and a pot of coffee. "It's cold this morning."

"Please," she said, not getting up until the maid had gone, though the smell coming from that tray was heavenly. When breakfast was a memory, and she had washed and tidied herself at the basin—the pitcher held warm water, so the maid must have delivered that even before she delivered the breakfast—she made sure she had everything she needed in her reticule, and went downstairs, fully expecting to find Jacob.

She was not disappointed. He entered the front door of the inn as she was about to take a seat in the salon next to it. Without a word he offered his arm; she took it, and they went out to his waiting carriage. Evidently automobiles were thin on the ground here; she hadn't seen a single one since she arrived.

He drove himself, which she expected. It was a carriage large enough to hold almost a dozen, which she also expected—she had not been inventing his large family. Like himself, Jacob's wife was an Earth Magician—much weaker even than Miriam, but she had the blood—and Earth magicians tended to be fertile.

"Where are we going, Jacob?" she asked, when she was sure they would not be overheard. The little town was as bustling as such a small town could be, and everything neat, clean, and in good repair. Whatever else was going on here, the town of Solace was prospering.

"I thought we'd look at the well first," he said diffidently. "It's the farthest out."

She nodded. It seemed reasonable. "At a farm, I presume?"

"Orchard," he said. "Miriam, how are you getting on since your father died?"

Well, *that* was an abrupt change of subject. "You know that father and I were never close. If I were to say I still mourn him after two years, I would be telling lies."

Never close was a typical New England understatement. Miriam and her father had lived like cordial neighbors after her mother died. There was no rancor, but they simply had very little in common other than her mother. Her father, like Jacob, was an Earth magician who had shared his peculiar gift of speaking with all Elementals with her. Her mother had been Fire and also merely a magician. Air fed Fire, Earth supported Fire, and so her mother had been the bond in the household. When pneumonia had taken her, there had been nothing much to hold them together. Miriam had already been well aware that there was little her father, a fine carpenter, could leave to her other than the house, so she had long been apprenticed to a haberdasher, who had allowed Miriam to buy her out with the small inheritance she had gotten. By selling his tools and the contents of his woodshop, she had put enough in savings that she was doing no worse than when he had been alive. Of course, being able to fashion her own wardrobe had certainly aided that considerably.

"I was sorry when father died, of course," she added. "But you are aware that he and I had very little to talk about outside of magic. And under ordinary circumstances, there is little enough need of that hereabouts."

Jacob nodded. "I was more concerned with your financial well-being," he said.

She smiled. "Well, you can stop. Granted, my purse does not easily stretch to unscheduled jaunts into the hinterlands, but my shop continues to bring in what it did when Madame Alouette was behind the counter, and my needs are few. I enjoy my work, and it is the rare man or woman who is permitted the luxury of doing what they enjoy for a living. Please, do not concern yourself."

She could see that Jacob was bursting to say more—probably about not having a man to care for her and protect her, or perhaps asking her where she thought she would ever meet such a man when she was never out from behind that hat counter, but he didn't. Not that she would have given him a set-down, of course; he was her elder, his oldest son was almost her age in fact, and it would not have been proper for her to speak to him with impertinence.

It did rankle a little to know that had she not been an Elemental magician, he probably would not have hesitated in speaking those unspoken words. Those with the power were inclined to treat the women with it more like equals—probably because there was no "weaker sex" in a magician's duel.

Well, she was not going to be able to end *that* in a single afternoon, although the ghost of an idea began to float through the back of her mind, and she set it aside to ripen.

She was still getting the impression that there was far more going on here than just Jacob's fear there was a renegade Water Magician about. Nevertheless, something told her to remain silent about that, and observe. Air Mages were nothing if not highly intuitive. Not terribly empathic, but intuitive.

The road began to pass through what was obviously an apple orchard, and it was just as obvious that every hand was out getting in the harvest. Miriam was glad she'd had that good breakfast; otherwise the mouth-watering aroma of ripe apples and the sharp, sweet smell from the cider-presses would have made her stomach growl in a most unladylike manner.

Jacob stopped the horse once to get out and speak with a man up a ladder—the farmer, she presumed—then came back and set the horse in motion again. It didn't take a genius to guess he'd probably gotten permission to go look at the well. Very wise, as well as polite. You never knew which men were likely to meet you with a rifle and which with a cup of coffee and a slice of pie.

"I told him you were a water-witcher," Jacob said. "He's been asking me to find him one so he can dig a new well."

She nodded; that was a good excuse and not even much of a fib, much less a lie. It wouldn't take her long to find a water source if it had to come to that.

He pulled the carriage into a neat farmyard, and waved to the red-faced and exasperated-looking woman who was carrying water to the house with an old-fashioned yoke and two buckets. "I hope that's the watah-witch yah've brought, Jacob!" she called, without altering her course in the least.

"It is, Martha!" he called back, and the woman lost a great deal of the exasperation from her expression.

"Then welcome, and theyah'll be pie," she replied, and without another word, proceeded into her kitchen.

The people of Maine, especially in the country, tended not to waste words.

Jacob helped Miriam down out of the carriage. The well head was obvious; and the farmer was prosperous enough that it was not an old-style chain-and-bucket, but a fine pneumatic pump. There was probably its double in the kitchen. No wonder the farmwife looked annoyed.

That the well was dry was obvious to her; not a sight nor a sign of a Water Elemental anywhere about, and they generally tended to brood about wells, even closed ones like this. Luna had kept pace with them this entire time, and she flitted about, examining everything, showing no signs whatsoever that there was any inimical magic in the area.

In Miriam's experience, you could not possibly dry up a well with magic unless it was dark. The lives of too many people depended on wells . . . and often you had to disperse the Water Elemental that guarded it.

Well, then. . . .

She might not have had much in common with her father, but that didn't mean they didn't speak, and generally when they did, it was about magic. One of the things she had brought with her was part of her breakfast. A johnnycake soaked in butter ought to tempt just about any Earth Elemental.

Even the best garden generally has a spot that for one reason or another has been left to go wild, and this one was no exception. It looked as if the blackberry vines had been a little more enthusiastic than this Martha had been prepared for this year; she'd probably prune them back after the first hard frost, but for now, they were a bit of a jungle.

She stepped over to it, broke off a bit of the johnnycake, and placed it on a rock.

And waited.

Earth Elementals hereabouts, if they hadn't come along with some immigrant Elemental family or other, tended to still be the native creatures. So Miriam was not at all surprised to see a huge toad hop out of the tangle of vines and scoop up the johnnycake with its fat tongue. The toad looked up at her.

"Well, sister-of-power," it croaked softly. "I see you have more of that tasty man-food. May I have it?"

"Will you answer me some simple questions, brother-in-power?" she asked politely. "If you will, I shall give you all. If not, I must save it for one who will."

The toad croaked a chuckle. "Ask, she who is both polite and cautious."

"Has one-of-power dried up the planting-folk's well?" she asked, in a straightforward manner. Earth Elementals liked things simple and direct.

"Ai-ha! You ask me something easy! No, no one of power has done it. Not long ago, there was a man with strange sticks up above in the hill. He planted them in the earth and ran, and the earth spoke and rocks rained.

He did not find what he was looking for after that violation, and went away. But the spring at the bottom of the well was sealed."

Miriam glanced aside at Jacob, who wouldn't look at her. "And can it be reopened again?" she asked the toad.

"Easily. Dig a little farther down. It has found a new channel." Miriam bent and put the rest of the cake on the rock, and the toad went to breaking off bits and licking them up with obvious glee.

"Thank you, brother-in-power," she said as she straightened. "For your straight answers and your courtesy. May you sleep safely while the breath of the cold one freezes the world."

The toad grunted his reply, since his mouth was full of cake. Miriam pointedly ignored Jacob and marched up to the farmhouse door to give Martha the welcome news.

It was only when they were in the carriage, with two fine pies wrapped in flour-sack towels for safety and cooling under the seat behind them, that she turned on him.

"You knew that!" she accused.

"I guessed it," he corrected. "I couldn't get the Earth Elementals to talk to me without forcing them." He rubbed the back of his head with a rueful expression. "I didn't know that trick with the johnnycake. Your father teach that to you?"

"Yes. And the cellar that flooded is downhill of that well, isn't it?" She pinned him with her glare. "The increased pressure when the spring was stopped up is what caused the water to seep into the cellar, isn't it?"

"Very likely," he agreed, "since the cellar is where you suggested. But before you storm at me, come look over the lobster situa—"

But she was already waving Luna over to the carriage. The little sylph happily flitted over when she brought out a stoppered vial of lavender oil, her favorite. "Luna, go down to the docks and talk to the sylphs there, would you please? I want to know if there are two fishermen who have a quarrel with each other. And find out if one went out secretly and broke the lobster pots of the other."

Sylphs might not be empathic, but they were wildly curious about anything that would make humans act in interesting ways. If there was a quarrel going on, they'd know about it, and they were probably sitting around it like children at a circus.

She had not specified that the two fishermen were brothers, because if she did that, the sylphs were likely to take her literally and not look for anything *but* brothers. It was always possible that someone outside the family had a quarrel with one of the men, but not the other.

Luna came flying back with the speed of a falcon, in a great deal of excitement. "Oh!" she exclaimed, so entranced with drama that she flew alongside in little circles rather than alighting on the carriage rail, *"Such* anger! *Such* hate! If he were Fire, he would scorch the sea itself!"

"Tell me slowly," Miriam said, coaxingly holding out the open vial of lavender, and grateful that she had mixed it with chamomile to add its own soothing powers to the tranquil essence of the lavender. Luna came closer and got a breath of the scent. Her eyes stopped dilating, and she finally landed on the rail in front of Miriam, perching like a sparrow and taking in great breaths of the scented air.

"There is one who is not a boy, but not yet a man," the sylph said. "His eyes are green, his hair is like yellowed kelp, and he has spots. He is clumsy in his speech, and slow in his movements. Most ignore him, some are scornful of him, and some make a mock of him."

Miriam nodded, feeling darkness steal over her spirit. If ever there was a circumstance designed to bring out the worst in someone, it was to be the butt of jokes and bullying. "And this is the Water Mage?" she asked.

"Master, and new come into his power," the sylph corrected. "Just as well, or he would be raising tempests and opening maelstroms rather than just making mischief. The cut net? That was his doing. The smashed traps his also. The first was because the fisherman told him he was to stop looking at the man's daughter. The second was because the lobsterman told him *he* was to have that same daughter, because *he* could provide for her and the other could not." Having emptied her store of information, Luna sat uncharacteristically still, and breathed in the flower-scent that was so rare at this time of year.

Miriam looked to Jacob, who shook his head. "I do not recognize the description of this lad," he said. "But then, I doubt that anyone but the fishermen involved would. What do you think he is doing?"

"I think," she said, "that he came into his power, perhaps when he was confronted by the first fisherman. I think that he is using the mermaids, coercing them, into taking revenge for him."

"That much I can deduce for myself," Jacob replied dryly. "But do you think he is doing so deliberately?"

She raised an eyebrow. "You are asking the wrong Element," she pointed out. "And at any rate, it will be for you to discover who he is. *I* certainly cannot be seen talking to random fishermen at the docks."

"No, no, of course not." Jacob flushed with embarrassment. "Well, let us go pay our respects to Julia and have luncheon. This boy is not going anywhere, and as yet he has harmed no one other than a little property destruction. We can discuss our options after we dine."

Miriam barely held herself back from giving Jacob a sharp rebuke. *Only* a "little property destruction?" Neither the lobsterman nor the fisherman would be able to ply their trade until their tools were repaired or replaced, and neither nets nor traps were cheap! But she held her tongue. Accidents happened. Presumably, the one young man's brother would help him, and no doubt the fisherman had other nets.

In the end, since there was little that Miriam could do in person, Jacob left her at the coaching inn and went down to conduct the investigation himself. There had been no use in actually going to the docks themselves until the fishing boats were in for the evening, so Jacob had given her the run of his library to while away the time while he conducted his business. But the moment she closed the door to her room, she had an uneasy feeling. It was nothing so strong as a vision, which she was rarely vouchsafed anyway, but it was certainly strong enough to be called a premonition.

So she didn't take off her hat or shawl, much less her gloves. She waited, instead, as the fog drifted in and the air darkened a little, and when the chambermaid tapped on her door she was not at all startled. She got up to answer it.

"Miss, the gentleman has sent a boy with his carriage

and asks if you would meet him?" The maid clearly had
no idea of Jacob's name, but a respectable carriage had
turned up with a message for her, and that was all *she*
needed.

Miriam nodded, as if this was something she had expected. And of course, the maid, seeing her already prepared for going out, assumed it was. "Please ask the
master of the inn to put back my dinner until eight,
would you?" she replied, and sailed past the girl, doing
her best to walk briskly and *not* run.

The carriage let her off at the docks, and Jacob was
waiting for her. "Can you feel it?" he asked, worriedly.
"Even I can feel it. His name is Samuel. Samuel Franks."

She nodded; of course they both would feel the wild
and dark strength out there at the farthest pier. Any
Master or magician would, no matter what their affinity.
This was a Master, with scarcely a shred of control, and
he was angry. "And you think he would respond better
to a woman than a man," she replied—because this was
one of the strategies they had discussed.

"In his state? I venture so . . . I fear that Angus Crocker
put two and two together with my questions and came up
with two hundred, and went to give the lad a dressing
down. He might even have described me—and I am an
old man." Jacob didn't have to say more. An untrained
Master was powerful *and* unpredictable, and Jacob was
likely to be overwhelmed by sheer, emotion-backed force.

"And if he can judge strength, he will know I am not
only weak because I am a woman, I am no match for his
magic." She nodded, and settled her shawl around her
shoulders. "I will see if I can speak sense to him. If nothing else, I can distract him before he calls a storm and
tears this town apart."

Without a backward glance, she set off briskly down the dock. It was getting dark now, and the boats that were tied up heaved uneasily at their moorings. She could feel the storm in the air. The boy was powerfully wrought up. There was no telling what he might do.

Her footsteps betrayed none of her unease, none of the chill of fear that went down her backbone. Her sylphs—her three particular, special friends, whirred around her in a protective circle.

She could see him, dark against the end of the pier. And she could hear the mermaids, see them in the water, thrashing their tails and keening with pain. "Sam?" she called out.

He whirled. She stopped a few feet away from him. His face was white, but with anger, not fear, and splotchy. He was not the answer to any maiden's prayers, part of her noted dispassionately. "Are you Sam Franks?" she asked.

"Who ahr you?" he rasped, in the Maine drawl that was typical of this town. "What d'ye want?"

"My name is Miriam," she replied, clasping her hands on the shawl at her throat. "And I think you know what I want. Please, Sam, you have to stop this. You are hurting them—" she gestured at the writhing mermaids below the water. "You hurt the fishermen whose tools you had them ruin. But most of all—"

She was going to say *most of all, you're hurting yourself,* but he interrupted her, a wild look joining the rage on his face. "Ye mean—I *did* it? I smashed that bastahd Arson's pots? I ruined Crockah's net?" He threw his head back and laughed. "Ye mean, theyah *real?*" He threw his arms wide to indicate the mermaids. "I ain't crazy? The powah—it's real?"

"It's real, and it's dangerous, Sam," she said, and made her expression as pleading as she could manage. "Now, set aside your anger. Let your wrongs go. Release those poor mermaids, and come with me. I shall bring you to a teach—"

"No!" he bellowed, as the waves lifted and the boats began to pitch wildly. "No more *teachers.* No more *bosses.* I'll be tha boss now!"

Miriam looked into his eyes and saw what she had feared most to see. Not the bullied, but the bully. Not the oppressed, but the oppressor. He had not greeted her words with joyful relief, but with gleeful rage.

He took a threatening step toward her and her sylphs bristled at him, hissing and showing claws. "And you won't be stoppin' me, Missy," he snarled, and grabbed her wrist. "I'll be wipin' this stinkin' town from the coast, and I'll be havin' all the wimmin and good things I want from now on, and there ain't *nothin'* you can to do stop me!"

"No," she sighed, and let out a single sob. "Only take your breath away."

And she stole all the air from his lungs.

He made a strangling sound, and let go of her wrist to clutch at his throat. She stepped back out of reach, just in case he somehow got control of himself long enough to lunge at her, but instead he stumbled back another couple of paces—

And released from his coercion, the mermaids surged forward in a wave of white arms and gray tails. A dozen hands seized his ankles. Two dozen hands jerked his feet from under him. He could not even scream as they pulled him off the dock. The last Miriam saw of him was a glimpse of terrified, green eyes in a stark, white face.

And then he was gone.

The sea smoothed to glassy stillness.

She went to the edge of the dock and peered over in the dusk.

There was not even a trail of bubbles to show where he had gone.

"I'm sorry, Miriam," Jacob said, unaccustomed humility in his tone.

"So am I," she sighed. "I had hoped he was only troubled, and not evil."

Jacob handed her case to the coach driver, who was paying no attention to anything either of them were saying—largely because he had been tipped generously by Jacob, more than enough to purchase a supreme lack of curiosity. The driver stowed her traveling case inside the coach for her and got up on the box.

"I must apologize. I was testing you," he continued.

Now she gave him a look of annoyance. "I am not *dim,* Jacob. I realized that as soon as we got to the farmhouse. I also know you didn't expect a renegade, newly awakened Water Master."

"You dealt with him better than your father could have," Jacob told her, flushing. "Even better than I. I hope you will consider joining the White Lodge. . . ."

Oho! So there is *a White Lodge hereabouts!* She knew about the White Lodges and their Huntmasters, in theory, of course—and everyone with a touch of magic knew about the great Lodge headquartered in London—but this was her first confirmation that there was such a thing here, and that Jacob and probably her father had belonged to it.

She thought about leaving him hanging. Then thought

better of it. The other members of the Lodge would go out of their way to make sure she was financially solvent, no matter what happened. And she would be *paying* for that with her magical service.

And she had certainly proved she was up to the job. . . .

"Thank you, Huntmaster," she said, allowing the coachman's assistant to help her into the carriage. "I accept."

About the Authors

Ron Collins has appeared in *Analog*, *Asimov's*, *Nature*, and several other magazines and anthologies. His writing has received a *Writers of the Future* prize and a CompuServe HOMer Award. A collection of his science fiction, *Picasso's Cat & Other Stories*, was published in 2010. A year later he published *See the PEBA on $25 a Day*, a baseball fantasy novel. He holds a degree in Mechanical Engineering and has worked developing avionics systems, electronics, and information technology. He lives in Columbus, Indiana, with his wife, Lisa. The obligatory cat's name is Keiko.

Samuel Conway holds a doctorate in chemistry from Dartmouth and currently lives and works in the environs of Philadelphia, Pennsylvania. When he's not doing research, he serves as the chairman of Anthrocon, the world's largest anthropomorphics convention, which is held annually in Pittsburgh. Somewhere between the two he finds time to write. This is his second published work beyond the small-press circuit, his first having been a short story in Mercedes Lackey's *Flights of Fantasy*.

Dayle A. Dermatis' short fantasy has been called "funny (and rather ingenious)," "something new and something fresh," and "really, really good!" Under various pseudonyms (and sometimes with coauthors), she's sold several novels and more than a hundred short stories in multiple genres. She lives and works in California within scent of the ocean, and in her spare time follows the rock band Styx around the country and travels the world, all of which inspires her writing. To find out where she is today, check out www.cyvarwydd.com.

Rosemary Edghill's first professional sales were to the black & white horror comics, so she can truthfully state on her resume that she once killed vampires for a living. She has worked as an SF editor for Avon Books, as a freelance book designer, as a typesetter, as an illustrator, as an anthologist, and as a professional book reviewer. She has written Regency Romances, historical novels, space opera, high fantasy, media tie-ins, and horror, and collaborated with authors such as Marion Zimmer Bradley, SF Grand Master Andre Norton, and Mercedes Lackey. *Mad Maudlin*, her third Bedlam's Bard collaboration, was a 2002 Voices of Youth Advocates (VOYA) selection as one of the best Horror and Fantasy novels of the year. You can find her on Facebook or Dreamwidth when she ought to be writing.

Tanya Huff lives in rural Ontario, Canada with her wife, Fiona Patton, and, as of last count, eight cats. Her 27 novels and 73 short stories include horror, heroic fantasy, urban fantasy, comedy, and space opera. She's written four essays for BenBella's pop culture collections. Her Blood series was turned into the 22-episode *Blood Ties* television show, and writing episode nine allowed her to finally use her degree in Radio & Television Arts. Her latest novel is *The Silvered* and her next will be the third Gale girls book—untitled as yet. When not writing, she practices her guitar and spends too much time online.

Cedric Johnson was born and raised in Lincoln, Nebraska, where he began writing short stories and poetry at an early age. While attending Lincoln Southeast High School, Cedric was a top-placing contributor, layout editor, and senior year editor-in-chief of its multiple award-winning annual literary publication *From the Depths*. Cedric currently resides in Commerce City, Colorado, where he continues to write while working with other forms of digital media, including 3D modeling and virtual world communications.

Michele Lang is the author of the *Lady Lazarus* historical fantasy series, set in a magical Budapest during World War II. Michele's most recent book in the series, *Dark Victory*, was released in January, 2012. The next book, *Rebel Angels*, is coming in March, 2013. Please visit Michele at www.michelelang.com.

Jody Lynn Nye lists her main career activity as "spoiling cats." She lives northwest of Chicago with one of the above and her husband, author and packager Bill Fawcett. She has written more than forty books, including *The Ship Who Won* with Anne McCaffrey, *Don't Forget Your Spacesuit, Dear!*, a humorous anthology about mothers, and over a hundred short stories. Her latest books are *View From the Imperium* and *Myth-Quoted*.

Fiona Patton was born in Calgary, Alberta, Canada, and grew up in the United States. She now lives in rural Ontario with her partner, Tanya Huff, two glorious dogs, and a pride of very small lions. She has written seven fantasy novels for DAW Books, and is currently working on the first book of a new series entitled *The King's Eagle*.

Diana L. Paxson first worked with the four elements in the Chronicles of Westria, including *The Earthstone*, *The Sea Star*, *The Wind Crystal*, and *The Jewel of Fire*. She has written two dozen other fantasy novels, mostly with historical settings, such as the Avalon series, which she took over from Marion Zimmer Bradley. She is also the author of several nonfiction books, most recently *The Way of the Oracle*.

Gail Sanders and **Michael Z. Williamson** are married veterans who live in Indianapolis, Indiana. Gail is a veteran combat photographer and contracts as a value-added paper pusher for the US Army. She graduated Basic Combat Training a week shy of her 36th birthday. Mike is retired from the military and is a full time writer, researcher, and consultant. In addition to writing, he tests and evaluates disaster preparedness gear and occasionally consults for TV shows and military exercises.

Kristin Schwengel lives with her husband and the obligatory cat (named Gandalf, of course) near Milwaukee, Wisconsin. Her work as a massage therapist affords her just enough time for writing and enjoying her hobbies of knitting and killing garden plantings. Her short stories have appeared in several of Mercedes Lackey's Valdemar anthologies, among others.

Elizabeth A. Vaughan writes fantasy romance. Her first novel, *Warprize*, was rereleased in April, 2011. The Chronicles of the Warlands continues in *WarCry*, released in May, 2011. You can learn more about her books at www.eavwrites.com. Her story is dedicated to Moira Cameron, Yeoman Warder of Her Majesty's Royal Palace and Fortress the Tower of London.

Elisabeth Waters sold her first short story in 1980 to Marion Zimmer Bradley for *The Keeper's Price*, the first of the Darkover anthologies. She then went on to sell short stories to a variety of anthologies. Her first novel, a fantasy called *Changing Fate*, was awarded the 1989 Gryphon Award. She is now working on a sequel to it, in addition to her short story writing and anthology editing. She currently edits the *Sword And Sorceress* anthologies. She also worked as a supernumerary with the San Francisco Opera, where she appeared in *La Gioconda, Manon Lescaut, Madama Butterfly, Khovanschina, Das Rheingold, Werther*, and *Idomeneo*.

About the Editor

Mercedes Lackey is a full-time writer and has published numerous novels and works of short fiction, including the bestselling *Heralds of Valdemar* series. She is also a professional lyricist and a licensed wild bird rehabilitator. She lives in Oklahoma with her husband and collaborator, artist Larry Dixon, and their flock of parrots.